ELLIPSES

ELLIPSES

A Novel

VANESSA LAWRENCE

DUTTON

DUTTON

An imprint of Penguin Random House LLC

penguinrandomhouse.com

LIBRARY OF CONGRESS CATALOGING-IN-PUBLICATION DATA

has been applied for.

ISBN 9780593472774 (hardcover)

Printed in the United States of America
1st Printing

BOOK DESIGN BY ALISON CNOCKAERT

To my parents, who never pressured me to
become a doctor or a lawyer.

ELLIPSES

Prologue

. . .

REPUTATIONS CAN BE a nightmare to maintain. New York's inhabitants should know. For decades, they had lived in a city that supposedly never slept, an expectation that requires perpetual exhaustion. Not every neighborhood complied in upholding this image. On a Wednesday night just past two A.M., the Upper West Side residents along a stretch of Amsterdam Avenue were all deep into their Ambien dreams. A plant shop and a Thai joint and a liquor store were unlit. The bright pink neon sign for a dive bar was the only marker of the city's wired status.

Though no traditionalist, Lily was as wide awake as she had ever been. She stood across from a church on Amsterdam Avenue and stared resolutely at her phone's screen. She willed the rideshare car she had requested to move a little bit faster. Lily hadn't planned to leave the apartment at this hour; she should have been in bed like her fellow Upper West Siders. Tomorrow was an important day. But an overwhelming restlessness had built in the pit of her stomach for weeks, months; if she was honest, for over a year. This desire—this need—had compelled her out of her pajamas and into a pair of jeans, a camisole, dirty white sneakers, and a hooded parka to shield her from the November cold.

This need had wrested control of her fingers, tapped out the address into the rideshare phone app. And it had instructed her to slip down the many flights of stairs to her building's front door.

Never before had Lily been so excited to dress for an evening out. This was the night that would mark Lily's future days as indelibly After.

Hours earlier, Lily had sat, cocooned in a blanket in the armpit of her sofa, and contemplated her notepad, cluttered with story pitches, display-copy ideas, and content rubrics. Her pen had hovered over the page, waiting for another spark. Her eyes had drifted over to her laptop screen, to the pages and pages of text she had dreamed up from the raw material of her imagination. This was where her mind yearned to be. Lily had shoved the pen and notepad aside and drawn her laptop in closer. Its keys had click-clacked with the vigor of her efforts. She had unwrapped herself from the confines of her blanket and tossed that out of the way, too.

For months, Lily had subjugated her instincts to B's directives. Lily had shushed her intrinsic reticence, the better to manifest B's signature self-assertion. She had done all that B had commanded. In the process, Lily had watched the pointer of her inner compass spin frantically, as though possessed, until it threatened to snap off in the whirling vortex of B's special storm. After so many sacrifices in the name of self-actualization, Lily had finally reached a decision. Her next chapter was six miles of dark streets away. She knew the exact words that would usher in the life that was hers to make.

Lily's fingers had flown across her keyboard. The page count on the document had grown and grown. With each additional paragraph, Lily's posture had lengthened. A brisk energy had coursed through her arms and legs. When she had determined that she was finished, via an inner mechanism whose logic made sense only to her, she had closed her laptop and bounded toward her closet. Outside, the dark night beckoned her to a pivotal choice.

A tremor ran down Lily's torso as a black car approached her street corner. The license plate matched the one listed in the app, so she opened the door and leaned in.

"Who are you picking up?" she asked the young guy—the app claimed his name was Chad—seated behind the wheel.

"Lily," he replied, and she got in.

The car reeked of lemon-scented disinfectant; the leather seats were immaculate. A warmth spread through Lily's chest and her pulse quickened in the curve of her neck.

"Mind if I open the window?" she asked.

"Go for it," Chad replied.

Lily stared out the window as the car sped toward its downtown destination, few obstacles in its path on the gaping streets. Chad headed along Ninety-Sixth Street to the West Side Highway, a clogged artery during the daytime. Now theirs was an unobstructed vehicular endeavor, as though the barriers to Lily's future happiness had parted with the tap of a finger. The Hudson River and New Jersey's shore rushed by in a blur.

A tingling buzz filled Lily's stomach and lungs and head. She uncrossed her legs and planted her feet firmly on the car's carpeted floor. The mere possibility that B had sensed her movement through some telepathic intervention nudged Lily to check her silent phone, in the pocket of her parka, for any notifications. Lily ignored this impulse. Patiently, she waited for the real deal.

Lily could remember a time before B, a time when a phone was a means of communication instead of a chasm of unreciprocated attention. When a dinner with a friend was a chance to catch up, not a distraction from the endless wait for a reply. When her waking hours were for charting her future course, not for plotting ways to follow someone else's path. B had been in charge all along. And she had no compunctions about keeping Lily at arm's length, to a degree that made Lily question why B bothered with her at all.

In fact, B had informed Lily, early in their text correspondence, of the motive behind her digital outreach. "I love to mentor young women," she had typed, after doling out a nugget of empowering advice. "It's a passion." Which, of course, had made Lily wonder how many other young women B was simultaneously mentoring. How widespread her self-described passion ran. And then a few months of tough-love pep talks had swept away these concerns before Lily pondered, again, why a woman of B's stature would have chosen Lily as a receptacle for her wisdom. Squeeze and release. Squeeze and release. The pressure-valve turns of their rapport could have put a metronome out of business.

Lily had tried to explain her strange pull toward B to her best friends and even to herself. Everyone else saw B's poise and power. They watched her navigate boardrooms and public appearances with preternatural ease. They charted her ascension to the highest ranks of corporate America as an organic progression. Lily snuck a peek behind the velvet curtain. She had unfettered access to someone most people could only reach through a magazine or a screen. Well, to be fair, Lily went through a screen, too, but her screen was different; her screen was more transparent than everyone else's. Her view was closer. And tonight, she was going to break down any remaining walls.

Chad exited the West Side Highway at Canal Street and headed southeast toward Tribeca. He made a few circuitous turns around the neighborhood's uninhabited streets before he stopped on Duane Street in front of an industrial building with a cast-iron façade.

"This is you," he said.

"Thanks," said Lily.

"You take care," said Chad.

"Yeah, be well," said Lily, and shut the door behind her.

She examined the illuminated panel of buzzers for each of the building's apartments. Lily pressed the bell for the penthouse and stepped back a few feet. If she stood too close it would telegraph her overeagerness.

"Hello?" came a voice from the buzzer's speaker. "Who's there?"

"It's me. Lily," said Lily.

"Lily?" came the voice. "What the fuck are you doing here? Are you crazy?"

"Maybe. I don't know. Are you really that surprised?"

A pause. Lily waited for B to say something. She could feel B plot her next move.

Lily wasn't a natural gambler; she had never had a taste for putting it all on the line. She was always methodical in her quest for what she wanted. She believed in legwork and progressions, not divine windfalls. But it was no longer good enough to wish for an ideal hand and let the cards steer her in whichever direction they chose. She had waited for the perfect moment to place her bet, to unleash the full force of her ideas and desires on the right person, the right job, the right circumstances for success. She had bided her time, so as not to go bankrupt for the wrong opportunity. But stasis carried its own set of risks. And now her stores of skills and experiences were on the verge of becoming meaningless, her coffers devalued by a change in currency. Whatever amount she had left demanded to be used. Go big or go home. Except home just wasn't an option.

The door buzzed. Lily pushed it in quickly. Once inside the elevator, she headed up to the penthouse. Like many loft residences, B's building had one apartment per floor. The elevator reached the penthouse and the door opened into B's foyer.

B loomed a few feet from the door, where she blocked most of the entrance. She wore loose men's-style pajama bottoms and a white T-shirt; her shoulder-length brown hair streaked with gray highlights was wrapped in a haphazard half loop. Her brow was furrowed.

"I still don't know what the fuck you're doing here," she said by way of greeting.

Lily stepped into the room. "I have something I need to tell you," she said.

"And you couldn't just send me a text?" B asked.

"It needs to happen in person," Lily said.

B stared at her intently. The corners of her mouth tugged outward, in a grimace or a smile, it wasn't clear. She moved to the side.

"Come in."

1

. . .

One year and eight months earlier

LILY AVOIDED HER own reflection in her office's smudged bathroom mirror. No amount of artful eyeliner or strategic concealer or shimmery highlighter could impart the illusion of vivacity after a ten-hour workday, certainly not in the green-tinged fluorescent lighting. There was no hairdresser on hand to coax her dark strands into some semblance of elegance. There was no stylist or date to help zip up the back of her dress. All Lily's hopes for a successful transition from sad cubicle dweller to black-tie event attendee were pinned on the delicate fabric of her borrowed gown. And its tiny zipper pull refused to budge. Lily contorted her arms into a broken pretzel and tugged at the pull as her face reddened with frustration.

In forty minutes, theoretically, at least, Lily would head to an iteration of the twice-annual An Unforgettable Evening gala in support of Alzheimer's disease research. The gala's slug line was extremely questionable, but the occasion was otherwise par for the course of Lily's professional social life. A magazine style writer with a partial society beat, she attended the odd cocktail party or dinner or jewelry luncheon from the sprawl of events that keep tony calendars full across the spring and fall seasons in New York. And then she wrote about these outings the following morning so that the people who had gone to them could read about them—because no one else read these stories beyond the people who had been at the parties—and relive their experiences through the lens of cultural validation. It was an IRL version of two-factor authentication: First one lived the thing, then one made sure it had been real and worthy by consuming someone else's narration of it. Check, check. A person's authenticity was intact.

In preparation for the ball, Lily wore a strapless floral dress whose voluminous skirt ended at her ankles. The designer look was a sample that Lily had eyed, a few months ago, as it swished down a runway in an industrial warehouse in the Brooklyn Navy Yard. What was a gown on Lily had been a cocktail dress on the model who had worn this exact sample in the show. A person paid to write about society events could not afford the high-end wardrobe the lifestyle demanded; a decade of squeezing herself into borrowed outfits a size or more too small had trained Lily's eyes to reconfigure designer collections to her non-mannequin proportions. She would sit in the fifth row of a fashion show and mentally eliminate looks worn by models with particularly tiny rib cages or waists. Anything that hit a model below her knees was a no-go for Lily, who was many inches shy of five foot eleven. Fabrics with stretch were ideal but rare. And a long line of wedding-gown buttons was an instant dealbreaker. No twenty-first-century woman, save for a member of royalty, had the time or handmaids such useless garment closures required.

These borrowed designer dresses were the closest approximations of a Cinderella fantasy that Lily had achieved in the many years of her partygoing employment. Fairy godmothers, though, knew how to tailor their looks before directing their future princesses to don them. Still, the opportunity to wear for a few hours an exquisite item of fashion, however wrongly sized, had not lost its allure, not entirely. Real-life fairy tales did not manifest without a certain amount of sacrifice.

The zipper's boxy carriage would not move further along its metal tracks. Lily dragged it down to its place of inception, near her sacrum, and restarted its upward journey.

Ever since she had turned thirty, two whole years ago, Lily had striven to rid herself of this partial society beat. It was exhausting and repetitive work, like being stuck in a Groundhog Day of high school winter formals with more expensive venues and equally ruthless mean girls. For the most part, Lily had extricated herself from this nightly grind; there were always younger, eager assistants who had yet to learn that partying with strangers was not the same thing as going out with one's friends. However, tonight's Unforgettable Evening had an unusual twist that Lily had felt unable to refuse. She had been specifically invited by one of the gala's chairs. Normally, Lily was dropped like dirty laundry onto a vacant dinner seat by a PR person for the event. This evening, Lily would sit at one of the gala chairs' tables, which meant that she was expected to devote extra attention in the next day's copy to her gracious benefactor, Annabelle Jones.

The zipper carriage of Lily's gown had reached its earlier sticking point. With one hand, Lily pressed the two tracks together, while she urged the carriage along with her other hand and some prayers for good measure.

A onetime assistant creative director turned handbag designer, Annabelle had recently married her husband, Jonathan, who was nearly thirty years her senior. Together, they occupied prime real estate at the intersection of international jet-setting and New York society—or at least what constituted its desiccated contemporary ranks. Annabelle hawked her overpriced clutches by day in the pages of glossy magazines and on various social media platforms. By night, she armed herself with the same goods and swanned around the city's various disease-oriented galas—heart disease one night, cystic fibrosis the next, and enough cancers to stock an all-you-can-eat buffet—and showed them off to her genetically blessed cohorts. She had met Jonathan at a mutual friend's birthday party at an Upper East Side cabaret. Within a year of their tricoastal relationship across Jonathan's homes in London, New York, and Malibu, the couple was engaged. They announced their impending union via a photo posted to social media, in which Annabelle stood behind a topless Jonathan. Her fiery red curls fluttered over his bare shoulders as she covered his eyes with her porcelain hands, on whose left ring finger a blinding five-carat whopper flashed.

With a final, firm yank, Lily tugged the zipper pull up its last stretch of tracks. Her arms ached from their prolonged contortions; she did some careful, small shoulder circles to loosen their kinks. She pinched a seam at her waist and hoped that silk jacquard had a propensity to stretch. Lily brushed her hand across the floral gown and admired its elegant sheen. Wrapped in so many green and blue buds, she looked like a field of wildflowers. Her feet were bound in black strappy sandals, an act of optimism or foolhardiness given that outside, icy ground awaited her.

It was March, and a surprise snowfall, like an uninvited guest crashing a dinner gathering, had blanketed the city in heaping piles of white. Lily had watched it flutter down, with an internal groan, from the windows of her glass office building. Within hours, the crystalline fluff had soured to a mottled sludge, the festive remains of canine walks and vehicular exhaust. Temperatures plummeted low enough that dark spots appeared on sidewalks, their blackened gleam the only warning of slippery danger.

Enough time had passed since the city's de facto rush hour to allow Lily to hail a cab a couple of precarious blocks from her office building. The Alzheimer's gala was taking place at an events space in Midtown across the street from Grand Central Terminal. Like many of the arenas for tony social gatherings, the events space was a former bank; now it housed moneyed people and their outsized revelry instead of merely housing their outsized accounts. Black-tie partying was its own form of currency.

The bodice of the sample dress tightened its grip on Lily's rib cage as the taxi maneuvered Midtown streets. She inhaled shallow breaths to prevent the inconvenient expansion of her lungs and focused her attention on the shiny folds of the dress's skirt.

Lily had met Annabelle a couple of years earlier when Lily's editor had assigned her a story on Annabelle and her latest handbag collection. Annabelle had been pleased with the piece, and as a thank-you, she had invited Lily out for drinks in the hushed lobby of a trendy SoHo hotel. People in Annabelle's world always thanked someone by imposing themselves on that person's schedule, since there could be no greater expression of gratitude than the opportunity to share a table with them.

Still, Annabelle was kind and generous, and Lily had found her company entertaining. And while Lily wouldn't have called them friends without a self-deprecating qualifier—"You know, when she has no one else to spend time with . . ."—the two stayed in regular touch. In the aftermath of her wedding, Annabelle decided her first social outing would be as chair of the Alzheimer's gala, a cause she chose not out of a personal connection but rather for expediency: It always kicked off the spring season after the rounds of international fashion weeks ended. At twenty-five years old, Annabelle also boasted the crowning achievement of being the youngest woman ever to grace the event's cochair list. Even in the realm of degenerative disease charities, youth trumped all.

At Forty-Second Street, Lily exited the cab and entered the cavernous event space; a vortex of power, money, and aesthetic preoccupation greeted her at the door. A string quartet created ambience for the cocktail hour. Magnolia branches, flaming candelabras, and still-life tableaux of artichokes, crocus bulbs, and green grapes anchored the dinner tables. It was spring equinox chic at its finest, an unforgettable assemblage, so long as one did not suffer from the very disease the gala's fundraising sought to cure.

Lily's first stop was the coat check station, just off the room's entrance. A small line had formed. Lily joined it and stared at the back of an elegant lady. Like Lily, this woman was petite; they would have been the same height if not for the woman's vertiginous footwear. This was where any overlap in their appearances ended. The woman's hair was brown streaked with gray and pulled into a tight chignon above the nape of her slim white neck. An unidentifiable scent of musk, perhaps, or leather or sandalwood, emanated from her skin. Unlike many of the other ladies in the room, the woman wore a lean pantsuit, the color of freshly popped champagne. It fit her like it had been designed and cut and sewn expressly for her body, which, to go by the size of the diamond-and-emerald islands that sparkled on her ears, it very much had been. Lily tugged at her gown, at its waning and suffocating glamour, in uncomfortable reply. Anyone who looked at her could tell this was not a dress from her closet. By this point, she was one large intake of oxygen away from splitting its seams. Lily had never attended one of these events in her own clothes, let alone a piece as utterly suited to her physique as this woman's ensemble. Whoever she was, this woman was at home in this room and in her physicality in a way that Lily would never be.

It was the woman's turn at the front of the line. She passed the plush camel coat draped over her arm into the waiting hands of the coat check woman and slipped her numbered tag into her black silk evening clutch. As she turned to her left, toward the red carpet and its waiting step-and-repeat backdrop, littered with the event's many corporate sponsors, and the cluster of photographers huddled near its border, ready to snap pictures of the rich and notable, the woman's face came into full view. Lily recognized her in a flash.

Billie Aston was the president and chief creative officer of one of the most prominent beauty companies in the United States. She was the product of staunch New England privilege and had been nourished with a diet of boarding school and the Ivy League, institutions at which she was a legacy. Billie had complicated this cookie-cutter success narrative by striking out as a makeup artist after graduation, a choice that demoted her golden-girl position to the black sheep level in the eyes of her parents. Her rise through the corporate ranks, from a twenty-something makeup artist who mixed lipstick shades over her kitchen sink to the creative executive in charge of product, retail, and marketing decisions for a stable of brands, had been followed almost as feverishly as her distinctive personal style. A fixture at charity galas, many of which her company sponsored, fashion shows, and arts events, Billie dressed the part in sharp suits, custom shirts, and killer footwear, all of which seduced American women, and perhaps a few men. Such adulation translated into higher beauty sales.

Billie was perennially single, a status she justified to those who felt it merited explanation with a gesture at her workaholic hours, which left no room for romance. For much of her early career, her sexuality had been a whispered point of curiosity and derision, from those who described themselves as "traditional," that both Billie and her employer refused to address. A few years back, tired of the gossiped speculation and recognizing a potential change in social tides, Billie had confirmed her queer sexuality, with her employer's full "blessing," in the splashiest way possible: via an acceptance speech for a corporate-trailblazer honor she received at an awards ceremony. Billie emerged from her revelation a brighter star, a champion of social progressiveness at the corporate level, and a queer icon, to boot. So long as sales responded well, she was free to be herself. In the wake of her awards speech, Billie had continued to fly solo, at least so far as the public knew.

Lily had observed Billie from afar when they had crossed paths at the rare cocktail party or breast cancer awareness fundraiser, breast cancer being the preferred cause for Billie's company. She had always considered Billie an intimidating presence. Part of it was that, like other women in their fifties and older, she radiated self-possession. Women of this demographic had a confidence that stemmed not from being the prettiest or smartest or thinnest person at any gathering, but from knowledge of their individual worth, and, equally important, from acknowledgment of their weaknesses, for which they refused to apologize. Lily wondered what that would be like, not to feel the need to qualify every action and statement with "Sorry." She spent half of her days in a state of apology for her mere existence. Even at thirty-two, she tended to downplay her presence, like an internal dimmer switch.

Billie's dark gaze drifted over to Lily. For a second, she and Lily seemed frozen in place staring at each other, Billie mid-step in one direction, Lily in wait to take her spot at the front of the coat check line. Billie's eyes lingered on Lily's face, then drifted slowly down Lily's neck, chest, waist, skirt, as though they were collecting data and formulating a judgment about every facet of Lily's appearance. Lily sucked her soft abdominal muscles in tightly and begged her lungs not to expand. Billie's gaze was like bug-detection software; all Lily's many flaws were exposed through the exacting force of Billie's stare. Lily searched Billie's keen face for an expression of disgust. Instead of disapproval, a sly playfulness tugged at Billie's lips as her eyes landed on Lily's bare toes.

"You must have a high tolerance for suffering," Billie remarked. "It's thirty-five degrees out."

Lily's default was to confirm Billie's comment with a polite smile and a nod. Some combination of gnawing hunger, physical discomfort, and curiosity inspired uncharacteristic daring. She was seized by a desire to impress Billie, who sparked a latent stirring in Lily's chest.

"Says the woman in five-inch stilettos on a snow day," Lily replied. "On the scale of suffering, I prefer almost hypothermia to a potential broken limb."

"A high heel has far more impact than a bare toe. When you're our size, you need to pick your sacrifices more wisely," said Billie. "Besides, my driver would never allow a broken limb or hypothermia to happen."

"Ah, so you didn't risk anything. You were going to win either way," said Lily. "Where do I sign up for those odds?"

A smirk curled across Billie's lips. Lily braced herself for a cutting reply, but Billie just continued her movement toward the step-and-repeat. She winked at Lily and uttered, "Batter up." Then she dissolved into a scrum of clicks and flashes. And it was Lily's turn at the coat check.

2

. . .

THE COCKTAIL HOUR of a gala was when Lily hunted for notable people from whom she could fetch a quote or two for the purposes of her next day's story. Once Lily was seated for dinner, she was essentially trapped with the same people for the remainder of the event; she was completely beholden to the sound bites, or lack thereof, from her table-mates, who were, more often than not, near the bottom of the social food chain, since Lily was generally parked in its lowest depths. A PR person had emailed her a tip sheet of expected VIP attendees in advance, so Lily could plan accordingly. Annabelle would comprise the bulk of her quoted copy, by virtue of her invitation to Lily and the extra media attention it implied as thanks. Unfortunately, Alzheimer's events did not attract the higher-wattage actors and musicians that breast cancer, lymphoma, and leukemia ones did. Lily scanned the cocktail crowd and set her sights on a model slash cookbook author slash yogi, who stood by one of the many bars in wait for a beverage.

The room was stuffy and tight, despite its majestic sixty-five-foot ceiling. Lily squeezed past black satin tuxedos and tiered chiffon gowns as she tried not to spill the glass of ice water in her hand. Champagne was out of the question; who knew what mayhem carbonation would wreak on the suction of her dress's bodice. The model slash cookbook author slash yogi was blond and tan in a way that spoke of surf trips to Costa Rica as opposed to the pigmented interventions of a bottle of bronzer. Her long, shimmery dress was aquamarine and its abdominal cutouts left little question as to the effectiveness of her yoga routine. Lily introduced herself, including the name of her magazine, to the young woman, who was in her early twenties, if Lily had to guess. As she did so, her peripheral vision registered a flash of champagne silk approaching from the right.

"What do you think of the food so far?" Lily asked the model. Billie Aston stood right next to them, behind the model, her profile now in Lily's line of vision. She appeared to order a gin martini. Lily's face flushed and she sipped from her glass of water.

"They really should have a vegan option, don't you think?" the model said. "It's discriminatory not to."

"Those crudités look vegan," Lily replied, and nodded in the direction of a plate of cut-up vegetables arranged around bowls of dips on the tray of a passing waiter.

The model tossed her head in obvious annoyance. "Vegans need more than just vegetables to survive."

"But isn't that, technically, all that you eat?" Lily pressed, eager to convert this conversation into something usable for her story. "I mean, it's called a 'plant-based' diet?"

"That's a gross oversimplification of veganism!" said the model, who, apparently, toted a rehearsed defense of her regimen as an accessory to parties. "We eat super-varied diets. We eat more diversely than many so-called omnivores. It's the subject of my new cookbook coming out this September. You should do a story on it for your magazine."

"I will definitely consider it," Lily said. Worst-case scenario, she could plug the model's book in her party coverage and frame it as "news" if her other quotes from the evening proved uninspiring.

"You should do a four-page story. Or six pages. With recipes. It's perfect for your magazine. I have a jewelry campaign dropping this fall. I could ask the brand about using outtakes in the story. I'll send you an advance copy of my book."

"That would be cool," Lily said. "What's your book called?"

"*Eating Your Way to Diversity: How Veganism Will Save the Human Race.*"

"Interesting."

"It's about how vegans are the most diverse people in the world."

"Do you have demographics to back that up?"

"We are naturally diverse. Because of the range of legumes and vegetables we have to eat to survive. This makes us better human beings."

"The argument being that veganism is nutritional DEI training?" Lily asked. "Will it save us all from microaggressions in the workplace, racial profiling, and unequal gender pay, too?"

A quick, sharp laugh came from the direction of Billie, who continued to stand behind the model, despite the drink in her hand.

"What's DEI?" said the model. "Is that the new superfood supplement coming out of Samoa?"

"No. It stands for 'diversity, equity, and inclusion.' You know, the training module that all big companies have their employees do so they can pay lip service to diversity without making any real changes. It was a joke."

Lily tried to make eye contact with Billie, but she slipped away, back out into the crowd of other guests.

"Never heard of it," said the model. "Anyway, give me your email and I'll have my publicist send you a copy of my book." The model brandished her phone and Lily typed her email address into the model's contacts. "Good talking to you."

The model strolled away. Once again, Lily stood on her own.

A gong—yes, an actual gong—ushered attendees to dinner. Lily was at table twenty-five. Annabelle was already there when Lily located it, with help from a seating chart.

"Lily!" she cried, and wrapped Lily in an embrace of tuberose and crêpe de chine. Like others of her ilk, Annabelle tended to greet people in a way that was hyperbolically disproportionate to how well she knew them. "You're next to me. We'll have plenty of time to chat."

Annabelle wore a black strapless gown that Lily recalled from a Parisian runway show six months ago by one of the industry's most famous and expensive designers. The dress likely cost more than Lily earned in six months. A cotton candy plexiglass evening clutch from Annabelle's latest collection popped against the gown's black austerity. As with many members of international society, the source of Annabelle's luxurious lifestyle was unknown. She did not have a recognizable surname that graced the sides of medical buildings and higher-learning institutions like the progeny of other famous families who partied alongside her in private London clubs and discos in Ibiza. She was from the middle of the country, a vast, shapeless locale that didn't exist in the worldview of most New Yorkers. It was the equivalent of saying one hailed from Antarctica.

The sales numbers of Annabelle's handbags, not that this data was publicly available, could not account for her six-figure wardrobe, her museum-quality jewelry, or her refusal to fly commercial. Even Jonathan's career—he was a former financier who'd cashed out and become a venture capitalist, focused on wellness and beauty start-ups—did not fully explain the couple's cushioned comings and goings. They were part of a perpetual New York phenomenon in which the upper echelons of the population remained mum about their inherited finances, the better to perpetuate the fantasy that their glamour was meritocratic. The ruse was that they had achieved their high social status not on the back of generational wealth or rich spouses, but as an extension of their intrinsic personal value. Their charity board seats were symptoms of their constitutional superiority.

Lily glanced at the place cards on the table. The one on her right read, "Billie Aston." Nearly as soon as Lily finished reading her name, the woman herself appeared. Billie received an effusive hug from Annabelle and turned to Lily and held out her pale, elegant hand.

"We haven't met. I'm Billie," she said.

There was no acknowledgment in her dark eyes of the footwear conversation at the coat check, nor the eavesdropping with the model at the bar. It was as if the last forty-five minutes of the event had happened to Lily but not to Billie. She must have made a habit of exchanging words with strangers and listening in on their interviews, then pretending otherwise. Or maybe Lily was so un-noteworthy, so deeply unimpressive, that Billie's brain had forgotten her, on instinct, as soon as Billie turned away.

Lily grasped Billie's cool hand, firmly but gently. It was well moisturized and callus-free, a hand more accustomed to dictating orders than mucking about in the trenches. The nails were short and squared off, with a crimson gloss. It was a look that revealed every nick and chip and thereby telegraphed its wearer's status as someone with the resources to maintain such an easily tarnished veneer. Lily wished she had been more diligent about her own hydration routine on this day. And her nails hadn't seen a manicurist in over a decade. She imagined how prehistoric her hand must feel in Billie's pampered grip.

"I'm Lily."

Billie's lips parted into a Cheshire cat smile. "Does Lily have a last name?"

"Michaels." Lily smiled, too. "Does Billie have a last name?"

One of Billie's sculpted brows cocked upward in surprise and Lily wondered if she had gone too far. This woman was famous in a substantive way, predicated on corporate accomplishment, not aesthetic perfection, though there was no way around the fact that Billie was physically stunning, too, by conventional standards. Her paleness was smooth and pink-toned, like the inside of a shell. Her nose was bony and strong. One could practically bungee jump off the sharp planes of her cheekbones. Her eyes were the one surprise: Where one expected something watery and blue to complete the portrait of peak whiteness, one instead found dark, molten orbs that were penetrating and opaque. They probed their subjects and gave nothing of themselves away.

Billie released that same quick, sharp laugh from earlier, and something inside Lily released, too.

"Aston," said Billie as she sat in her allocated dinner chair. Her posture was ramrod straight, almost to the point of arrogance. "But you already knew that, didn't you?"

Heat rushed to Lily's face. Billie took her reddened cheeks as an answer.

"Are you a big supporter of Alzheimer's research?" asked Billie.

"I'm here for work," said Lily.

"So am I."

"I think we have different definitions of work."

"How so?"

Lily wanted to point out that she had spent the cocktail hour interviewing a vegan about legume diversity while Billie had spent it drinking a gin martini. "Your earrings are stunning. Are they yours?"

"Of course they are. Who else's would they be?"

"There you go."

"I didn't have earrings like this when I was your age."

"And I doubt I'll have earrings like those when I'm your age."

"Surely your self-esteem is higher than that."

"I didn't say your earrings were on my to-do list. Just that they're symbolic of our differences."

"And what is on this important list?"

"A one-bedroom apartment. A week's vacation somewhere warm, preferably involving a beach. A story assignment that's longer than one thousand words. For example."

"I think you need to dream bigger," said Billie. "If you lowball yourself with your goals, no one is going to take you seriously. You may as well just give up and go home." Her gaze executed another scan of Lily's face and torso. Then Billie turned to her right, to her other dining partner, Matthew Blake, director of a well-known hedge fund, and never looked back at Lily.

Confusion washed over Lily as she picked at her plate of bland chicken and steamed potatoes and tried to pay attention to Annabelle's chattering on her left. Billie appeared to be annoyed at Lily's boldness. So much so that she refused to acknowledge Lily for the rest of the meal. And yet, Lily thought, the act of explicitly dismissing someone undermined the cool detachment that ignorance aimed to achieve. To turn a cold shoulder on someone required contorting one's body to avoid the other person; it confirmed that this someone had affected one enough to force a change. Billie's first impression of Lily may not have been what Lily had wanted, but she had made an impact nonetheless.

Dinner came to a heated conclusion with a live auction for an all-inclusive trip to the Maldives and a summer rental in Aspen. A band replaced the string quartet and it was time for inebriated black-tie dancing. Lily's flourless chocolate cake remained untouched on the table. No food would pass the threshold of her lips until her torturous dress was off her body and in a black garment bag. Fortunately, no one at this table or at any other table in the room would ever remark on Lily's lack of consumption, because they were too busy pushing their own food around in casual circles to cover their restricted appetites. Billie's cake was untouched, as well, and its owner stood next to Annabelle and kiss-kissed her good night. Then Billie swept past Lily, her unidentifiable musk the only sign that she had been there at all. Lily said her goodbye, too.

"Drinks soon!" Annabelle trilled, with full knowledge that Lily wouldn't hold her to this offer.

Lily retrieved her coat and stepped outside into the cold, sulky night. Midtown was ghostly at this hour; all the office workers were long gone, and no one seeking a good time selected a night out on East Forty-Second Street as their poison of choice. The rideshare car prices were astronomical, beyond what she could reasonably expense for work, so Lily trudged slowly west in search of a taxi home. The balls of her feet throbbed. Her exposed toes lost their feeling in the thirty-degree air. Thank god tonight's performance of forced frivolity was finally over. Even seated next to a cochair, at a high-ranking table as opposed to her normal spot in social oblivion, Lily was at odds with the proceedings that surrounded her. She would always be an approved outsider expected to appreciate the spectacle from afar without affecting the course of events. Her presence was necessary to reaffirm the heightened status of those around her through the contrast between her lot and theirs. She was an unassuming buffer and a quiet observer, but she was never, ever supposed to be an active participant.

Lily had hit Fifth Avenue when a dark town car pulled up beside her. Its rear window rolled down.

"Do you know where your children are?"

It was Billie. Wryness dripped from her voice.

"Excuse me?" asked Lily.

"Isn't that the PSA message that used to run after the evening news? 'Do you know where your children are?'"

"Am I the child or the parent in this scenario?"

"Do you have children?"

"No."

"Well, then . . ."

Lily was too cold and tired and hungry to banter. She was about fifteen minutes away from ripping apart the bodice of her dress and inhaling whatever greasy, carcinogenic food she could locate in Midtown at ten thirty P.M. Billie seemed to sense Lily's exhaustion. She opened the door to the car.

"Get in. I'll give you a ride home."

"You don't know where I live."

"So long as it's in the five boroughs, we're good. But if you live in New Jersey, I'm afraid you're out of luck. I can't do New Jersey."

"I don't live in New Jersey," Lily replied.

"Thank god. Now get in. It's freezing."

Lily clambered into the car as Billie slid over in the seat to make room.

"Where to?" Billie asked.

"Ninety-Fourth and Amsterdam," Lily replied. The driver turned on Lexington Avenue and headed south, the opposite direction from where Lily needed to go.

"I'm in Tribeca," explained Billie. "He'll drop me off first and then take you to the Upper West Side."

Lily didn't know what to say to that. Tribeca was six miles from the Upper West Side, a forty-minute drive with average traffic. Billie's lift had more than doubled the amount of time it would take Lily to get home—and more than doubled the ticking minutes until she could finally eat. Lily wished she could invent a gracious exit from this car. Instead, she adjusted her dress into a less excruciating alignment under Billie's amused gaze.

"Not yours?"

"We don't all have black-tie wardrobes at the ready."

Billie smoothed the fabric on the jacket of her suit. Her left leg was crossed over her right; her left foot dangled a few inches from Lily. "So, wear what you have."

"We both know it doesn't work that way."

"How do you know Annabelle?"

"I wrote a story on her a couple of years ago. How do you know her?"

"Her husband is the son of a family friend. Jonathan was three years ahead of me at Andover. So, you're a journalist."

Billie really didn't remember watching Lily interview the vegan during cocktail hour. Or this was all still part of her MO in which she pretended not to have noticed others. And now she was giving a ride home to a total stranger.

"A writer."

"What's the difference?"

"Journalists are ultracompetitive. It's all about getting the scoop first. I identify more with the storytelling aspect. I don't care about winning."

That amused expression returned to Billie's face. "Then what are you doing working for a magazine that produces journalism?"

Billie seemed to know the magazine where Lily worked; she must have overheard Lily mention it to the vegan. "How do you know where I work?"

"You work for a magazine, don't you? A newspaper girl wouldn't have access to that dress."

"Yes, I do. And magazines produce stories, too."

"Why not just take the journalism out of the equation?"

"Then what would I write about?"

Billie's expression turned thoughtful. "Is this what you always wanted to do?"

"Yes," said Lily.

It was. It wasn't just what she had always wanted to do. It was the only thing she had wanted to do. Lily had grown up immersed in fashion magazines and the supermodels therein. She had grown up with novels, too, but the literature she had read had seemed worlds away from her contemporary existence. Lily was eager for a road map. While she couldn't live in the literal pages of a book, she could, with some ingenuity, access the glamour contained in a magazine. The gatekeepers of fashion and beauty had tricked her into believing that aspirational womanhood was achievable with the correct accoutrements. It was true, according to magazines, that to be an ideal woman was to be tall and white and thin and beautiful and well-dressed. She would never be tall or white; the other three factors were slightly more malleable, through often unhealthy means. That realization arrived later. Magazines produced fantasies. If she worked at a magazine, she could be a part of that dreamworld. And who wouldn't want an excuse to get paid, albeit very little, to dream?

And yes, admittedly, the sparkle of that glamour had dissipated with time, case in point, the ill-fitting dress that squeezed the life out of Lily's body. The older she grew, the harder it was to insert herself, spiritually or physically, into the fantasies she helped perpetuate. Her body became less pliable, thanks to the effects of aging. And more important, she had become less willing. It wasn't simply the dress that didn't fit, it was the whole philosophy it represented: that she needed to change herself in pursuit of someone else's idea of who she should be. The glaring gap between how the models and actresses looked in the clothes and how Lily and other so-called normal women appeared had always been there; it had taken Lily longer than it should have to notice it. Youth had draped a scrim across her field of vision. She was hardly "old" by any standard except, for example, the peak age of female fertility, as she was constantly reminded by egg-freezing ads across social media. But Lily had been alive long enough that the scrim had worn thin. She didn't want to strive for physical beauty. She wanted to be valued as she was. No magazine could give her that. Lily had yet to figure out what could.

"How old are you?"

"Thirty-two."

"You're a baby. What you want will change."

"Maybe it already has," said Lily as she smarted at the word *baby*.

Billie's face widened with a grin. "And what about your personal life? I don't see a ring."

"I'm in a relationship."

"And do you think he'll propose soon?"

"It's a she and I doubt it. We don't live together."

"She?" Billie scanned Lily's body as though in search of evidence to support Lily's romantic status. "You don't look gay."

"I'm not. But my girlfriend is. Like that T-shirt slogan."

"I thought that slogan was supposed to be ironic."

"Irony can also be true."

The one downside to these older, self-possessed women, the queer ones, too, was that they had a different understanding of the world, one that often contradicted their surface sophistication. Narrow-minded beliefs like theirs were part of the reason why Lily had explored her sexual fluidity in an online space, where her unabashed normative femininity proved less a point of contention than it did in real life. Online she managed to secure a steady stream of dates with poets and nonprofit workers and a struggling painter who eventually decamped for the Florida Keys to teach arts and crafts to retirees.

Determinedly, Lily had worked her way through this idiosyncratic array until she stumbled upon her current and first girlfriend, Alison, a history buff turned corporate devotee. While Lily had chased her childhood dreams of glamorous womanhood over the course of her twenties, Alison had spent that same period building a more secure, though highly competitive career as a management consultant. Lily's twenties had been a montage of borrowed dresses, late-night lounges, and on-deadline interviews; Alison's first adult decade had been marked by PowerPoint presentations, conference calls, and dingy hotel rooms in middle-of-the-country states to which she flew round-trip weekly for months at a time. Alison had chosen pragmatism over the fantastical, and she had the savings account, airline mileage, and hotel points accrual to show for it. Lily and Alison had been dating for just over two years now. They were settled into a cozy and effortless routine, one divided amicably across separate apartments and social lives. Lily was an introvert forced into gregariousness by professional circumstances; Alison was an introvert encouraged to bear down on her seclusion by unyielding work hours. Together, they were a perfect pair.

"I suppose it can," Billie replied. "So, what did you think of tonight? Did you have a fun time?"

"Fun is sort of beside the point for me," said Lily. "These parties are a job."

"Only thirty-two and already so jaded."

"Did you have fun?"

"I did. That man next to me, Matthew Blake, gave me some interesting investment tips. Who knows, I might even have made a future profit off tonight."

That was the difference between Billie and her. Billie had potentially made a killing from this event, and all Lily had gotten was a stomachache and a car ride that could have taken her to New Jersey by the time it was over.

"Careful with Matthew," Lily told Billie. "I've heard he's on the hunt for wife number three."

One of Billie's eyebrows rose skyward. "Safe to say I'm not his type."

"And he's not the type of man to be halted by something as pedestrian as unreciprocated desire," said Lily.

"How do you know all this?"

"I spent more of my twenties at these parties than I did with my own friends. You'd be amazed how much you can learn by sitting around with your mouth shut."

"And do you write about all this in your stories?" Billie asked.

"Of course not," said Lily. "I'm not a gossip columnist."

"Maybe you should add some of these tidbits in. You might expand your readership."

"No, thanks," said Lily. "People won't tell you things if they think you're going to publish them online the next morning."

"It's a question of integrity, then?" asked Billie, her tone clearly mocking.

"Printing gossip is uncreative," said Lily. "It's low-hanging fruit."

"I think you should reconsider your position on that. With media the way it is now, you need to do whatever it takes if you want to succeed."

"Then maybe I'm in the wrong lane," said Lily. "Besides, I barely attend these things anymore. This was a special occasion."

Billie seemed on the verge of saying something, but the driver interrupted her to announce his arrival at her block. Lily noted the industrial building on a quiet Tribeca street.

"Nice," she remarked.

"Yes," said Billie. "I'm in the penthouse."

"Well, thank you so much for the ride," Lily said. "You saved me from the cold."

"I love saving other women," Billie declared. "Say, send me a link to your story on tonight. I'm curious to see how it turns out."

"Sure. Where should I send it?"

"I'll give you my number." Lily handed Billie her phone, and Billie entered her name and number. Lily texted Billie so she had her contact info, too.

"Don't worry, your quotes are off the record."

"Feel free to write about me all you want," Billie replied. "I don't turn down free press."

Lily watched as Billie exited the car and strode to her building's glass doors. She barely looked up as she typed in her security code, she was so buried in her phone and its long line of unread messages.

3

· · ·

NATURALLY, THE FIRST thing Lily did at work the next morning, after filing her party copy for the magazine's website, was plunge herself headlong into research on Billie Aston. She was familiar with Billie's general background, but it wasn't until she typed her name into a search engine that she realized exactly how prolific and, frankly, iconic this woman seemed to be.

Lily scrolled through an onslaught of sycophantic headlines and article abstracts. "Top Female Beauty Executive Makes Forbes Ones to Watch List for Sixth Year in a Row." "The Eyes Have It—and So Does Beauty Executive Billie Aston at the International Beauty Awards Gala." "Billie Aston on Professional Achievement, No-Makeup Makeup, and Her Epic Pantsuit Collection."

There was Billie front and center in a feature story in *Harper's Bazaar,* in which she waxed poetic about her Pilates routine, her daily water intake, and her obsession with matcha green tea flown in weekly from Japan. In the accompanying portrait, she wore an haute couture tuxedo, complete with a ruffled white button-down shirt and French cuffs. A business piece in *The Wall Street Journal* trailed Billie over a day at the office, during which time she approved color choices and names for a new lipstick line, counseled the marketing team on potential slogans for their next magazine insert, advised the product development team on the sheer finish of a tinted moisturizer, and somehow found time to mentor a group of visiting teenagers from an underprivileged neighborhood on how to impress potential interviewers when they applied to college. This woman operated on a different human plane.

One photo from the *Wall Street Journal* story was seared onto Lily's brain. Billie was seated at the head of a long conference table. Every chair at the table was filled with employees in blouses and cable-knit sweaters. The outer perimeter of the conference room was bursting, too. Men and women leaned against the wall and contorted their bodies to squeeze into nonexistent space. The room was as crowded as a rush-hour subway car. Unlike the constituents of that irritating scenario, this cohort shimmered with anticipation. Every pair of eyes in that photo was focused on Billie. A bomb could have exploded right outside the conference room and not a single person in that meeting would have turned away from her. Billie's mere presence commanded respect.

Lily couldn't elicit the consideration of an editorial assistant when she asked for help with some light fact-checking. Interns barely registered Lily when she wondered if they could do a quick and completely professional errand as opposed to the endless coffee runs other colleagues requested. It took Lily days to work up the courage to have a perfectly banal conversation with her executive editor, Theresa, about a change in her story or a concern she had about an upcoming interview. There was no galaxy in which Lily would ever reach the heights that Billie had scaled. And she wouldn't wish for that level of power, either. Some stars hang lower in the sky; they remain stars nonetheless.

Still, the effect of the previous night's proximity to Billie persisted. Lily couldn't understand why Billie had offered her a ride; why she had handed over her cell phone number; why she had, essentially, ordered

Lily to send her the Alzheimer's gala story. Billie couldn't possibly be so thirsty for coverage that she would deign to fraternize with a nobody like Lily on the off chance it would garner her some press. Surely a woman of Billie's stature had publicists on retainer to do that dirty work for her. Billie wasn't exactly hurting for attention.

Yes, in addition to the many corporate profiles rhapsodizing about her business acumen, there were also articles in Lily's research that wove a different tale, one in which Billie emerged as a "diva extraordinaire," in the *New York Post*'s words, with all the cattiness such a term insinuated. There was the rumor that she refused to sit next to people she didn't know on airplanes, even in the roomy quarters of first class. Whenever she traveled, her assistant had to buy the seat next to her, too; apparently, an early assistant of hers had been unaware of this transportation requirement and Billie had flown from Los Angeles to London, many years back, next to a man she described as "in desperate need of head-to-toe depilation and a full-body hygiene overhaul." The assistant in question left New York not too long after and never returned.

One tale that fascinated Lily and unsettled her in equal measure dated back to ten years ago. Billie was in her early forties and on the cusp of achieving her current position as chief creative officer. Everyone in beauty media said her promotion was a done deal. Another, small beauty start-up, focused on "natural" makeup and skin care, began to take off, particularly with younger customers who cared more about the origins of their cosmetics than their predecessors had. None of the companies in Billie's roster could compete with this sheer buzz factor. The start-up's founder was a yoga lover and a tree hugger and happened to be extremely photogenic; her dewy face was plastered across every magazine and blog. People murmured that the start-up founder was the next Billie.

In response, Billie reached out to her younger rumored doppelgänger. She courted her, heavily, over meals at East Village macrobiotic cafés and in the sweltering confines of infrared saunas. Billie convinced the start-up founder to sell her brand to Billie's company. The start-up founder was so seduced by Billie's pitch, she declined to negotiate a legal protection for her role. "It's so amazing when women support other women," she told journalists at the time. She sold her brand to Billie's company. And six months later, Billie toppled her from her leadership position and installed an accommodating and, yes, less photogenic executive in her place.

This image of Billie annihilating her competition with merciless cunning made Lily shiver. Of course, Billie had encouraged her to sprinkle gossip across her pieces for the sake of extra eyeballs. This was a woman who held zero compunctions about dismantling another, younger threat. She had the mentality of a general; no cost was too high when the prize was her professional survival. Then again, Lily knew that older women executives, heck, all women, period, were held to a different standard of achievement than men. Behavior that was de rigueur for men was deemed overly aggressive from women, who were supposed to be friendly and nurturing. Billie's slicing and dicing of her competition was likely the same action a man would have taken to little fanfare. The headlines decrying Billie's ruthlessness could simply be discomfort with woman leadership masquerading as character assassination.

After all, the detail that attracted the highest journalistic word counts, more than Billie's supposed take-no-prisoners attitude, was her prevailing conviction that she would never marry. Or have children. She had stated as much point-blank years ago, without any detailed defense. "Not for me," she told a reporter at the time. "And I don't believe I should have to justify that." Yes, one of the twisted side effects of progressivism was that a gay woman was no longer immune to the heteronormative pressure to launch a family.

If Billie didn't believe in marriage or children for herself, why had she asked Lily about her personal life during the car ride last night? Perhaps Billie assumed that she was singular, which she was, by most accounts, and that all other women were focused on these goals, that Lily would be on this path. Well, she wasn't, necessarily. Billie and her cohorts had been raised with the notion that marriage and child-rearing were a woman's sole purposes. Lily and her women friends had been fed a different, but still damaging, narrative: They weren't *allowed* to have it all, the "all" being a career and a family; they were *expected* to have it all. Anything less than simultaneous procreation and corporate advancement was a disappointment to all womankind. And Lily was struck by how rare it was to encounter another woman, a Billie, willing to admit—proud to admit—that she wanted something different from what was demanded of her.

Everything about Lily's interactions with Billie—the way Billie noticed her, then ignored her; the way she eyed Lily's borrowed dress; her reaction to Lily's job—made Lily dizzy with its opacity. It was not a bad dizziness. It was a dizziness that buzzed.

When a digital editor, Marc, emailed Lily a link to her Alzheimer's gala story, now live on the magazine's site, Lily did what she had been told to do, as always, and texted Billie the link, with a message.

Lily: As requested, here's the piece. Hope you like it. Thanks again for the ride home.

In the end, she had mentioned Billie but had not quoted her; none of Billie's sound bites made sense for her story anyway. Lily had also selected a photo of Billie with Annabelle and ensured that it ran prominently in the piece. Lily meant what she had texted, that she hoped Billie liked it. By the same measure, she never expected to hear from her again. Billie was busy, busier than Lily had ever been or would ever be. There was little chance she would bother to text Lily back.

4

· · ·

THE OFFICE WAS as cold and quiet as a morgue. That was the simile that crept into Lily's mind as she sat and typed at her desk at work, not that she had any familiarity with morgues. Though it was now a temperate April beyond the building's imposing glass façade, its interior spaces were frigid. Cold air wafted quietly but perceptibly from metal vents scattered across the walls. Many of the women workers—and the magazine staff was predominantly women—had blankets and shawls draped over the backs of their chairs, with which they regularly cloaked themselves against the arctic temperatures, and, it could be argued, against the chilliness of interactions with their colleagues. The magazine's physical environment was a manifestation of its operational ethos: effortless, coldhearted perfection. It functioned on fantasies, after all, the most pernicious of which was that coolness, in fashion, in demeanor, in platonic same-sex relations, was an ideal that everyone should strive for at the expense of their bodily and emotional well-being.

The cold didn't bother Lily as much as the quiet did. She owned a blanket, and she was so accustomed to wrapping herself in its thick expanse that it became a veritable appendage. She was happy for a frigid ecosystem that extended her an excuse to spend her workdays swaddled like a newborn child. The quiet, however, was disconcerting, mainly because of the point of contrast it provided between how her career had begun and where it currently stood. In the golden pre-digital time of Lily's early work years a decade prior, her office had been a site of chaotic cacophony. Bullpens bumped up against bullpens, packed with reporters yelling into phones, yelling at each other, yelling across each other, anything to get the story done. These days, people typed their aggression, passive or otherwise, into messenger apps and cell phones and emails. They did interviews over email, too, in part because their subjects and their subjects' public relations representatives wanted as much control as possible over the content of their stories. All this lent the office the unnerving silence, hissing air vents and humming computers aside, of a landscape in purgatorial calm before an inevitable apocalypse.

In this cold and nearly silent dystopia, Lily picked up the handset of her phone and dialed into an interview. She insisted on speaking by phone when possible. Her call was with the star of a new streaming show about high schoolers in a small Pennsylvania town that just so happened to be the epicenter of a cataclysmic extraterrestrial invasion. The actress was twenty-nine years old, but her character on the show was seventeen years old. Thus, the actress's PR person had already warned Lily not to ask any questions that might overemphasize the actress's real-life maturity and thereby alienate the teenage audience the show courted. Lily assumed the PR person would listen in on the call, something that journalists, not that Lily was a journalist, always pushed against but were often powerless to stop. She could only hope that the PR person, who had argued her case to Lily across the twenty-three emails and five phone calls it had taken to confirm this interview, would back off and allow the conversation to flow.

A beep on the phone conference system signaled that both the PR person and the actress were now on the call.

"Hi!" Lily said, careful to ensure her greeting bubbled with excitement, though to her mind, she sounded manic. Everyone in media spoke and wrote in a state of perpetual exclamation as a counterpoint to the industry's reputational snobbery.

"Hi!" said the actress, who, apparently, followed the same greeting protocol as Lily.

"I'm so excited to speak with you," Lily said, in case she hadn't established her point in her initial "Hi!"

"Me too!" said the actress.

"Great! Why don't you start by telling me what attracted you to this role?"

"I relished the opportunity to dive into these teenage years. And the alien invasion gives the show an urgency that is in keeping with the way adolescence functions in our society. It really is the most important time in a person's life."

"I see. And did you have to do any specific research to get into the mindset of your character, Betty?"

"I'm going to have to stop you there!" said the public relations person. "That feels like a leading question suggesting that my client had to research being a teenager."

Lily had made it a whole ninety seconds before the interruption, practically a record.

"By 'mindset' I was referring to Betty's responsibility to defeat the aliens and save the world from destruction, while juggling a full course load, not to her specific age."

"Okay . . . ," said the PR person. "Well, you should be more specific about what you're asking next time."

"I did," said the actress, who ignored her PR person's outburst. "I read nonfiction books about heroic personalities who have historically battled injustice. I think of Betty as an activist, advocating on behalf of the human race and, of course, teenagers. And I have a younger sister, and I took her and her friends out to lunch and asked them what it's like to be a teenager in today's world."

Lily paused to let the PR person reprimand her client for broaching a verboten topic. When she didn't interject, Lily took it as a sign that she could proceed.

"Were there any specific insights you gleaned from that conversation?"

"This is your final warning!" the PR person snapped. "Any more questions of this kind and I am going to end this call!"

"She brought up the conversation with her sister and her friends," Lily pushed back, as the actress, once again, stayed silent. "If she opens the door to that topic, I should be allowed to ask a follow-up. And if she doesn't want to answer, that's totally fine."

"I don't care if she says that she's twenty-nine and graduated from high school eleven years ago and just got engaged to her forty-year-old boyfriend, which is *off the record* even though she posted it on social media yesterday. You are not allowed to ask her anything about her age or being an adult or not being a teenager. Are we clear?"

"Yes," said Lily.

And she covered her mouth with the inside of her hand and squeezed her eyes shut, anything to keep herself from screaming.

To soothe the frustration of the PR person's bullying, Lily met Alison for dinner at a local sushi haunt on the Upper West Side. Partway through their meal, she felt her phone vibrate in her handbag, which was hooked over the back of her chair. She reached into her bag for her phone to check the notification. The message was from Billie.

Billie: Thanks for the story. Your writing is quite readable. Appreciate the photo op — but where's my lengthy sound bite? Surely you had enough material to work with.

Lily inhaled sharply.

"Who was that?" asked Alison.

"Billie Aston."

"Who is she?" Alison plucked a piece of salmon sashimi, effortlessly, from the shared platter between them, dipped it gently in a tray of soy sauce, and slipped it into her mouth. For a white, blond woman from Connecticut raised on tuna salad sandwiches and Sunday night steak, she was quite adept with a pair of chopsticks. "Could you pass the wasabi?"

"The beauty executive." Lily passed Alison the dish of wasabi and pulled up an online encyclopedia page devoted to Billie on her phone. She showed it to Alison. "I sat next to her at the Alzheimer's gala three weeks ago. Remember, I told you she gave me a ride home?"

"Right." Alison glanced at the screen, then back at the platter of food. "A powerhouse. Good-looking woman, too. Why did she text you? Do you mind if I take the last piece of yellowtail?"

"Go for it. She asked me to send her a link to my Alzheimer's story. And I did." Lily sipped from her mug of tea. "And she just texted thanks."

"Three weeks later?"

"She's super busy, I'm sure." The tea sent heat to Lily's face. She pushed up the sleeves of her sweater.

Alison watched. "You're warm? It's freezing in here."

"It's the tea."

"What did she say?"

"Thanked me for the story. Said she liked the photo we ran of her. Do you think it's weird if I text her right away?"

"Why would it be weird?"

Lily shifted her weight in her seat. She was still warm, so she drank from her glass of water. "I don't want to seem overeager. She's a good contact to have."

"How is she a good contact? You don't want to work in beauty." Alison placed her chopsticks down and leaned back in her chair. A piece of corn silk hair fell across her face and she brushed it behind her ear.

"No, but you never know. And she knows everyone. Maybe she could pass my name on to someone for a future job or something."

"So, text her back."

Lily typed out a reply.

Lily: I'm afraid I don't take editorial direction from my subjects. But glad you liked the story. Thanks for the compliment on my writing.

She placed her phone back down on the table and bit into a sliver of pickled ginger; it was sharp and bright in her mouth. The restaurant was hushed, with a sober Tuesday night crowd. Its austere white and tan décor had a silencing effect on its patrons.

"Do you want to go to that show in Brooklyn this weekend?"

"Sure."

"Maybe we could get drinks after at that new place in Greenpoint?"

Buzz buzz. Lily checked her phone.

Billie: Not even from me? That's too bad. I don't normally give out good advice for free.

Lily: Did you have more specific feedback to offer?

"Is that Billie again?"

"Yeah. She wants to give me editorial advice."

"Maybe you should take it. As you said, she's hooked up." Alison drained her water glass and smiled at Lily expectantly. "Should we get the check? Your place or mine?"

Buzz buzz.

Billie: About the story or something else?

"Yes. Yours."

Lily: I'll take whatever you have to offer.

ELLIPSES

. . .

THE FOLLOWING MORNING, Lily sat at her desk and typed away at a transcript for the interview with the forever-young twenty-nine-year-old actress. After the PR person's second interjection, things had avalanched downward—fast. The actress had brought up the fact that she was not a teenager approximately six more times over the course of the remaining eighteen minutes of the call. And Lily had, per the PR person's enraged dictate, declined to pursue any of these openings. The result was a conversation that sounded like it had taken place between an interviewee eager to cooperate with any and all queries and an interviewer who asked questions completely unrelated to the previous answers and who had, one could surmise, recently consumed a heavy dose of tranquilizers that rendered her incapable of linear thought. And, of course, the story based on the interview was due tomorrow.

Lily had become the go-to person on the features staff for last-minute stories. She reasoned that it was a compliment of sorts, a testament to her ability to write quickly and well on deadline. It was deeply frustrating, though, to watch other writers receive a luxurious two weeks to turn around four-hundred-word pieces, while she was extended a measly week on longer ones, or, in this case, five days for what the magazine's executive editor, Theresa, had deemed "so easy, you could write it in your sleep." Lily didn't believe that she had the leverage to push back. She was still too junior, she thought, to have a say in the circumstances of her workload. She earned very little; it would be easy to find a replacement for her if she became "difficult" to work with and therefore expendable. Lily's value to the magazine, to any workplace, was more than that of an obedient mule, happy to drag around the deadweight no one else wanted to touch. But, she reasoned, if she earned her keep, then she would have a stronger foundation for negotiations in the obscure future, whose arrival was always postponed by her self-effacement.

Lily continued to transcribe her interview. And as dread filled her throat upon consideration of how impossible it would be to transform this lobotomy of a conversation into an engaging story, she wished she had the courage to ignore the PR person's threats and write whatever she wanted. She wished she had some—not all—of the ruthless drive that she had witnessed in her research on Billie. A woman like Billie would never have caved to the PR person's interference. She would have yelled back and bulldozed her way toward the interview she deserved. She would have charmed the figurative pants off the twenty-nine-year-old actress until she had a document of perfectly extracted sound bites. And then she would have dished that feast of evidence into a colorful, smart piece.

Billie hadn't replied to Lily's acceptance of her feedback offer at the sushi restaurant. It was against text etiquette to probe Billie further when the burden of response lay in her hands. Desperation inspired an unexpected boldness in Lily, and she pecked at her phone's flat screen.

Lily: How would you handle a story where someone is blocking you from doing your job?

As Lily resumed her transcription, her brain began to spin. Billie likely wouldn't reply until after the deadline for Lily's story had passed. It had been a waste of her time and Billie's to bother her with such an inane question. Billie would read Lily's lame words and roll her dark eyes and toss her phone to the side. Internal footage of Billie's reaction played out for Lily in real time.

And yet, ten minutes later, buzz buzz went Lily's phone.

Billie: I need more details.

Lily: Story is on a twenty-nine-year-old actress playing a high school character.

Lily: PR person has ordered me not to mention this discrepancy.

Lily: But I can't write about the actress's prep for the role without this background.

Lily stared at her phone's screen for an interminable two minutes as she waited for Billie's reply.

Buzz buzz.

Billie: Why do you care what a PR person says?

Of course someone in Billie's position would assume she could behave however she wished, though she probably had people on retainer to do exactly what this PR person had done on Lily's call: intimidate others into submission.

Lily: Because she represents a lot of top actors. And if I piss her off, she'll retaliate by withholding future interviews from me.

Billie: And if you give in, she'll know that in the future she can make you do her bidding.

Billie: Don't you have power, too?

Billie: You can refuse to do stories on her clients.

Lily: It doesn't work that way. We need her clients more than she needs us.

Billie: Trust me. I know what I'm talking about.

Billie: It's what I wanted to tell you about your party story.

Billie: You need to express your opinion on what you experience.

Billie: Have a voice.

Lily considered a rebuttal. She wanted to tell Billie that her point of view was that *An Unforgettable Evening* was a ridiculous and problematic name for a gala raising funds for Alzheimer's. And that this oversight clearly demonstrated that the event's priority was not altruism, but the appearance of altruism as a justification for superficiality and status one-upmanship. And that furthermore, she didn't understand why these galas were necessary at all. Couldn't rich people just donate money to needy causes without the requirements of catering, a tuxedo, a string quartet, a five-piece band, copious amounts of alcohol, and a live auction of luxury goods? Lily couldn't write any of these opinions or raise any of these questions because, first off, her magazine wouldn't print them, and second, Theresa would accuse her of biting the hand that fed her, though it fed her very little, and jeopardizing the crucial relationships the magazine maintained with the corporate sponsors and cochairs of the event. Also, there was the minor issue that without these galas and the people who threw them, Lily's magazine would cease to exist. And Lily would be out of a job.

Lily: Okay.

Lily: I get what you're saying.

Lily: Thanks.

Billie: My pleasure.

Billie: I love to mentor young women.

Billie: It's a passion.

The eager face of the start-up founder, the young woman whom Billie had seduced into her fold only to exile her the second she lost her utility, flickered across Lily's mind. She swiped this image away, like it was an errant pop-up window on her phone's screen. Lily was not the start-up founder; she offered nothing of worth to a woman like Billie. Any transaction between them would be a one-way street that favored Lily.

Billie: Write your story.

Billie: Explain everything to your editor.

Billie: And put this PR person in her place.

Billie: Let me know how it goes.

Self-empowerment in Billie's words was so easy and risk-free. Lily never should have reached out to her. If she ignored her advice—her directive, actually—Billie would decide that Lily was a coward, a spineless hack who waved a white flag for bullies to stomp all over her. Surely, that would end this short-lived mentorship. And if Lily followed Billie's command and it exploded in Lily's face, as she was convinced it would, she would suffer professional consequences and Billie would continue to rise, unchanged. There would be no apology for having led her astray. The kind of woman who made her assistant book out spare seats on airplanes and sent them packing when they failed at this task was not someone who handed out mea culpas to anyone, least of all a random young woman to whom she owed nothing.

Lily twisted her fingers together in tense indecision. Maybe she should give Billie's idea a chance. She could at least write the story the way that she, Lily, wanted to and run it by Theresa. Leave the decision up to her executive editor, whose job it was to make these calls. She had no doubt that if things went south, though, Theresa would not only throw Lily under the bus, she would drive the vehicle herself at top speed.

Still, Lily had operated in this fog of resignation for so long. It had earned her nothing. She required a new methodology. Here was her chance. The full motivation behind Billie's interest eluded Lily, but their exchange bestowed on her the sense that she had been chosen, except for what, she couldn't say. All she knew was that she desired to learn more.

She wrote the story as she knew it should exist. It was in Theresa's queue by the end of that day. Lily included a note in the file that explained the exchange with the PR person so that Theresa had context.

Two days later, when Lily logged in to the editing software on her work computer, Theresa had sent her back the forever-young twenty-nine-year-old-actress story. There was a note from Theresa at the top of the piece: "Good job. We don't negotiate with terrorists. And I'll tell the terrorist that the next time I speak to her." Lily exhaled deeply. Her body seemed to lift a few inches out of her desk chair. It was without exaggeration the most supportive thing Theresa had said to her in years. For once, Lily didn't require her thick work blanket for comfort. And she had Billie to thank for this rare occasion for occupational satisfaction. Lily grabbed her phone from her bag.

Lily: I did what you said. And my editor loved the story and said she had my back. Thank you so much, Billie. For the great advice.

The story file was dotted with questions from Theresa about quotes and word choices, none of them divergent from the norm. Lily opened her transcription document to find the quotes in question. Buzz buzz.

Billie: Not surprised at all. Happy to have helped.

Billie: And you can call me B.

Billie: Like my friends do.

Lily thought she might float out of her seat altogether, out of the building, and into the stratosphere. Billie considered her a friend. Lily pulled up Billie's—B's—contact in her phone and changed its name to just "B." As in *boss*. Or *bigwig*. Or, yes, there was another, less flattering word that came to mind, too, but obviously that descriptor had no place here, especially not after B had bolstered Lily with such selflessness.

Her head a fluffy marshmallow, Lily placed her phone back on her desk. And she returned to the edit of her story.

5

· · ·

MAY ARRIVED AND the city was awash in bouquets of cotton candy. They formed cloud-shaped configurations across the landscape of every park and square. When a strong wind gusted, delicate petals danced through the streets and settled into pastel piles at crosswalks, in drainage systems, in the crevices of cobblestone slabs, like the sugar-bulked icing on cupcakes. Cherry blossoms and magnolias bloomed with such alacrity, one could be forgiven for thinking that this was how life was always supposed to look. New York was trapped in an endless wedding weekend, whose pink detritus never encountered the activities of a broom and dustpan—or of a divorce lawyer's inner sanctum.

For weeks following the newly dubbed B's pep talk, Lily's phone remained vibration-free, so far as her self-appointed mentor was concerned. Theresa assigned Lily a story on a ballet-inspired fitness class and its graceful founder and instructor, Julie Turner. After a decade-long career as a soloist at a top ballet company, Julie had experienced an epiphany of sorts at a dinner during the ballet company's annual spring gala. The donor who sat next to her had leered at her jutting clavicles and sinewy back and remarked that she would make a killing financially if she could find a way to "bottle her body" and sell it to all the ladies at the gala in question. Julie was exhausted by her stagnant advancement at the ballet company and the uninspiring roles she was generally asked to dance. It was time to capitalize on whatever allure she possessed.

Julie quit the ballet company and started to teach fitness classes for women with no formal dance training who wanted to look like ballerinas without the punishing rigor, athleticism, and talent that the profession required. Her sessions became a phenomenon, particularly among women who already boasted long and lean physiques that merely desired fine-tuning.

As research for her story, Lily planned to attend a group class one morning before work. Julie had opened a new Upper East Side studio. Uptown women provided an ideal crossover demographic of low body fat percentage and well-endowed balance sheets. And Julie was hosting a series of "friends and family" classes to break in the space. Lily generally preferred workouts where the end goal was sweaty exhaustion as opposed to dewdropped refinement. She approached exercise as a form of exorcism. The prospect of passing an hour first thing in the morning with a group of hungry women in leotards and tights and with no perceivable sweat glands held little appeal.

The night before the class, Lily headed to Alison's apartment, a sleek postwar place that straddled the border between the Upper West Side and Hell's Kitchen. Alison's consulting offices were in Midtown West; if the weather was temperate and she wasn't traveling for a client, Alison would often walk to work. It was the one moment in her day that wasn't assaulted by the slides and text boxes of her team's PowerPoint presentations. Where Lily's apartment had a sliver of a street view from the small window in her sleeping alcove, Alison's living room and bedroom both enjoyed sweeping vistas of the Hudson River. Lily's apartment was a mishmash of what could generously be called "vintage" furniture but was in reality a grouping of hand-me-downs from various family members. Alison loved modern seating and clean lines; her living room had a pale blue Italian sectional that resembled a high-end pool floatie, and her countertops and tables were all dove-gray granite accented with chrome. Her apartment, with its lack of clutter and freshly painted walls, evoked cleanliness; it luxuriated in blankness over accumulation. Lily's home looked like a theater set, with all its attendant tchotchkes and dashes of quirk. It was a place that took the phrase *lived in* quite literally.

On her walk from the subway to Alison's apartment, prickles began to stab at Lily's neck. A shift in the air on her skin suggested that someone was approaching from behind. Lily didn't need to glance over her shoulder to confirm the story her clenched stomach and iced veins already narrated. She had two choices. She could pick up the pace and hope to lose her tail. Or she could slow to a grinding halt, pretend to peek into a shop window, slip into the nearest grocery store or bodega as she had done so many times before. Like countless women in this city, Lily was accustomed to earmarking random businesses she passed on her regular routes, under the assumption that she would have to use them for this very purpose on an undisclosed future date. That time had arrived.

It was a few minutes past eight P.M. and the sidewalks were brisk with fellow commuters, so Lily stopped at a brightly lit supermarket window. She peered through the glass, as though mesmerized by a display of cartoonishly red apples. She could smell her own sweat waft up from the armpits of her bomber jacket. The man was about to pass her. His navy quilted arm was less than a foot away from brushing her left shoulder. He pulled over next to her and maintained two feet of space between them. The supermarket's garish lighting illuminated his pasty face. His cheeks were cherubic and he had some sandy brown strands, but what remained of his mane didn't look long for this world. He faced Lily now and stared at her unabashedly. She stepped back in alarm.

"I didn't mean to startle you," he said.

Out of the corner of her eye, Lily watched as the traffic light across Ninth Avenue flashed to Don't Walk. She figured she had maybe ninety seconds before she could make a quick dash to the other side of the avenue without the risk of a car accident.

"I saw you on the subway and . . . ," he continued.

"And you thought you'd follow me out of the station?" Lily shot back. Her indignation won out over her pragmatism.

"You're so exotic. Could I just walk with you for a couple of blocks?" The man's voice went up in pitch, like he was pleading.

Lily's breath was hot and tight in her throat. "Get the fuck away from me or I'll scream."

The man's face folded in on itself at her suggestion. "Really? And what are you going to tell people: that some guy came up to you on the street to tell you how sexy you are? You ungrateful cunt."

The man stalked away back in the direction of the subway.

Lily exhaled a sizzling release. She edged through the supermarket's open automatic door and stood in the produce section; the scent of bananas and oranges and lemons closed in on her. Lily remained there for minutes that passed like hours. She let the store's industrial-strength air-conditioning solidify her molten insides. Then she exited the supermarket and walked slowly toward Alison's apartment, as she glanced over her shoulder every few seconds to make sure the disgruntled man no longer followed her.

In the open kitchen that extended from her living room, Alison seared steaks for dinner as Lily was curled up tightly on one corner of the sectional, her dark hair in a messy ponytail. The smell of black pepper and browned fat drifted across the room. It enveloped Lily in a domestic comfort that she hoped might snuff out the lurking creep of the pasty-faced man. Here, within the walls of Alison's apartment, she was temporarily safe — safer. Lily hadn't wanted to ruin their evening by sharing with Alison the details of her fraught commute. At what age would the pasty-faced men of this world finally evaporate? What number of gray hairs or wrinkles would repel these men for good? Though of course, no amount of visible aging would change the so-called exoticism that drew their beady eyes and then bore their fury when disinterest confronted their desire. No relief would come so long as traces of otherness remained.

Julie, the former ballerina, had made a preemptive exit from her industry because of ageism, and here Lily sat, fantasizing about growing old as a partial salve for another type of ism. Julie's calling demanded the buoyancy of physical and aesthetic youth. And so, she had pivoted. There was no pivot available from the consequences of otherness. In a professional arena, though, Lily was not so different from Julie: She stared down her own impending obsolescence every day, in the faces of the twenty-something actresses she interviewed and at the hands of encroaching digitization. She was almost too old for a job that worshiped girlish femininity and she was never old enough to escape perpetual fetishizing. The former scenario was one she could attempt to remake.

B knew something about career longevity and the sacrifices it required. Her last piece of encouragement had ended so well. Lily wouldn't mind a second morsel from B's banquet of knowledge.

Lily: I'm doing a story on a former ballerina who was forced to pivot to fitness because her career stalled.

Lily: Makes me wonder if I should do the same.

Lily: Not fitness, I mean. But pivoting. Since I'm kind of stalled, too.

Lily pressed send, and instantly, consternation seized her. None of her messages were technically questions, which could dissuade B from texting back. And further, Lily worried that she had been too forthcoming about her own career concerns. B had offered herself as a mentor, not a therapist. Lily had strayed too far into potentially needy territory.

To distract herself, Lily switched on Alison's television and searched one of the streaming services for a show to watch.

"You should try that movie I texted you about last week, *Maiden Voyage*," Alison called out from the kitchen. "I thought it wasn't so bad."

"Such high praise," Lily replied as she clicked on *Maiden Voyage* nonetheless.

Lily and Alison were always on the lookout for films or shows about queer women couples. When possible, they tried to see these movies in a theater; this meant that in a good year, they spent fifty dollars each on a pair of films. Alison had a higher tolerance than Lily for the painful dialogue and borderline-offensive plot points that often characterized stories about queer women. This was the product of Alison's optimistic nature and general desperation for something, anything, that depicted a romantic relationship between women. The films that did generally involved either incredibly graphic and anatomically unsatisfying sex scenes or near-Victorian expressions of ardor that relied on long, meaningful stares and fingers that accidentally-on-purpose brushed against each other beneath tablecloths.

One woman—or both—was always in a preexisting, extremely committed relationship with a man, whom she would have to forsake to fully embrace her new queer love. Bonus points if she had children whom she would also have to abandon to fulfill her selfish true nature as a woman-loving deviant. The films generally ended when one of the two women changed her mind, as one does; left the city, country, or continent in which the story was set, forever and with no plans to return; or better yet, dropped dead, thereby rendering the question of ethical decision-making a moot point. Lily couldn't wait for the movie in which the two women were separated in the final moments not by conventional travel or pedestrian mortality, but by intergalactic realms: One woman would end up an extraterrestrial from a long-lost planet and would have to teleport back to her home before she disintegrated into dust.

According to the abstract blurb on the streaming service, *Maiden Voyage* was a queer twist on an iconic cruise ship love story, in which two women from different social classes, one wealthy and there with her fiancé, the other a stowaway, fall for each other on the high seas. Instead of a nude-model drawing scene, there was a musical instrument moment; the stowaway teaches the rich engaged woman how to play the flute. Lily's hopes for *Maiden Voyage* were not particularly exuberant, but she clicked on the movie anyway. Three minutes into her viewing, her phone buzzed.

B: Interesting story. But not sure I agree with your premise.

B: If the ballerina couldn't cut it anymore, that's on her. No one forced her to do anything.

B: Careers stall because the people behind them aren't pushing hard enough.

B was not a font of compassion, it seemed. Even she must have experienced a setback that was beyond the grip of her control.

Lily: Maybe it's not that she couldn't cut it, but that she was held to an unrealistic standard.

Lily: Or the demands of her medium changed.

Lily: If someone doesn't feel valued in their office, is that entirely their fault?

It was the meet-cute moment for the two women in *Maiden Voyage*, which in this movie was code for the beginning of the end. The stowaway woman borrowed some fancier clothes and snuck into a black-tie dinner. There, she spied the rich woman across the ballroom; she spent the rest of the meal on a quest to meet her. Buzz buzz.

B: Change is the only constant.

B: The ballerina should have accepted that sooner.

B: The same applies to you.

"Dinner's almost ready," Alison said. "Could you grab some plates?"

"Of course." Lily typed out a quick reply to B.

Lily: Maybe the company didn't value any other skills she had to offer.

Lily: And as for me, the system is pretty stacked.

Lily: Women are set up to fail. If we're too flexible and compliant, people take advantage. If we push back, we're labeled bitches. Or worse.

Lily: At a certain point, why bother?

Plates and forks and knives in hand, Lily set the table for dinner. For the meantime, the fate of the *Maiden Voyage* characters remained on pause.

· · ·

THE DAILY COMMUTE had barely begun when Lily left Alison's apartment the next morning to attend her dreaded ballet-not-ballet class. The studio was on the second floor of a town house on a side street in the upper sixties between Lexington and Park Avenues. Large windows welcomed in southern light, while the parquet floors shone with a recent application of polish. Julie had installed floor-to-ceiling mirrors and a ballet barre around the room's perimeter. Various white women of indeterminate ages lay strewn across the floor on rubber mats. They contorted their bony hips and legs into a range of discomforting positions. Julie sat with her back to the windows dressed in a tomato-red leotard and pinkish-white tights. Her flaxen hair hung down to her waist in long wisps.

Lily chose a spot near the back of the room and planted her phone next to her mat so she could type any notes as the class proceeded. Julie led the group through a warm-up of various gyrations and a round of wide-legged pliés, then told them to lie on the mat for a series of excruciating and endless leg lifts. Buzz buzz.

Lily reached across the mat and behind her for her phone.

B: You need a serious attitude shift.

Lily: What are you talking about?

"Okay, now we're moving on to clamshells. Everyone start by lying on their right hip, facing me, please," said Julie.

Buzz buzz.

B: When it comes to your career.

Lily: Okay, how?

"Thirty-nine, forty, forty-one . . . keep your hips squared off, no opening up, you'll feel it too much in the lower back."

Buzz buzz.

B: Stop blaming the system.

Some advice B gave.

Lily: The system is the problem.

Buzz buzz.

B: Individuals have power. Free will.

"Seventy-one, seventy-two . . . just a few more. Looking great, ladies."

Lily: Sure. That doesn't mean there is no collective responsibility.

Buzz buzz.

B: Life isn't fair. For women.

B: If you keep internalizing that unfairness, you'll never get ahead.

Lily: It's not just internal if other people are using it to minimize me.

B: You can't control other people. The only thing you can control is yourself.

Lily: Where does that leave me?

"Okay, time for the other side. Everyone flip over to your left hip. You should be facing away from me, toward the back of the room now."

Buzz buzz.

B: You're clearly sleepwalking through life.

B: You need to fight for what you want. No one is going to hand it to you.

B: If your career isn't where you want it to be, then that's your fault.

"Could the lady in the black tank top please put down her phone? This is supposed to be *you* time!"

Sleepwalking through life. All Lily's fault. The words jumped off her phone screen and slapped her in the face. She had no one to blame but herself. Her job, at which she churned out endless stories on bullshit deadlines dictated by those above her, that was on her. Not on a corporate office that sucked humans dry and then searched for more sustenance. Not on a magazine world that encouraged food-starved women to fight to the death to come out on top. Not on a larger culture that saw women without fertile eggs or children as devoid of purpose. No, Lily's dissatisfaction was a product of her emotional weakness and her bad attitude, according to B. And the solution was for Lily to become a carbon copy of B, a woman devoid of compassion for a struggling ballerina, a woman who had no problem excising a younger competitor like a cancerous tumor. Some mentor B was. Lily should cut off ties this instant. She could seek salvation somewhere else.

Lily looked to Julie for diversion. Julie lay on her back at the front of the room, her flaxen hair fanned out behind her on her mat, as she demonstrated an abdominal exercise that made her resemble a metal protractor. The muscles in Julie's arms and legs were rippling and alive. She performed these exercises with ease; the tilt of her mouth and the glaze in her eyes telegraphed her utter boredom. It was so evident that this woman's body was capable of far more than her own class demanded—and of far more than the larger world would let her demonstrate. And yet, the very thing her body had been trained to do, the art that it had devoted its life to perfecting, was out of reach. Forever. A pang echoed in Lily's stomach. It wasn't from the abdominal exertion.

Julie had dreamed of the highest echelons of artistry; now she was a fitness instructor for pampered Upper East Side women and could barely stay present in her own class. She couldn't have changed the inevitability of physical decline, but maybe her pivot could have been less disappointing. This was the eventuality from which B was trying to save Lily. Her words had been harsh, yes. B's bedside manner could use some refinement, not that she concerned herself with other people's feelings. The content, though, was there: Lily needed to decide her own fate before someone else did it for her. In delivering such a brutal, but otherwise warranted, message, B had expressed her care for Lily's future.

The class came to a merciful end and Lily shrugged on her jacket and laced up her sneakers. She couldn't approach Julie in her current state. They could meet over the phone and she would omit the fact that she had been the uncoordinated texting culprit who interrupted the class. Lily walked south down Lexington Avenue toward the closest subway station. A block away from the subway, she veered off onto a side street and leaned against an apartment building. Its rough brick façade provided hard reassurance. She pulled out her phone.

Lily: That is tough to hear.

Lily: But I get that your intentions are good.

She shoved her phone back in her bag and closed her eyes. Buzz buzz.

B: Change takes time.

B: Don't give up just yet.

The PR person's bullying hadn't earned Lily's defeat. She wouldn't concede her career so easily, either. She required patience — and power. Neither of those traits manifested instantaneously. Whatever advancement Lily stood to gain from her connection with B required time. B deserved more time.

Lily: I won't. I promise.

B: Good.

Lily: I don't surrender that easily.

6

...

A DECADE OUT from graduation, Lily and her close friends Marissa and Jordan were as existentially intertwined as they had been during their school years at the small New England college they had all attended. On a Friday evening in June, the three friends gathered for dinner at a sleek Mexican restaurant in SoHo.

Marissa had been in Lily's sophomore fall American literature class; they had bonded over their mutual love of coming-of-age stories and their shared disinterest in chauvinistic minimalism. Jordan had been a member of a *Hot in New York* viewing club that Lily had joined that same semester. The club had met once a month in the dowdy basement of a student dorm to screen and discuss episodes of *Hot in New York* as a stress-relief technique from the pressures of academics. *Hot in New York* was a show that followed four women protagonists navigating love, sex, and work. Jordan and Lily had watched the series on their own throughout middle school and high school. While they both took issue with various aspects of the show, its unrelenting whiteness and straightness, its insistence that grown women structure their lives around the romantic pursuit of men, for example, they also loved the glamour and genuine friendships at the heart of the storylines. And they refused to deny themselves these latter pleasures in protest of the show's systemic disappointments. Their relationship with the series, as with all art that appeals to but ignores entire populations, was complicated. That joint complication became the basis for a budding friendship.

One night during the reading week preceding fall semester finals, Lily had invited Marissa to a viewing night with the club as a break from studying. Marissa had sat in between Lily and Jordan, and by the end of the episodes, the three of them were inseparable.

On this June evening, the trio of friends sat at a table along the restaurant's glass-windowed façade. The cars and pedestrians of Lafayette Street whizzed along next to them. Sharp lime and sweet agave wafted by as servers carried dishes and clusters of margaritas to other tables. Plates of cauliflower tacos al pastor and freshly made guacamole lingered in front of them.

After college, they had all moved to New York—Lily back to New York—to pursue their careers. Marissa had worked for a couple of years, then moved away for law school. She was now permanently in New York, where she practiced corporate law, an ideal match for her reason-oriented brain—and her competitive streak, hidden beneath a placid exterior. For the past three years, Marissa had dated Luke, a fellow lawyer at another firm whom she had met in law school.

Jordan had jumped around from field to field through his early and mid-twenties before he settled on a job as a public relations coordinator at an art gallery in Chelsea. His work provided a dose of glamour via the gallery's show openings and their accompanying downtown guest lists, though, like Lily's profession, it came at the cost of financial and lifestyle security. Jordan was perennially single, mostly happily so, he claimed, but Lily suspected his declared contentment was at times a defense mechanism rather than a lived reality.

Marissa was in the middle of an anecdote about Luke's latest fitness adventure, a grueling twenty-mile trail run in upstate New York, when Lily's phone, facedown on the table, vibrated.

"Sorry," she said, and picked it up to scan the notification. It was a text message.

B: Had a window to check in. Haven't heard from you in a few weeks.

Lily flushed with the pleasure of being missed.

"Was that Alison?" asked Marissa. She sipped her tequila.

"No," said Lily.

"Then who was it?" asked Marissa, who leaned forward in her seat. "You're blushing."

"It's the mezcal," said Lily. "You know, Asian flush."

"Nice try," said Jordan. His arm brushed against Lily's as he reached for another tortilla chip.

"It's a new industry friend I made," said Lily. She shifted her position. The chair's wooden seat was suddenly harder than when she had first sat down. "She's been offering me professional advice. Over text."

"Who is she?" asked Jordan.

Lily explained to them who B was and how they had met at the Alzheimer's gala. How B had offered her a ride home. How B had asked Lily to send her a link to her story the next day and then had texted her feedback. And now she and B touched base every few weeks.

"That's so Mr. Bold of her!" said Jordan of B's town car maneuver, similar to one employed by a recurring and toxic male love interest in *Hot in New York*. "She even has the same first initial."

"What do you talk about in your texts?" asked Marissa, ever the lawyer.

"Mainly my struggles at work." Lily shrugged. "She gives me advice on what to do."

"On a Friday night?" asked Marissa.

"She's super busy. She can only text when she has a free window."

On more than one occasion, Lily had wondered about B's sustained interest. Lily's incentive was clear: to absorb as much of B's essence as possible, the better to manifest Lily's own next step, whatever that might be. But B was not a person with considerable spare time. In an interview B had done with *Women's Wear Daily* a few years back, she had described her daily meetings schedule as so intense, comprised of upwards of ten a day, that her assistant had to remind her to eat lunch by placing the meal in front of her midmeeting. It was curious that she would waste her meager leisure moments texting a random thirty-two-year-old woman.

B was also quoted in that same interview as declaring, "I still consider myself an outsider," on the topic of her corporate stature. This kind of faux self-effacement from those at the top of their field always rang disingenuous to Lily's ears, similar to when supermodels posted "awkward" photos of themselves from elementary school in which their alien-like beauty shone from every pore. Yes, B had forsaken family approval when she ventured into cosmetics after college. Yes, she was one of the few out queer women at the top of the corporate food chain, and in beauty, no less, an industry entrenched in conventionally straight feminine norms. But she was a leader now. She was power incarnate. Not to mention, a white beauty icon. That hardly constituted the marginalization that defined outsider status.

I'm probably nothing more than a charity case to her, Lily thought. A cognitive tax write-off. She swooped a lone chip across the chunky surface of the guacamole.

"I think I've heard of her. I read about her in *Forbes* or something," Marissa said. She searched for B in her phone's browser and pulled up a picture of her in a black tuxedo and silver snakeskin pumps, her lips a glossy tangerine. "Yeah, she's pretty iconic."

"Let me see," said Jordan. He glanced over Marissa's shoulder at her screen. "Yes, she looks like a boss. With a capital B."

"She's crazy successful," said Lily. "I honestly don't know why she's texting with me. I have nothing to offer."

A quick glance passed between Marissa and Jordan.

"Maybe she thinks you're attractive?" said Jordan.

"And young," added Marissa.

"No, that's crazy," said Lily. "She probably feels sorry for me."

"Mentors are very hot right now. Everyone wants one," said Jordan. "I heard the front desk woman at work the other day talking on the phone to a friend about how she needs a mentor so badly or she'll never have her own gallery by the time she's thirty."

"I had a mentor for a couple of years," said Marissa. "When I first started at my firm, they set all the newbies up with partners and did some big event where we had drinks together."

"Was it helpful?" asked Lily.

Marissa tucked her wavy hair behind her ears. "Not really. I had lunch with her maybe twice over the first six months. I called her once with a question about a client. And then I let it peter out. I felt like I couldn't trust her."

"Why?" asked Lily.

"That client I asked her about was this pretty difficult guy. Like, he wasn't very cooperative, but he earned the firm a lot of money. We billed so many hours to him. And I was careful not to complain about the client, but I did ask for suggestions on how to handle him. A week after my call with my mentor, I was in a meeting with a different partner and he goes, 'I hear you're having trouble with Dan. Maybe we should put someone else on him.'"

"Yikes," said Jordan. "Your mentor sold you out."

"Yeah, she definitely did. So, I told that partner, 'No, I'm good.' And he let me stay on with Dan. And it all worked out fine in the end. I figured out on my own how to navigate his mood swings."

"Have you worked with her since then?" asked Lily.

"No. We've never overlapped on a client. I'm pretty sure that's on purpose. I pass her in the hallway all the time. She never says hi or even acknowledges me. It's like I don't exist. The whole thing makes me sad. She's supersmart, was top of her class at Harvard Law, editor of the law review. I could have learned so much from her."

"I was going to say that I wished I had a mentor, too, but now I'm not so sure," said Jordan. "Seems like I'm better off alone."

"It's different for men," said Marissa.

"Yeah," said Lily. "You're not fighting for the same minuscule sliver of space."

"I'm sure my mentor—ex-mentor—had to trample every woman and man on her way to the top. She didn't have a choice. I just wish she could relax a little now that she's there. I'm not a threat."

"Maybe you are," said Jordan. "You killer."

Buzz buzz.

B: Tick tock, my window's almost up.

B: Cat got your tongue?

Lily switched her phone to silent mode, stuck it in her bag. She swallowed some mezcal. The smoky, peppery liquid left a pleasant burning sensation on the roof of her mouth.

"Careful there," warned Marissa. "Make sure she's really on your side."

"I will," said Lily. "Thanks."

•   •   •

THAT WEEKEND, LILY camped out at Alison's apartment. An early summer heat wave smothered the city in unexpected humidity; on Saturday evening, after Alison shut her work laptop down until Sunday night, the two women cooked dinner together in Alison's kitchen. As Lily sliced cherry tomatoes and tore pieces from a salty ball of mozzarella for their pasta meal, she watched Alison oversee a skillet on the stove. In a faded gray T-shirt and striped drawstring pants, her pale blond mane in a loose ponytail at her nape, Alison set a covered pot of water on high. She sprinkled a handful of salt into its contents. The furrow of concentration on her face as she taste-tested a strand of spaghetti cut a sharp line of affection through Lily's chest.

This was her person. Alison was everything she had dreamed she might find in another human being. This relationship they continued to build from the fragments of their respective emotional baggage was the biggest source of goodness in her life. She loved Alison the way one loves their favorite sweater, a garment of endless comfort and reassurance. One sinks their face into its knitted expanse and they are enveloped in the memories of snowy afternoon walks and mulled cider and sizzling radiators and nightcaps in the booths of sepia-toned bars as frigid winds gust outside. Alison was happiness and affection and compassion all woven into one startling human being.

About a year into dating, Alison had timidly broached the topic of cohabitation. Her lease on the apartment she had at the time was up. She had recently been promoted at work to a project leader role, whose bump in salary meant she could upgrade to a nicer place. And she and Lily were together four or five nights a week as it was. What did Lily think? Lily's heart began to thump and a pool of dread filled her stomach. She loved Alison; they both said as much to each other on a regular basis. Alison was allergic to nagging. Living beside her would be ease personified. But Lily couldn't move—her body or her possessions. This was her first serious relationship. To move in together would merge her distinct shape into Alison's; their individual silhouettes would cease to exist. That was the goal of cohabitation, to declare to the world that never again would someone be a person, singular, but instead they would be in perpetuity a couple, plural. It was commitment to a specific version of an ideal life. That untarnished stage in which solitude was all that a person needed for fulfillment would be gone for good.

Alison had grown up in an idyllic nuclear unit in Connecticut. She had played field hockey and lacrosse and spent summers with extended family amid the cottages and wildflowers and sandy dunes in Nantucket. Her parents had been married for decades. They belonged to a local country club. Alison had shown Lily a photo of the four of them, including Alison's younger sister, on her phone early into their relationship; in their preppy, primary-colored outfits, Alison's family looked like one of the stock images that come nestled into picture frames. To Alison, domesticity and the security of romantic partnership weren't ideals for which she should strive; they were expected facets of life.

It wasn't simply fear of codependency that held Lily back from this astonishingly mundane step in their relationship. For most of her life, Lily had fought against the encroachment of other people's beliefs about who she was or who she was supposed to be. At home, alone in her tiny apartment, where no one could stare at her through their lens of misperception, that was the only time when Lily could truly be. Living with another person, even a person she loved fiercely, didn't simply require that she share a space and reveal her flaws; it meant accepting that she could never escape someone else's version of who she was. Lily was not willing to relinquish herself to that all-consuming gaze. She told Alison she wasn't ready for them to move in together. And they drifted into their current configuration.

Lily smiled at Alison.

"What?" asked Alison, her pale cheeks flushed from the steaming pots on the stovetop.

"Nothing," said Lily. "The pasta smells amazing. Is it almost ready?"

The weekend, cuddled up with Alison, muted the buzz of Lily's phone. It was merely a device, after all, and so was everyone in it, B included. Reality beckoned. Though the ninety-degree temperatures discouraged all forms of movement, Lily tried to convince Alison to explore a new exhibit at an uptown museum.

"Their air-conditioning is exceptional," she explained.

"So is the air-conditioning in my apartment," Alison responded. "And it comes with the bonus of not requiring clothing."

Alison usually won these banal disagreements. Her consulting job required twelve-hour days and work on the weekends—and not the type of work that happened in a borrowed cocktail dress. Currently, she had escaped, for now, the drain of constant travel to Kansas, Indiana, North Dakota, etc. Alison was managing a team on a case for a New York–based telecommunications company. Local hours were still exhausting, and for Alison, the tidy, clean confines of her modern apartment were the best reward for her corporate consignment. She had chosen a career that paid a good salary so that she could build an adulthood similar to, albeit in Manhattan and sans offspring, what her parents had given her as a child. Her chief goal was existential reproduction. .

Instead of a museum outing, Lily and Alison watched reruns of old sitcoms and cooking competition shows between plates of scrambled eggs and leftover pasta grazing. They made microwave popcorn and dumped the hot, fluffy kernels into a glass mixing bowl. Sip after sip, they emptied a bottle of chilled red wine, in defiance of the humid weather. After they tired of the television and the snacks, they found pleasure in each other, burgundy-stained lips and smooth skin merging together in tangled bedsheets until they had enjoyed their fill.

When Alison had met Marissa and Jordan for the first time, she and Lily had arrived at the planned drinks outing straight from bed. It was four months into Lily and Alison's courtship and they were fifteen minutes late to the weathered Village bar Lily had selected for its unintimidating atmosphere and nondescript patrons. There was no laminated binder of whiskey selections, no seventeen riffs on a martini. It was scratched wooden banquettes, sticky cardboard coasters, and a soundtrack stuck somewhere between World War II and the invention of the birth control pill. Straightforward, that was how Lily wanted her ambience, and the exchange between her girlfriend and her best friends. Then Alison had shown up at Lily's apartment peony cheeked and aglow, and they had barely made it to Lily's bed. Fifteen minutes past their arranged meeting time, they walked into the bar, ruffled and pink, or in Lily's case, burnished coral.

"We were wondering where you were," Marissa said as she hugged Lily and gave Alison a discreet once-over.

"Did you come straight from the gym?" asked Jordan. He tried, unsuccessfully, to restrain a smirk.

"Sorry, sorry," Lily said, though she wasn't the least bit apologetic.

The heat from their pre-drinks activities remained on Lily and Alison as they sat, bare legs touching, arms and hands intertwined, on one side of the banquette. The bar was temperate, not cold, and it smelled like late nights and poor decisions. Its one concession to solid food was bowls of complimentary semi-stale peanuts. Jordan ordered a round of double whiskies with glasses of ice on the side.

"You're from Connecticut?" Jordan asked Alison.

"Yes."

"Whereabouts?" asked Marissa.

"Greenwich."

Lily squeezed Alison's warm, soft hand in encouragement.

"Good luck getting this one up there," said Jordan with a head tilt at Lily.

"We're going next week," said Lily.

"Are you getting some dainty pastels for the occasion?" Jordan asked Lily.

"Why? It's not like you have any you can loan me."

"Actually, I have an old baby-pink blazer with mint-green piping. An ill-advised purchase from college, back before I had taste. I can't tell you the last time it was laundered, so that's at your own risk."

Marissa watched Lily and Jordan's repartee with amusement, while Alison rubbed a salty peanut back and forth between two fingers. Jordan turned to Marissa to discuss the latest painter at his gallery and Lily squeezed Alison's leg.

"Hey," she whispered.

Alison turned her gray-green eyes on Lily. In her crisp white T-shirt, her blond hair fluffy and buttery, Alison was transcendent.

"Is it going okay?" Alison whispered back.

"Of course," said Lily. "How could it not be?"

"You don't have to come next weekend if you don't want to."

Again, Lily applied pressure to Alison's smooth leg. "Of course I want to come. I can't wait to meet your family. We were just kidding about pastel clothing. Jordan loves Greenwich. There are some great galleries there. He'll probably ask to come, too."

Alison leaned closer to Lily. "Your cheeks are still flushed."

"Are they?"

"Yes." Alison smiled. "I think we should have a sequel when we get back."

Now Lily shifted closer. "Okay."

"Hey, you two," said Marissa. "We're still here."

"Sorry," said Lily. She kept her hand on Alison's thigh and turned back to her friends. "What did I miss?"

7

· · ·

A STALWART FEATURE of Lily's job was the interviews she did for the magazine's "Up Next" column. Every month, the staff selected one young woman to photograph and profile. The subject was always pretty and thin and had an intriguing creative project and/or a noteworthy lineage; the latter happily stood in for the first few determinants in the always equitable world of glossies. Lily wasn't sure how or why she had been deemed the person to write this column month to month—perhaps her part-time, occupational forays into New York society were the culprit. She had no major objections to the assignment. The women she interviewed were generally excited to have been chosen for this honor, which made them compliant interviewees. Every so often, Lily wondered about the effect that cycling through fresh young women every month had on her experience of time. After years of these short profiles, her subjects were an attractive but interchangeable blur. Lily might reach fifty without knowing it and glance up from her computer, only to realize she had spent most of her adult life trapped in the heads of wealthy, comely twenty-something women, with no sense of what real womanhood, and its accompanying struggles, actually looked like.

This month, a twenty-three-year-old art school dropout demanded Lily's focus. The art school dropout had amassed two hundred thousand followers on a social media photo-sharing app with images and videos of herself drawing caricatures of her model friends. She happened to be an occasional model herself. As Lily typed away at a draft of the story, Theresa approached her desk.

"How'd the interview go?" she asked.

Lily removed her headphones. "It was fine. She didn't have a ton to say, but I'll make it work."

"Good. Listen, we're adding a last-minute story to the issue and I want you to take it. It's a first-person beauty piece on lipsticks." Theresa narrowed her eyes. She was one of those people who hated cosmetics, as they only enhanced the attractiveness of the average woman. White and wiry in the manner of a lifelong athlete who was perennially on a restrictive diet, Theresa resented the idea that physical appeal was for sale. She saw it as a matter of absolutes. In her world, one was either a supermodel, with sharply honed cheek and hip bones, or one was a woman, with jiggly thighs and a soft midsection, and should remain indoors, out of sight. Beauty wasn't a democratic commodity that could be purchased by anyone with enough cash and motivation. It was an extremely rare luxury, whose possession was for the chosen few at the exclusion of everyone else. "Go liaise with Lindsay. She'll give you the products and any press releases. But basically, it's eight hundred words. And I need it by next Tuesday."

"Okay, got it."

Beauty stories were not Lily's normal beat. But they provided unexpected opportunities for sociological exploration, as beauty was a rather loaded topic for any contemporary woman with an ounce of cultural awareness. So, Lily was enthused about the assignment, deadline notwithstanding. She made her way to Lindsay's desk, which, being the home of a senior beauty editor, was generally covered in an array of creams, lotions, and perfume bottles that wouldn't hit store shelves for months.

An olive-skinned brunette who was slim to the point of ephemeral, Lindsay explained to Lily that the story was a roundup of the best red lipsticks for fall from some of the top beauty companies. Many of the lipsticks boasted technologically advanced formulations that promised anti-feathering, long-wear color, and boosts of hydration. One lipstick, cheekily called Lipjection, claimed it could increase one's lip poutiness by 50 percent.

"It irritates your lips with cayenne, causing them to swell temporarily," explained Lindsay.

"Jesus," said Lily. "Is that safe?"

"So long as you don't have a cayenne allergy it is," said Lindsay.

Red-painted mouths had been all over the fall runway collections, shown in February and March of the current year. Lily was asked to test-drive the shades, Cherry Pie, You've Got the Beet, Heart on a Sleeve, etc., at any events she could scrounge up and write about the experience.

"Have fun!" Lindsay trilled.

The assignment held a certain irony for Lily because red lipstick was one of the few cosmetic products in which she had never dabbled. Timidity was partially responsible. Lily opted for a minimal touch when it came to her daily look. The goal was to look nice enough to shield her from negative glances, but not so pretty as to elicit unwanted interest. Red lipstick was the opposite of subtlety. The lightest application screamed its intentions.

There was a deeper layer to Lily's reticence, too. There was the fact that red, in general, was a stereotypical Asian color. And there was the additional fact of racial fetishizing. While red lipstick on a white woman could denote classic beauty, in the mold of a 1960s movie star or a 1990s supermodel, red lipstick on an Asian or other nonwhite woman could add fire to an already flammable situation of hypersexualization.

And Lily had enough to deal with in that department; she didn't need to feed things further with some clichéd Dragon Lady maquillage. It was hard not to wonder if part of the reason she had received this assignment in the first place was, however unconsciously, because of her ethnicity, not that she would have dared raise the possibility with Theresa.

Lily hardly expected B to grasp this element of her concern; B was whiteness personified. She imagined, though, that as a woman of an older generation, B had at some point confronted a handout over which she was conflicted. And she wondered how B had justified her decision-making.

Lily: Got a new assignment at work.

Lily: It dovetails with your area of expertise.

Lily: But I think I got the story for a bogus reason.

Lily: What do you do in these situations?

B's reply was swift. Lily's phone had hardly been on her desk for five minutes before it buzz-buzzed.

B: What area of expertise is that? I have so many.

B: I've never received something I didn't deserve.

B: Why do you think you got the story?

Of course B wouldn't question the steadiness of the rungs on her corporate ladder. Every step she took was confident and unapologetic. She had probably never encountered the insecurity that afflicts much of the larger population.

Lily: I think it may have something to do with my identity.

Caution nibbled at Lily's fingers. She didn't want to open this door too far for fear that B would say something off that would color their future conversation. Buzz buzz.

B: I see.

B: Well, your identity isn't going anywhere.

B: Seize any opportunity you can. And make the most of it.

B: That's my advice. Take it or leave it.

B: But as always, I suggest you take it.

And that was exactly what Lily did.

Over the next week, she frolicked at hastily arranged cocktail meet-ups and dinners, in the dead of July, with various public relations directors and third-tier socialites, the better to workshop a panoply of crimson pouts. She was struck by the power embedded in something as decorative as a swipe of lipstick. She was more self-conscious, yes, more aware of her presence in a room. But a layer of liberty hovered beneath that bold slash of red. It was a declaration of one's intent to be seen and, therefore, a refusal to hide in the quiet, dark recesses of social interactions. It was defiant: I will not be silenced. I will not be diminished. I will not disappear.

True, this was a lot of significance to heap on an amalgam of beeswax, oils, and dyes. Lily finished writing her story in time for the deadline and sent it to Theresa for editing. In her text, Lily dutifully recorded her experiences with the various lipsticks, but she also included some more personal feelings around the topic of makeup and stereotypes. She recognized that Theresa probably hadn't envisioned her beauty roundup as a hybrid think piece. And this was the first time Lily had broached the topic of identity—her identity—in the context of a story. She wondered if she had invested the assignment with more heft than its flimsy conceit could withstand. Lily had to dig for meaning wherever she could, though. And B had instructed her to jump on the opportunity at hand.

Three days after Lily submitted her copy, Theresa called her into her office to discuss the edits. As Lily grabbed a pen and notepad, her phone buzz-buzzed on her desk.

B: I have a few minutes free.

B: How did the story go?

Lily: Fine. Sorry. My editor's about to give me changes.

B: Good luck.

Theresa's windowless office was comprised of an anonymous desk, some built-in bookshelves, a couple of uncomfortable desk chairs, and a sliding glass door. Lily lowered herself into one of the chairs.

"I think you did a nice enough job," said Theresa. She made a point to follow the editorial dictum that one should always lead with the positives before they unloaded the harsh critiques. "It needs some cutting. The graf about red lipstick and Asian stereotypes: You need to lose that. It's a bit distracting."

"Distracting?"

"Yes. It distracts from the main thrust of the piece, which is about red lipstick as empowerment. How can it be empowering if it's also a stereotype?"

"Well, can't something be both? The whole point I was trying to make was that I found unexpected power in something I had avoided because it was a stereotype. It's a complicated relationship."

"Yes, exactly. I think it's a bit too complicated for this story, for our readers."

"I think you're underestimating our readers."

"Excuse me?"

"Our readers are capable of understanding complication. You might even have some readers who have experienced it themselves."

Theresa's eyes narrowed just as they had when she first assigned Lily the story. "As executive editor of this magazine, I know our readership better than you do. Make the changes. Then send me back the story."

"Okay."

"But that's not the only reason I asked you in here. We were going to use an archival image as art for the story, you know, like a tastefully erotic sixties portrait or something, along with product silos. But after reading your piece, I think it might be nice to run an image of you wearing red lipstick."

Theresa beamed. She was convinced she had played her trump card. There wasn't a young woman on the planet who would turn down the offer to have her picture in a magazine. Certainly, Lily's ego wasn't above such ministrations. She couldn't help but observe the disparity here: Her writing on Asian stereotypes was a distraction; a photograph of her exploiting said stereotype was not.

B wouldn't accept this obvious bribe for her cooperation. And neither would Lily. She couldn't control the exact opportunity, but she could negotiate its terms.

"Okay," said Lily. She inched forward to relieve the pressure on her leg. "But not my full face. Just my lips."

Theresa cocked her head in surprise. "Oh. Okay."

"Okay."

Back at her desk, Lily's phone went buzz buzz.

B: So.

B: Don't leave me hanging. How did it go?

Lily: Okay.

Lily: She didn't really get what I was trying to do. But I guess we sort of compromised.

Buzz buzz.

Alison: We still on for dinner later?

Lily: Definitely.

In the lipstick story's file on her computer, Lily scrolled down to the paragraph where she mentioned the reasons why red lipstick might be a more loaded makeup item for an Asian woman versus a white one.

Buzz buzz.

B: Did you fight for your position?

Lily released a sigh of exasperation.

Lily: I tried to push back.

Lily: I didn't get exactly what I wanted. But I got a concession.

Buzz buzz.

Alison: Can't wait.

On her computer screen, Lily highlighted the paragraph in question, clicked delete, and began to type a smoothing transition sentence.

Lily: Me neither.

Buzz buzz.

B: Something is better than nothing.

B: Good girl.

B: I knew I chose well.

A glow of praise fell upon Lily, even if it came couched in diminutive terms.

Over the next hour, Lily finished her editor-mandated story changes. She reviewed the revisions one last time before sending them back to Theresa for her blessing.

"Do you have a second?"

It was the beauty editor, Lindsay, who stood in front of Lily's desk, her eyes dark and serious.

"Of course. What's up?"

Lindsay's gaze flittered down Lily's chair and then back up; she seemed reluctant to hold eye contact.

"Did something happen with your lipstick story?"

In her role, Lindsay focused on the selection of products for the magazine's beauty pages and the maintenance of beauty advertiser relationships; she didn't edit any pieces, including Lily's, despite what her title might suggest.

"Theresa had some edits. And I'm making them now. Why?"

"Susan claims Theresa told her you were being 'antagonistic and militant' about her changes. And that you had some agenda. Of course, she came running straight to me."

Susan was the magazine's features editor. She was two steps beneath Theresa on the masthead, which meant she primarily edited stories, occasionally Lily's, and wrote longer pieces herself. Susan was that person in any office who through the sheer force of her unpleasantness managed to avoid all tiresome assignments. If anyone on the staff could be deemed "antagonistic," it would be Susan. But, of course, not all women were punished to the same degree for expressing a "difficult" opinion.

Lindsay narrowed her eyes and continued, "Anyway, I'm sure it isn't true. And Susan is probably making it up. But I thought you should know. And be aware."

A singeing flame rose up the back of Lily's throat and she swallowed hard to force it down. When she had begun her current job at the magazine, a few acquaintances had warned her of Susan's rough temperament. "She's just awful," one person had confided. "Her bark and bite are equally terrible." Lily had shrugged off these cautionary asides. She preferred to make up her own mind about people.

At first, Lily went out of her way to be friendly toward Susan. But then Lindsay, a digital editor, and a fashion market assistant had approached Lily separately with different anecdotes about Susan maligning Lily and her work behind Lily's back. Though Lily was skeptical of these individual sources' motives—they seemed a little too eager to tell Lily how awfully Susan had disparaged her—taken collectively, the data was impossible to ignore. And these days, Susan didn't simply dis Lily covertly; she also did it to her face.

Lily's immediate reaction to this information on Susan was hurt. Though she had never expected to forge a friendship with Susan, Lily had hoped for a consolation prize of approval. Susan was a seasoned and smart editor; her respect for Lily's work, however begrudging, could have given Lily a minor support system in her workplace. From hurt, Lily swiftly moved on to relief, tinged with the embarrassment of having been naïve enough to believe she could break through a barrier where no one else had succeeded. Susan was exactly as awful as Lily had been warned. And Lily had specific evidence, souvenirs she had collected on her own roundabout journey to the same conclusion that everyone else had reached more directly. Hence, Lily was liberated from caring about Susan's opinion. Betrayal has its perks.

This time, Lindsay appeared genuinely uncomfortable to pass on this latest Susan tidbit, which may or may not have originated with Theresa. Lily wanted to tell Lindsay that there was no need to share future details of Susan's trash talk. That Lily already operated under the assumption that Susan said terrible things about her regularly. And there was little Lily could do to stop it. But Lily smiled at Lindsay.

"Thanks. I really appreciate you telling me."

* * *

THE ISSUE FEATURING Lily's red-lipsticks piece debuted a few weeks later and the magazine posted the story to their site. A few of the lipsticks Lily had worn belonged to brands that B oversaw in her chief creative officer capacity, a fact that had not been lost on Lily. It had thrilled her to think that she and B were linked in the print magazine, too, and not only in the confines of her phone. B had urged on Lily's self-assertion with Theresa. And Lily's writing had merged with something of B's creation.

At the thought that B's ideas and decisions had influenced something she put on her body, heat caressed Lily's face. It was as though B had touched her by proxy. How did it feel to have the power to decide what millions of women applied to their skin every day before they presented themselves to the world? It must be heady and heart pounding, like black coffee on an empty stomach.

While Lily was tempted to send B the link to her lipstick story, as she had the night after the Alzheimer's gala, she decided to give B a few days, to test how deep her investment in her story and in Lily really ran. It was the height of maturity. If she heard nothing, she would eventually text B the link.

Days after Lily's piece was published, she was out to dinner with Alison at a Mediterranean restaurant on the Upper West Side when her phone pinged with a notification. It was an email from the magazine's editor in chief, Timothy Jacobs, on her work account. In her more than five years at the magazine, Timothy had never emailed her and had exchanged hardly any words with her in person. The message was characteristically short.

"I sat next to Billie Aston earlier tonight at the lymphoma gala. She went on and on about your lipstick story, how much she loved it. She particularly liked the photo of your lips. Well done. And with an advertiser, no less."

Lily inhaled sharply.

"What is it?" Alison asked. She placed her fork down on her plate. In the warmth from the food and the restaurant's open kitchen, she unbuttoned the cuffs of her white shirt and rolled the sleeves up to her elbows.

"It's an email from my editor in chief."

B had not only read her story, she had praised it to Lily's boss.

"All okay?"

"That lipstick story I wrote. It went over well with an advertiser. My editor in chief was congratulating me."

"Oh wow. That's so great, babe."

"He's never emailed me before. Since I started working there."

"I know, this is so good. You're on his radar now. I'd toast, but we're drinking seltzer."

"B was the advertiser who gushed about my story to him. At a dinner tonight."

"B?"

"Sorry, Billie. You know, from that gala?"

"Right." Alison dabbed at her rosy lips with her paper napkin and sipped her seltzer. "That's nice of her."

"Yeah."

It was the stuff of Lily's most self-involved daydreams. This went beyond polite tolerance of a random stranger. Lily basked in this moment of unadulterated pride for a few minutes before she texted B her gratitude. She didn't want anyone's reaction, including B's, to dim the brightness that beamed from her every cell. But really, no one else's opinion mattered when someone of B's renown had marked her as unequivocally worthy.

"I'm going to text her and thank her."

Alison picked her fork up and nudged the remains of her grilled chicken.

Lily: I can't believe you told my boss that you loved my story!

"You know, I was thinking about how Theresa asked you to take out the stuff about red lipstick being an Asian stereotype."

Buzz buzz.

B: You're welcome.

"Sorry, one sec."

Lily: How did you know those were my lips? We didn't ID them in the caption.

"What about it?"

"Maybe she didn't realize you were Asian until you wrote it into the story. And she found it awkward and confusing. And that was part of it."

Buzz buzz.

B: Of course I knew they were yours. You have very distinctive lips.

"Wait, what?"

Lily: Oh, well, thanks.

Lily: Maybe we could have coffee sometime.

"Are you listening to me? Who are you texting?"

"Yes, sorry. You think Theresa didn't know I was Asian? Seriously?"

"It's possible."

Buzz buzz.

B: Totally.

Lily: To talk more about career trajectory.

"Sorry, what makes you think that?"

"Because I didn't know you were Asian when we first started dating."

Buzz buzz.

B: Sure. Let's do it.

Lily silenced her phone and set it facedown on the table.

"What do you mean you didn't know I was Asian?"

"You're only half-Asian."

"Thanks for the reminder."

"And you looked white in your photo online."

"What?"

"And then on our first date, I wasn't sure until you mentioned that your mother was from Shanghai."

"Wow."

"It's not a bad thing."

"Is it a good thing?"

"No! I mean, it's not bad or good. It's just what happened."

Lily drained her glass of seltzer. "I'm pretty sure you're the only person who's ever thought I was white."

Alison fingered her glass. "I don't think I am. But it doesn't matter. I'm trying to say that something that seems obvious to you might not be so visible to others."

"Meaning to white people."

"I guess."

A server came by to clear their bowls and plates. Lily and Alison split the check and then stepped out onto Amsterdam Avenue.

"Your place?"

"Sure."

The women walked in the direction of Lily's apartment. Lily's body had frozen solid. To contain multitudes in a world that had decided she could only be one thing was a scenario Lily knew very well. To have her potential life partner see only one thing and not the multitudes, this was new. To have her look at Lily and see only the thing that made her more palatable, like white sugar to help that medicine go down, that was a revelation.

The frost in Lily's chest wasn't disbelief or sorrow. It was guilt. Because Lily's confusion quickly gave way to something alarming. She had experienced a pang of pleasure at Alison's admission. Lily was proud, momentarily, that she had fooled Alison without trying or truly wanting to. Lily was a chameleon who could be one thing to one person and an entirely separate thing to another. No one would turn down a gift like that. Yet, her prize was not without a steep cost. She knew that the enjoyment of such trickery, however minute, was wrong. It was shameful. And there was this, too: Next to the person with whom she might be closest in the world, she was still unknowable and alone. And who would want to unwrap that present?

8

. . .

THE END OF the sticky summer lumbered along. The email from Timothy Jacobs manifested no noticeable rewards for Lily at work. Another way of saying this was that Lily had failed to translate her editor in chief's brief compliment into something concrete. The day after Timothy Jacobs's email, Lily had arrived at the office high on expectations. He must have forwarded his note along to Theresa with the directive to assign Lily more, meatier stories. Or if not a forwarded note, he must have mentioned it to her in passing. But Theresa said nothing to Lily. And Lily declined to share the editor in chief's email with Theresa. To do so felt like a boast or a violation of the editor in chief's privacy, neither of which was ideal. The hours of that expectation-ridden day trickled by, and eventually Lily departed the office deflated, like the email had never existed.

When it came to B, Lily had also struck out. She had tried, subtly, to pin B down to an in-person meeting. On each occasion, a phone call, a shower, a prior engagement, reared its head and cut their text conversation conveniently short. After three tries, Lily gave up. The odd thing was that B never directly rejected Lily's invitation for coffee. She bobbed and weaved where a simple "I'm too busy" would have sufficed. B did not have a history of confrontation avoidance. Lily couldn't puzzle out why this was a moment when B selected coyness. All Lily knew was that the potential buried in B's praise and in her editor in chief's email had fizzled. And somehow, it was entirely Lily's fault.

One afternoon in late August, Lily texted Alison a link to a social media page for her latest "Up Next" interviewee.

Lily: T minus twenty minutes.

This month's column subject was a social media star named Katrina Smith. She was twenty-four years old, originally from Charleston, South Carolina. She had recently transitioned from a small-town model to a full-time influencer with six hundred thousand followers and a slew of contracts with French and Italian luxury houses. The recipe for her success was distilled in her milky complexion, whose pallor she maintained by fastidiously blocking out the sun with various over-the-top accessories. She posted selfies of these eccentric ensembles and the images had garnered increased traction, more so than anything she shot for athleisure websites. If one typed "Katrina Smith street style" into a search engine, as Lily had in the course of her probing research, they would be gifted a bounty of paparazzi images of her strolls through Tribeca, the West Village, and SoHo, where she now owned an apartment. She always carried a rotating array of parasols, whose varieties ranged from crocheted confections that wouldn't have been out of place in a 1930s musical to dark gothic designs that lent her the appearance of a Victorian widow in a mourning processional.

The latest installment of Katrina's success story was a capsule collection of parasols with a fourth-generation master umbrella craftsman in Bath, England, whose work was beloved by British royalty. She had also agreed to share her famous epidermis with a mass cosmetics company, reportedly for their forthcoming sunscreen campaign. And the crowning touch to her burgeoning empire was slated for release later this fall: a memoir chronicling her rise from unknown ingénue to solar queen of influencers. It was titled, appropriately, *The Sun Always Rises: A Tale of SPF Success.*

Katrina had rescheduled her interview time and date with Lily five times via her aggressively exuberant publicist, who offered the unapologetic "You should see her schedule!" with each cancellation. It was ten minutes past the hour for their call and Lily steeled herself for another change in plans.

"Sorry I'm late!" came the breathless voice on the other end of the phone when Katrina finally rang.

"That's okay. I know how busy you are. Tell me about your parasol collection. What was the inspiration for the design?"

"The parasol is an underutilized weapon in the war against premature aging. I wanted to make it fun and fashion-forward to encourage people to carry one."

"The price range for the parasols is $1,595 to $5,655. Who do you see as your target customer?"

Buzz buzz went Lily's phone on her desk.

Alison: Omg.

"Yes, well, it is a *capsule* collection. And with all the hand stitching, heavy silk and cashmere embroidery, and crystal embellishments, they're very well priced. I think they're for women like me, who want something special that also prevents wrinkles."

Lily: In the middle of the interview.

Lily: She's dropping a line of four-figure parasols.

Lily: Some covered in crystals.

"I'm not sure crystals are the first thing that come to mind on the subject of sun protection, but I see. Speaking of which, tell me about your upcoming sunscreen campaign. How did that come about?"

"I'm a spokesperson, not a model, to be clear. I was looking for my first major beauty outing. And it was the perfect match with my deep modeling heritage and my intense commitment to sun protection."

"Right."

"And they understood that I would help them spread their SPF messaging to a younger generation."

Buzz buzz.

Alison: Are crystals weatherproof?

Lily: Apparently.

Lily: She's also the face of militant sun protection.

Lily: Aka obsessive pallor.

"Where do you think your zeal for sun protection comes from?"

Lily's ear throbbed from the pressure of the plastic handset, sandwiched between her shoulder and face, which was sweaty from its prolonged contact with the mouthpiece.

"My mother always slathered me in sunblock as a kid. She used that intense zinc oxide stuff. I looked like I had face paint on every time we went to the beach. I burn super easily."

"I bet. But you could probably avoid a sunburn in New York City by wearing sunscreen and a hat. Where did the parasols come from?"

Buzz buzz.

Alison: She is super pale.

Alison: She probably burns every time she leaves the house.

"Obviously, they're a chic accessory. And they provide that extra level of protection. They also make a statement. Our society is so obsessed with tanned skin as a signifier of health. When, in fact, it's an expression of sun damage. The parasols really drive home my desire to counter that belief. That damage equals health."

Lily: She's white, not a literal vampire.

Lily: She hasn't mentioned cancer prevention or a family history of cancer.

Lily: Which would make her concern more understandable.

Lily: I think the parasol is performative, not medically necessary.

"I mean, yes, of course, the skin producing extra melanin can be a response to UV exposure. But do you ever worry that equating pallor with health is just as dangerous as encouraging people to have unprotected sun exposure for the sake of a tan?"

"Why would it be dangerous? Any message that keeps people out of the sun is great."

"Sure, but some people are never pale. Even when they stay out of the sun. Maybe there might be a way to divorce sun protection from paleness?"

Buzz buzz.

Alison: I'm going to start carrying a parasol everywhere.

Alison: Since I'm almost as pale as she is.

"I'm confused. What do you mean?"

Lily: And I will fully cross to the other side of the street if you do.

Lily: She also has a memoir coming out.

"You know what? We're running low on time. And you haven't told me anything about your memoir. Were there any specific challenges you've faced that you identified while working on this book?"

"I know what it's like to feel frustrated by the path ahead of you."

Unexpected vulnerability from the self-centered influencer: It was Christmas in August.

Buzz buzz.

Alison: No.

Lily: Yes.

Alison: About what?

"How so?"

"Well, I've never told anyone this. But I'm actually a natural blonde. I know, right? But I've been dyeing my hair brown since I was fourteen. To make me seem more relatable in photos. I was too *intimidatingly pretty* as a blonde. And then I kept it when I transitioned to influencing.

But now, I'm like, is this who I have to be for the rest of my life? Someone who lies about her hair color so she can have a good career?"

"What you're saying is that you know what it's like to feel . . . trapped. By circumstances."

"Exactly. I know what it's like to feel trapped by circumstances."

It was like spoon-feeding a hungry baby.

Lily: The challenge of being too intimidatingly pretty.

"Great. Well, it was so nice chatting with you. Thanks for your time."

Buzz buzz.

Alison: You're kidding.

Lily: No.

Alison: Have fun writing the story!

Lily placed the phone's receiver down and rolled her head in a few circles to release the cramping in her neck. She marveled at the energy required to navigate these interviews. On the surface, it should have been a simple discussion of a new accessories collection, a skin care campaign, and a book release. And for Katrina, this was the conversation she had just had. Lily's jaw throbbed from her efforts to suppress her deeper feelings on Katrina's anti-solar fanaticism.

An SPF acolyte, too, Lily often found herself interrogating how much of her sun avoidance was a product of health versus cultural brainwashing over the desirability of pale skin. She could recall multiple visits to an always very white dermatologist wherein Lily would sit in the examining room and watch a look of pure disapproval cross the doctor's face as she eyed Lily's browned limbs. *I wear SPF fifty every day and I've never sunbathed a second in my life,* Lily would tell the doctor each time. *I could tan in a dark cave; this isn't irresponsible behavior, it's my natural state of being.* Baseball cap shading her face, Lily would leave these appointments and feel like a walking billboard for melanoma, despite her sun precautions, which exceeded any that her white friends took.

Katrina's declaration that a tan was a false, universal signifier for health ignored the fact that only pale people, like her, enjoyed cultural rewards for browned skin. Meanwhile, society devalued those who came by the look organically and encouraged them to minimize what paler folks sought to replicate. It was madness.

The worst part in this was that through her interview and story, Lily would help spread the appeal of a Katrina and all that she represented. The Katrinas of the world were clickbait. Breathless coverage of their multimillion-dollar homes, fashion choices, and beauty looks were sure-fire hits for a publication, Lily's included, even if they yielded little to no veritable content. People wanted to know about them because everyone else wanted to know about them. People saw them everywhere, on magazine covers and in social media posts and on reality shows. And somehow, instead of getting sick of them, they wanted more. In fact, the insubstantiality of Katrina and her ilk was the driving force behind their perpetually trending state. They were the sugar-free pieces of gum everyone kept chewing. People hoped for some remnants of flavor when all evidence suggested there were none to be had.

And Lily was unable to deny her part in perpetuating the cultural dominance of these subjects. Every month, she helped anoint a new Katrina to the halls of the hot, enviable, and empty. Even if she didn't partake of the sugar-free confections herself, Lily was responsible, in her own way, for the chewed-up wads that marred the undersides of subway seats and that latched on to the soles of a favorite pair of shoes.

• • •

CENTRAL PARK WEST was vacant and sweltering the next morning as Lily walked east into the park for a run. She hadn't technically begun her workout, but sweat beaded across her chest and dripped down her back in the August heat. On the walk to the park, Katrina loitered in the alleyways of Lily's mind. She couldn't shake the conclusion that Katrina was who Lily was supposed to be. Or rather, who Lily was supposed to want to be. Katrina was an early-aughts It Girl and a golden-age magazine editor smashed into one terrifying hybrid. She had combined the worshipped status of the former with the story messaging power of the latter and spun them into a livelihood whose self-promotion was both its reason for existence and its means of production. Katrina was the newest, most convincing road map for womanly success.

Katrina's iteration of a road map did not have the same seductive hold on Lily that magazines had exerted when she was a teenager. Maybe Lily had toiled in the proverbial sausage factory for too long to salivate over the goods. She admired a certain bravery on Katrina's part that distinguished her from her analog predecessors. Katrina had planted herself front and center in her narrative. Unlike an editor, Katrina didn't and couldn't hide behind the glamour of a glossy magazine employer; she would succeed or fail based on her own image. And, god knew, there were so many images from which to choose. How exhausting that must be, Lily mused, to constantly thrust oneself, albeit in a highly filtered form, before hundreds of thousands of strangers, knowing that the devotion of these strangers is the sole determinant of one's accomplishment. Lily wondered what would happen to Katrina should her followers eventually flock to someone else. Her whole life was predicated on other people's likes; she might not understand how to exist for herself. At least the former ballet dancer, Julie, had specific training and skills to fall back on when her dance company lost interest in her.

Though B and her career were continents apart from the trajectory of a Katrina, they shared a common thread: a willingness to spotlight themselves for the sake of advancement. This thrusting of the self appeared to be the only reliable mechanism of achievement.

Lily wanted to pose this exact theory to B. Perhaps it was the heat or her general frustration with the past couple of months, but before she could second-guess a six A.M. text, she dropped her message into the ether.

Lily: Do you think self-promotion is necessary to a successful career?

Her phone zipped in the back pocket of her running shorts, Lily ran south along the rolling hills of the drive's west side past a rowboat pond. There were no rowers out at this hour. She was about a mile into her run when her pocket vibrated.

B: That's quite the early morning question.

B: Why do you ask?

B was awake at this hour. Lily jogged off to the side of the road.

Lily: I interviewed an influencer yesterday.

Lily: And her entire career is based around exploiting her personal lifestyle.

Lily: She's not promoting a product, like a model with fashion. Or an actor with a film.

Lily: She's not creating art, like a painter doing a self-portrait.

Lily: There's no larger goal besides promoting her existence and her pale skin.

Lily returned her phone to her pocket and resumed her movements south. The flat, wide Sheep Meadow lawn yielded to softball fields. Buzz buzz.

B: Interesting.

B: And you think your career has stalled because you don't promote yourself enough?

Again, Lily pulled over to a curb that ran parallel to the park drive. She swiped at the sweat on her forehead and upper lip with the inside of her forearm.

Lily: I don't know.

Lily: There's always a danger in putting yourself out there.

Lily: Like, did you worry at all that your sexuality would affect your career?

This time, Lily waited a couple of minutes before she stuffed her phone away and restarted her run. Again. She looped around the park's southern tip, framed by Art Deco hotels and the hubristic Jenga towers of Fifty-Seventh Street.

Buzz buzz.

She was partway up an interminable hill. She crested the top and jogged over to the side. Her lungs inhaled the air greedily. Lily retrieved her phone. Never again would she text B first thing in the morning.

B: Giving people new information about you will always create change.

B: That change can be for the better though.

Lily: Yes. And it can also be for the worse.

Lily: Fashion and magazines appear progressive. But a lot of what they perpetuate about women is harmful.

Lily: I cut my hair into a bob a couple of years ago.

Lily: And one of my colleagues told me, "Men only like women with long hair. You don't want to look like a dyke."

B: You can't make decisions about your life based on what other people think.

B: Especially people who are that dumb.

Lily: I get that.

Lily: But a lot of people in this industry believe that sexuality overlaps with aesthetic taste.

Lily: They hire you based on your taste. Even if you're a writer.

Lily: Straight women and queer men have taste. Queer women and straight men don't. That's their thinking.

Lily: Anyway, you still haven't answered my question about your experience.

Five minutes ticked by as Lily waited for a reply. Her breathing returned to its regular cadence, and she stashed her phone away and ran north on the drive. A duo of museums blurred past her. Or the sites weren't the blur, but rather Lily's vision was, slurred with sweat and sunscreen.

Buzz buzz.

B: Well, obviously things worked out.

Forty-five minutes had dragged by since Lily had begun and she was barely four miles into her run. She really should silence her phone. But she couldn't stop until she knew B's answer to her question. And B's ongoing deflection only heightened Lily's determination.

Lily: Yes, but were you concerned? That things wouldn't.

B: It was a risk.

Lily: And how did you decide that it was a risk worth taking?

B: Stasis is also a risk.

Lily: Okay.

B: I chose the risk with the greatest potential reward.

Lily: Isn't the risk with the greatest reward also the one with the biggest potential downside?

When her phone remained vibration-free, Lily stored it and continued on her way. She increased her pace now that she had burned through so much time waiting on the sidelines for messages that might never materialize.

Buzz buzz.

B: Of course.

B: But at a certain point, you have to decide if you're going to focus on downsides or rewards.

B: And I prefer rewards.

Lily: Good to know.

B: You owe me a cup of coffee.

Lily: And you owe me a date on your calendar.

Two minutes trickled by. Lily's phone was as unmoved as B's conscience, it would seem. Buzz buzz.

B: One minute.

Silence, again. Lily's skin was slick with perspiration; her sweat glands had doubled their efforts during the period of her extended inertia. Buzz buzz.

B: Sorry. My assistant has been texting me.

B: And now she's calling me.

B: Gotta run.

As far as dopamine spikes went, this was one of Lily's lowest. With her unintentional multitasking, she had somehow sabotaged the natural high she earned from exercise and the spiritual one she gleaned from her repartee with B. And how was it that Lily could be fully aware of B's deception—that casual reference to a coffee meet-up that B clearly had no intention of actualizing—and continue to actively participate in her own manipulation?

B's avoidance of Lily's questions provided answers in and of themselves. She was pro-self-promotion no matter the cost because her rewards were so staggeringly high. Lily's goals were not nearly as inflated as B's. And Lily didn't know how to reconcile her continued draw to B's swagger and arrogance with her intrinsic self-effacement.

She remembered a weekend when she was at Alison's apartment, a few months into their relationship. She had helped Alison clean out and rearrange the items on her bookshelf. And there was a file box on the floor that contained old college papers and homework, notes from lectures, syllabus handouts, etc. Lily had rifled through these papers and come across Alison's college transcripts. She had received straight A's across all eight semesters and had been awarded an American history honor for her thesis.

"You got straight A's in college?"

Alison had turned around from the pile in front of her and glanced at the transcript.

"Oh yeah," she had said. "I did."

"You never mentioned it."

"When or why would I have mentioned it?"

"I don't know. You must have graduated with honors."

"I was salutatorian."

"That's a huge deal."

Alison had shrugged and turned back to her pile.

How someone with such a casual approach to her own achievement could end up a consultant at a company of puffed-up egos, Lily couldn't fully explain. It cemented her kinship with Alison. They were people who existed in professions where the expectation of constant self-promotion was at odds with their unassuming natures. Success, as it was defined by their two competitive industries, was a mirage. One day a person was at the top; the next they had been supplanted by someone younger and more hyped. Modesty was the only reliable protection against such a mercurial system. If one never built their confidence from the standard wood planks of accomplishment, they didn't have to worry that a competitor would huff and puff it away. Stick to one's own proprietary brick blend and one's house will stay intact. Lily had always believed this. She had never dreamed that she would find someone who lived this way as fervently as she did.

And now Lily sought increasingly frequent counsel from someone who believed, just as fervently, in the opposite. Someone who had built a life with many, many, many wood planks that no one could ever obliterate. B was untouchable—literally. Lily's conversations with B were barely real. They were a bunch of loose fragments hanging out in the digital ether, impossible to touch or feel. They were nothing. This was all pure nothing.

9

. . .

ONE OF THE most reliable principles of an office building ecosystem was that the only people one would ever encounter in an elevator were the exact people one wished never to see in person at all. An elevator encapsulated that wonderful contradiction: a deeply impersonal space rendered uncomfortably intimate by a paucity of square footage. Feelings of inferiority only upped the chances of unpleasant interactions. If one was underdressed or tardy or hungover, the likelihood of an unfortunate tête-à-tête increased exponentially. At that point, it was advisable to take the stairs.

In the chilled and austere lobby of her office building, Lily entered one of the elevators to discover another occupant, Cynthia Park, already there. Lily was neither underdressed nor tardy nor hungover. On this early September morning, she was simply the recipient of some bad luck.

"Sorry," Lily said as she pushed the button for her floor, which would thankfully come after Cynthia's stop. Cynthia pushed the close button and waited impatiently for the doors to respond. "How are you?"

"Fine, thanks," said Cynthia in her clipped manner.

Cynthia was a features director at a beauty title owned by the same parent company that oversaw Lily's publication. She was in her early forties and Ivy League educated. She and Lily had overlapped at enough socialite-hosted events for high-end workout gear and cosmetic accessories, including a luncheon devoted to a line of jade rollers, that the two women had a level of mutual recognition that would commonly prompt a cordial greeting. That said, Cynthia terrified Lily. She couldn't pinpoint the exact source of her nervousness around the woman; it was more a general sense that Cynthia disapproved of Lily in some way for reasons that were beyond her command.

The first seconds crawled along during the agonizing journey to their respective floors. Cynthia stared at Lily across the few square feet of the elevator with unapologetic disdain. The light in the elevator was starkly bright with green-blue undertones. Every pore and blemish on Lily's face was under a microscope as Cynthia's eyes penetrated deeper. Lily could feel heat slowly flood her face.

"How is your current issue going? You're on December now?" Lily asked. She would say and do anything to deflect Cynthia's attention.

"January. We like to work ahead," Cynthia said. "You have a good crease."

"Sorry?"

The trip from one to twenty-three had become practically transatlantic. And these elevators were supposed to be technologically advanced.

"Your eyes. The crease. It's a good crease."

"Oh. Thanks."

Cynthia stared hard at Lily. "You're lucky."

The elevator dinged. They were at twenty-three. The doors opened and Cynthia exited, without so much as a parting word. Lily slumped against the elevator's cold metal wall. She pressed the pads of her fingers to her flushed cheeks. That's right, she was terrified of Cynthia Park in the way that she was terrified of any fully Asian woman who looked at her with unmitigated resentment. Lily would catch a random Chinese or Japanese woman, say, staring at her across a train car on a subway ride home, and instantaneously her pulse would begin to ricochet across her neck. She knew exactly what the woman was thinking as her glare grazed Lily's eyes and nose and lips and especially her neither-here-nor-there skin. It was the same thing Cynthia Park implied with her laser beam comment. *Traitor.*

• • •

LABOR ON THE December issue of the magazine galloped ahead. Theresa had assigned Lily six shorter stories in the magazine's "front of book," or FOB. These opening sections were generally comprised of pieces whose subjects were considered less weighty or deserving of print real estate. The stories in the FOB were the appetizers to the main courses in the magazine's center section, otherwise known as "the well." A subject in the well was something the editorial team—or an advertiser—had deemed worthy of deeper attention from a reader, e.g., a celebrity profile, an evocative fashion shoot, a probing travel feature. This deeper attention was acknowledged through the page count, the photography shoot budget, and the reputation of the writer assigned to the piece. The more numerous and elevated these elements were in a story, the greater its telegraphed impact. In essence, the magazine determined in advance how well a story would do and how likely it was a reader might connect with its writing and visuals based on its allocation of resources.

Six stories meant six mentions of Lily's name in the issue, so her industriousness wouldn't go unnoticed. For a couple of years now, Lily had asked Theresa, on multiple occasions, if she would consider her as a potential writer for a well piece. Each time Lily raised this topic, Theresa sniffed and pressed her thin lips into a wan smile and replied with, "But you're doing such a good job with the stories you write now. The magazine needs your work," as though she believed that this hollow flattery would satiate Lily's hunger. And Lily would nod okay and return to her desk equally dejected by Theresa's dismissal and by her own refusal to fight back.

One afternoon, ten days before the December issue closed, Theresa summoned Lily to her office. Lily assumed another last-minute FOB story was about to land in her quadrant.

Theresa sat at her desk, cloaked in a cashmere blanket that looked thick enough to travel from the office's arctic environs to the actual North Pole without losing its warmth factor. From the blank, vaguely annoyed expression on Theresa's face, Lily knew her assumption was correct.

"Take a seat," Theresa said.

Lily sat in the closest chair, as uncomfortable as ever.

"We've added a new story to the issue."

Here we go.

"And we would like you to write it."

Of course they would. She particularly enjoyed Theresa's use of the royal *we,* to deflect responsibility from her own role in this delegation.

"It's a profile of Antonio Russo."

Antonio Russo was an up-and-coming fashion designer based in Milan. All profiles were on up-and-comers or iconic veterans. The middle did not exist.

"Fifteen hundred words."

Okay, that was an unusual length for the FOB.

"In the well."

Lily's stomach tingled. Had she heard correctly? The well. Theresa stared off to the side. She avoided eye contact with Lily. It clearly pained her to offer Lily such a substantive assignment, though Theresa could take pleasure in the absurd ten-day deadline. The coordination of the interview alone would devour five days.

"That's great. Thank you, Theresa," Lily said. Emotion crept toward her voice, but she held it at bay.

"I'll connect you with Antonio's PR person." Theresa's gaze continued to linger on a point a few inches to the left of Lily's head. "Hop to it."

Lily was elated enough, she could have hopped. She settled for a controlled fast-paced walk back to her desk. A well story, finally. And she didn't even have to beg. All those pep talks from B on standing her ground continued to generate dividends. She knew her pursuit of B would pay off. She had to thank her right away. And then she would share the news with Alison.

Lily: Just got assigned my first well story for the December issue.

Lily: Out of nowhere!

She typed a similar message for Alison, and as she was about to press send, her phone buzz-buzzed.

B: On Antonio Russo?

Lily: Yes.

Lily: How did you know it was on him?

B: He's a friend of a friend.

B: I had dinner with him the other night when he was in town.

B: He mentioned the possibility of the story.

B: And I said he had to request you as the writer.

B: Glad it worked out.

Well, that explained Theresa's resentment. The assignment hadn't originated within the magazine's walls. It had emanated from B through Antonio. There was no way Theresa would push back on a writer request from a buzzy designer; she would be too eager to please him and claim him as one of the magazine's conquests. Lily hadn't earned this opportunity on her own. She had been gifted the chance by B.

And yet, Lily could argue in her head that she had earned the assignment, not through a traditional channel. Put differently, she had earned it through the most traditional channel there was. The greater part of the magazine industry existed atop a foundation of nepotism and connections, of daughters and sons with recognizable surnames and family friends in positions of power. Those who didn't enter the industry with an illustrious safety net did their best to weave one from every casual introduction they made. Networking wasn't a tool for professional development; it was a necessary instrument of survival. No one in this industry could get by on talent and hard work alone.

Introverts, like Lily, who struggled to construct this network with implicit ease were at a disadvantage. Finally, Lily had a secure loop in her fledgling net. She had earned B's respect and this had begotten the story. There were no limits to where else it might lead.

Lily: Wow, thank you so much.

Lily: I am forever grateful.

She meant every word of what she typed.

· · ·

ANTONIO RUSSO PROVED a delightful interview—charming, warm, and humorously self-deprecating. He had begun his career as an apprentice to another Italian designer, a famous one, directly out of art school. After a year as an apprentice, he had been promoted steadily up the ranks of the design house. It was rumored that he was being groomed as the successor to the current head designer and founder, an octogenarian whose recent bouts of illness had prompted many newspapers to keep drafts of his obituary on file.

And then there were the clothes. Antonio's contributions to the Italian fashion house were universally lauded. The founder had made his name on sharp tailoring and geometry. Antonio breathed airiness into the silhouettes while maintaining the rigorous lines that were the brand's signature. It was a feat of ingenuity; he made a preexisting aesthetic his own, without fundamentally altering its DNA. Antonio had a long career ahead of him, assuming the luxury conglomerates granted him ample time and opportunity to make good on his talent, never a certainty.

Another gift Antonio possessed was for the art of the thoughtful sound bite. Here was Antonio on his early love of fashion: "Beauty is one of life's great blessings. As a boy, I used to watch my mother get ready for a night out. I watched how her posture changed when she slipped on her opera coat. She seemed to grow inches before my eyes. I thought that clothing must be the most transformative medium out there."

Unlike the women who regularly wore his creations, Antonio was not judged first and foremost on how he looked. His rumpled attire, the beginnings of faint lines across his olive complexion: If anything, these were considered signs of his seriousness and life experience. His capacity to dream was unencumbered by societal demands for his physical perfection. None of this was to dismiss his talent or hard work. It was worth considering, though, that his definition of beauty as a blessing came more easily when he didn't experience firsthand its darker, twisted ramifications. He could imagine beauty in a purely positive light because he never had to embody it himself.

Lily was halfway through a draft of her story on Antonio when she landed on this quote from him about the deep, strong femininity embedded in his pantsuits: "Power is not a matter of fashion. It is not fashion's job or my job to empower a woman. It is fashion's job to enhance a woman's implicit power. And there is no better way to do that than to design a pantsuit." Antonio's quote made Lily want to rush to a store and purchase a pantsuit. It made her think of all the strong women, the politicians and CEOs and studio heads, who regularly wore pantsuits. It made her think of B.

For the next thirty minutes, Lily did everything she could to train her focus back onto Antonio's inspiration for the latest collection, his childhood love of his mother's trousers, his two best friends from art school who were similarly making waves at their respective design houses. Finally, she surrendered to her true inclination and opened a new browser window on her computer. She typed B's name into the image search engine and scrolled through the fruits of her harvest.

Here was B three years ago, front row at a charity fashion show for women and heart disease, in a scarlet pantsuit, her hair flat-ironed pin straight, sandwiched between an Oscar-winning actress and a twenty-two-year-old social media star. Another photo from that same year showed her on a red carpet in a black tuxedo, B's posture sturdy and proud. At the American beauty awards gala from four months ago, B stood next to a round dinner table in a ballroom somewhere in midtown; she wore a copper silk jumpsuit, a rare, subtle departure from her go-to pantsuits. Her lips were a dark burgundy and her brown-gray hair hung in soft, bouncy waves beside her sharp cheekbones. Behind her, lines of candelabras and floral arrangements petered off into the distance.

"Research for a story?"

Lily nearly popped up from her seat in surprise. It was Lindsay, who glanced curiously at Lily's computer screen.

"I was thinking of doing a piece on evening pantsuits," she stammered. Lily quickly closed the browser window to reveal her partially written Antonio story.

"Cool," said Lindsay. "She is the queen of the pantsuit, isn't she?"

"Yes, she is."

"She was at a blush launch I went to the other day."

"Oh?" Lily strove to keep her face impassive.

"She's crazy smart. Very intimidating. I hear she makes her assistants go to the farmer's market every morning to get fresh produce to puree in her smoothies. Every morning."

"That's intense."

"Don't tell anyone here, but I would kill to work for her. If anything ever opened up over there."

"Your secret is safe."

"I have such a girl crush on her."

Lily's chest thumped. "Doesn't everyone?"

"Totally. Anyway, I just came over to ask about your Antonio Russo text. We need to add a beauty note to the page for the models we shot in his clothes and I was wondering how long you thought your story would be."

• • •

FOR A MUCH-NEEDED long weekend, Lily and Alison booked a room at a bed-and-breakfast near the town of Cutchogue on the North Fork of Long Island. They met at Penn Station in Midtown on a Saturday morning. To avoid traffic they chose to take the train out and rely on rideshare services while in the area. Lily and Alison found a two-seater in an otherwise packed car. With duffel bags balanced on their laps, they were off. Their destination was Mattituck, a charming hamlet town bookended by the Long Island Sound and the Great Peconic Bay. The proprietor of the bed-and-breakfast had offered to drive them the four or so miles from the Mattituck station to their lodging. A few minutes' walk from the train station, on the earnestly named Love Lane, Alison spotted a café. They would lunch there before they called for their ride.

Seated at cramped wooden tables, they shared fish tacos and a Cobb salad. Two tall glasses of iced tea sweated daintily beside them in the mild fall air. They basked in the anticipatory glow of the three lazy days stretched out before them. There was nothing to do; there was nowhere to be, save for the three dinner reservations Alison had booked at some well-rated nearby places.

"Maybe we could go to a winery this afternoon. What do you think?" said Lily. She fetched a navy baseball cap from her duffel bag to shield her from the sun while they ate.

"Sure, that sounds nice. A glass of rosé. Maybe a cheese plate," said Alison.

"I brought three books with me."

"Great."

"I like to have options."

"I'm good with the option of sleeping as much as possible." The sun highlighted glints of wheat in Alison's hair, and her mint-checked shirt brought out the green flecks in her eyes, like sea glass speckled across a beach. "Do you think the B and B has a porch? I love a porch."

"A porch would be nice."

"Remind me why we live in the city?"

Alison adored the suburbs of her youth. She liked swimming pools and freshly mowed lawns and glasses of ice-cold lemonade. Her urban existence had buffed her love of these residential enclaves into full-bodied nostalgia. Lily could count on one hand the number of times she had been to the suburbs—along with the number of times she had felt the need to travel there.

"Are you serious?" Lily said.

"It's so relaxing out here. You have a charming small town. Space. There are hardly any people around. What's not to love?"

"Sure, it's nice for a long weekend, but then you'd go crazy. There's nothing to do. There's a reason so few people live out here and so many people live in the city."

"Crowding doesn't mean a place is more desirable. Anyway, I hope to live in the suburbs again one day."

Lily swallowed a forkful of tilapia. "You do?"

"I mean, yes, eventually. Your money goes further. And you get more room."

"I guess. But you're living in the suburbs. When were you going to tell me this?"

Alison sipped her iced tea. "I didn't think it was something that needed to be told. It's something I'd like to do. At some point in the future." Her eyes took in Lily, who raked her fingers skittishly through her hair. "The far-away future. Relax. It's not like we even live together."

The women paid for their meal and called the B and B. Twenty minutes later, a forty-something man in a red car drew up to where they stood. He stepped out of the car to help them with their bags.

"Hi, I'm Joe," he said, and smiled warmly. His full head of brown hair was streaked with gray and he wore a plaid shirt whose unbuttoned cuffs wafted loosely as he moved. His skin was a faded tan with red patches on his nose and upper cheeks.

The ride to the guesthouse carried them past vineyards and fields of corn, striated landscapes of natural growth bent into organized submission. Joe's wife, Amy, waited for them when they arrived. She exuded the same welcoming air as her husband and she led them to their room on the house's top floor. A four-poster bed was covered in a white crocheted spread. There were nightstands topped with blue and white lamps, and a white-linen-slipcovered armchair occupied a corner near the dresser.

"There's no TV, but we have an alarm clock with speakers for your phone, if you want to play music. And here's the thermostat for the AC," said Amy. She gestured at a dial on the wall. "We serve breakfast from eight to ten thirty every morning. And taxi service can be spotty, so we're happy to drive you anywhere close by. Just let us know."

"That's so nice of you, thank you," said Alison.

"I'll let you girls settle in," said Amy. She closed the door softly behind her.

"God, they're both so nice," said Lily.

"It's the suburbs."

The two women freshened up and strolled to a vineyard a few minutes away from the B and B. They ordered their tasting, sauvignon blanc, rosé, a chardonnay, and a Riesling mix called First Blush White, and lounged on a picnic bench that overlooked the vineyard's perfectly articulated rows.

A radiant satisfaction from the Antonio Russo story still enveloped Lily. The piece had turned out better than she had hoped. And Lily experienced the soft, warm happiness of having contributed, in her own small way, toward the success of someone deserving. Her story on Antonio would forever be a tiny step on his path to stardom. This had always been one of the major benefits of her job: the chance to help another person's dreams secure a foothold in reality.

B's assist had reminded Lily of this crucial fact. She loved what she did—it was a privilege. Or the opportunity to write an Antonio story was a privilege. It was the price she paid for that privilege, the PR bullying, the rushed and tiny word counts, the interoffice warfare, the proliferation of Katrina stories, and whether it was merited that remained up for debate.

B would never spend a long-weekend getaway second-guessing her choices. Lily imagined what it might be like to live the way B did. To act on her every desire. She imagined how B might look if she were in Lily's shoes in this very moment. She would wear a men's oxford button-down and bright white jeans. She would have on a giant straw hat to protect her alabaster skin from the sun; her lips would shimmer with the sheerest coral glaze. She would chat with her companion and read her book. When she was hungry, she would eat. When she was thirsty, she would drink. When she was bored, she would stand up and walk away. She would never, ever apologize.

Lily tried to feel the weight of B's importance in her bones. The sensation of taking up so much space without gaining an ounce in size.

"I'm going to walk out closer to the vineyards," said Alison. She slipped on her aviator sunglasses. "Want to come?"

"I'm going to stay here. I'll watch you," said Lily, momentarily jolted from her reverie.

Alison carried her glass and slowly waded out toward the line where the vineyards met the mowed grass.

With her phone, Lily snapped some photos of the scenery. She texted one to B.

Lily: Celebrating the Antonio story with a weekend getaway.

Lily: Thanks, again, for the assignment!

Two minutes later, her phone vibrated.

B: That's nice. Where are you?

Lily: Vineyard on the North Fork.

B: You there with your girlfriend?

Lily: Yup.

B: Cute.

B: How long have you been together again?

Lily: Two and a half years.

B: I see. And she's creative like you?

Lily: She's a consultant.

B: So, no.

Lily: She's creative in different ways.

Lily: And supersmart.

B: Of course she is.

Lily sipped her chardonnay. B's words mocked her, though it was so hard to tell over text.

Lily: What about you? What are you doing?

B: At a friend's house in the Hudson Valley.

Lily: Cool.

Lily: Would you ever move to the suburbs or country permanently?

B: Hell no.

Lily: But you grew up in a suburb?

B: Exactly.

Lily: Why not?

B: Because I need energy.

B: Excitement.

B: People.

B: I'd go crazy living anywhere else but in a city.

Lily: Yeah, me too.

"Who are you texting?"

Alison had returned from the vineyard's edge while Lily had been immersed in her phone.

"It's Billie."

"We're on vacation. Stop texting about work."

"She was wishing us a happy weekend."

"Oh. Where is she?"

"The Hudson Valley."

"See? It's all about getting away from New York."

"Right."

10

. . .

A MEASURED VOICE filled Lily's ears from the headphones crushed against her skull. She sat crumpled at her work desk with her hands clasped beneath her chin as though in prayer. The young blond woman on her screen spoke carefully from her perch on the witness stand. A defense attorney grilled her with questions; the young woman paused every so often for a sip of water. Her posture remained poised, even as the words that spilled from her mouth grew increasingly alarming. Her steadiness belied the immense hardship of her task. She was alone on that stage, as she had been in the pain she now described publicly. And she and everyone who watched her knew that as she shared her story, she forfeited her right to peaceful anonymity and possibly to future professional opportunity. She was forever changed in that moment. Every cell in her body radiated that sacrifice.

Lily's face was slick with tears. Clear rivulets pooled in her cupid's bow. She fished in her handbag for a tissue and dabbed at her eyes and nose. She wasn't the type to cry at her desk, but some circumstances eviscerated her emotional restraint. Lily would have assumed such testimonies would no longer rattle her. So many women had come forward.

So many stories of harassment and abuse and assault were piled up like the casualties of a world war. One would think such an unrelenting barrage would desensitize a person and that each revelation would leave less of a bruise. Sometimes, the reverse was true. One's façade was so weakened by earlier attacks that it could no longer withstand a lighter beating. Each successive story hurt more than it would have as an isolated incident. One resigned themselves to the idea of constant suffering.

This young blond woman had worked at a bank. The middle-aged brunette the previous week was formerly a lawyer. The younger brunette three weeks before her had been an aspiring film producer. They were "brave" and "so strong" and "warriors" and "whistleblowers" on social media. But in the real world, their careers were over. And none of their digital acolytes, who sang their praises across platforms, were going to materialize beside them and pick up the pieces of their shattered futures.

Lily blew her nose and closed out of the browser window in which the trial streamed. She pressed play on her digital recorder and transcribed an interview with an up-and-coming actress who had started a sustainable slogan–T-shirt company.

". . . the cotton is grown organically on these farms in the Turkish countryside and it's woven on looms twenty-five miles away. Then we ship that fabric to the US by boat so it uses fewer carbon emissions. That's why each shirt takes forever to make from start to . . ."

So engrossed was Lily in her transcription that she didn't notice the tall, sculpted figure, in a gray T-shirt, navy zip-up vest, and baggy jeans, who wound his way around the labyrinthine cubicles in the direction of her desk. It wasn't until he stood in front of her cubicle, wavy hair flopping across his unlined forehead, and stared at her expectantly with his blue eyes, that she realized she was no longer alone with the actress's voice in her ears.

"Hey, what's up?"

It was Marc, an editor on the digital side of the publication. His zip-up vest was a nod to the preferred stylings of his Silicon Valley idols. It was a horror-inducing eyesore to the magazine's staff, especially members of the fashion department. He rested his long, white forearms on the top of the dividers and leaned over them to peer at Lily. Marc was firmly out of collegiate circles. Yet he had the perennially gleaming appearance of a Division III athlete who was also president of his university's most popular fraternity. He was a young man who had never been forced to question his place in the world because wherever he went, he encountered enormous welcome mats and wide-open doorways. As such, Marc entered every room and approached every situation as though it were incomplete without his unmatchable presence. He and Lily were hardly close acquaintances, in any interpretation of this word; one wouldn't know this to go by the overfamiliarity with which Marc treated each of their exchanges.

Marc was a relatively new hire at the magazine, or rather, at the magazine's website, since the two entities were not one and the same, in the opinion of the print side. He had been at the office for less than a year. His hiring was part of an overall push across the magazine's parent company to build out the websites for all the magazines, to create online-only content, all of it offered to readers for free, that could capture the attention of an analog-allergic public and compete with the growing presence of social media. Marc had no previous editorial experience; his background was in marketing. Further, he was twenty-seven years old, but because of the structure of the digital staffs at the magazines—they were smaller than the print teams and skipped over the top tier of the editorial masthead to report directly to the editor in chief—he had the hyperbolic title of "executive deputy editor." The *executive* was a gratuitous flourish given there were only three people beneath him on the digital masthead: an associate editor, a photo editor, and a just-plain editor. Lily didn't understand how Marc had landed this job. He had no published articles to his name prior to arriving at the magazine. And his editing style, from what she had witnessed, involved cutting and pasting various words into different paragraphs for the sake of the algorithm. She imagined Marc must have marketed himself over and over again through the entire interview process. It was his specialty, after all.

"Just thought I'd swing by to say hi. I've been dying to tell you all about my vacation."

Lily paused her recording and removed her headphones. "Hi, Marc."

"Are you okay? You look like you've been crying."

"I'm fine."

"Well, this will cheer you up," he said. Marc walked around the divider and sat on the portion of Lily's desk not piled with papers and back issues of the magazine. Lily scooted her desk chair back to create as much space as possible between them.

"I was just in Rio de Janeiro. Remember I told you we'd been planning a trip there for months?" Marc continued. A thin gold band glinted on his left ring finger. He seemed not to have noticed Lily's movement.

Lily nodded in faint recollection.

"It's winter there, but it was still, like, in the high seventies the whole time. Beautiful city. Have you ever been?"

"Nope."

"It's magnificent. The dramatic views. Christ the Redeemer. That Sugarloaf Mountain. You should really go."

"I will keep it in mind."

"You'd love it. You'd fit right in."

"Sorry?"

"With the people there." Here Marc paused. He looked Lily straight in the eye and his mouth broke into a smirk. "All the women there look like you."

Lily swallowed hard. "I highly doubt that. I'm not part South Amer—"

"No. They do."

"If you say so."

Marc leaned forward a little. "Trust me. It's a good thing."

Lily's stomach tightened involuntarily. "I should get back to work."

Marc stood up. "Right. Well, feel better."

And with that, he ambled away.

Lily scooted her chair back to its position directly in front of her computer. She clenched and unclenched her fists in her lap and trained her gaze on the transcript document in front of her.

Behavior like Marc's was too common to bother with or complain about to the office higher-ups. Because what was a person supposed to say, "My male colleague who has no power over my career, but like every man can reduce me to a sexual object, leered at me and thinks I should be grateful to him for doing it"? It was like running to the doctor every time one's nose was stuffy. Somehow, it made more sense to make do with consistently less air.

Lily resumed transcribing in the hopes that its monotony would lull her into a stupor.

". . . finish. And then we also use dyes made from organic plants for our different color needs. We're planning to introduce some new slogans for spring just in time for International Women's Day. 'Be Aggressive.' You know, like that high school sports team cheer. And 'Assert Yourself.' A riff on Madonna, of course. And . . ."

Buzz buzz.

Alison: How's it going?

Alison: You still having drinks with Jordan tonight?

Lily: Yeah.

Lily: And I've been better.

Alison: Why? Everything okay?

Lily: That guy Marc. The digital editor. Just sat down on my desk and was all like, "I was on vacation in Brazil and Brazilians are hot and you look just like the hot women there."

Alison: Gross.

Alison: You told him to get lost?

Lily: I said I had to get back to work. And he walked away.

Alison: I'm sorry. So annoying.

Lily: The idiot didn't even fetishize the correct background.

Alison: Fetishize?

Lily: He made it specifically about race.

Alison: Just try to stay away from him.

Lily: Yeah.

Alison: What a creep.

Lily's drinks date with Jordan was in the east sixties, at a bar they had agreed upon for its quiet elegance, a palate cleanser from the aggressive cool of Jordan's and Lily's respective work environments. Situated in the back of a hotel, the place was, essentially, a gorgeously appointed living room that happened to come with a waitstaff, kitchen, and fully stocked bar. Arrangements of tan wool sofas and club chairs provided ample seating options, the coffee tables were piled high with art and fashion books, and there was a fireplace, which the servers lit on chillier nights. New York apartments, save for those belonging to the very wealthy, were known for their claustrophobic dimensions. Public spaces that exuded cozy domesticity like this bar allowed New Yorkers to experience, for a couple of hours and the cost of some overpriced cocktails, what it might be like to own acceptably spacious real estate. In essence, these spots conferred on New Yorkers the semblance of proper adulthood before their carriages turned into pumpkins and they trudged back to their glorified dorm rooms.

Lily chose two tiger-striped dining chairs that framed a large side table and ordered a gin martini. She preferred vodka, but she had read in one of the many interviews B had done that she only drank martinis with gin. "Vodka is for philistines," she had said. "It's for people who don't want to taste their alcohol. The only real martini is a gin martini." Perhaps she could sip some of B's aura.

Her martini was served ice-cold with two olives propped up against the coupe's ledge. Lily brought the glass to her mouth. The heavy, fruity smell of the gin hit her and she paused. Then she sipped cautiously. Compared to the vodka iteration she preferred, the drink was cloying, like she had swallowed a florist's entire inventory. Lily gulped from her tumbler of water to wash the flavor away. She glared at her martini, as though the drink was to blame. Lily really didn't like gin, but maybe she needed to try harder.

Buzz buzz.

Alison: What are you up to?

Lily: Waiting for Jordan.

Lily: How's work?

Alison: Okay. I'm training a new analyst.

Alison: I swear to god this kid has never used PowerPoint.

Alison: I feel like I'm teaching him how to read.

Lily: Ugh. I'm sorry.

Lily: Maybe you can punt him to another team.

Lily plucked a potato chip from a bowl on the side table and crunched it. Buzz buzz.

Alison: What are you drinking?

Lily: A martini.

Alison: Nice. Have one for me. I'm going to be at the office for a while longer.

Jordan arrived, a paragon of understatement in a gray sweater, a tan jacket, and crisp Japanese denim finished with an anonymous brown belt. Jordan's occupation relied on downtown edge, but his personal style was more in keeping with the bar's whispered surroundings, tiger-striped chairs notwithstanding. He resented the idea that flamboyance was expected to be his fashion language simply because of who he dated and where he worked. No trace of a colorful print or a fitted muscle tee had made contact with his body since his college years.

"I hope I'm not late!" he said. He wrapped Lily in his sturdy arms, muscles palpable but not visible beneath roomy gray wool.

"Not at all," said Lily. "I was just getting a head start."

Jordan eased into the chair across from her. He leaned forward and sniffed at Lily's glass.

"Is that gin? Since when do you drink gin?"

"Yes. I'm trying something new."

"Good for you," said Jordan as he scanned the bar's menu. "Shake things up."

He requested a double tequila with a glass of ice on the side.

"What's new?" he asked. "Besides your alcohol choice."

"Not much. How's work?"

"We're hanging that new show this week."

"The abstract painter from North Carolina?"

"That's the one. I'm excited. Her colors are so intense. I wish I could own one of her paintings."

Lily sipped another painful dose from the glass of gin. "Maybe one day you will."

"Not working this job, I won't. It's the great irony, isn't it? You and I got into fashion and art out of passion. And because we work in fashion and art, we'll never make enough money to buy anything from our favorite designers and artists. We can do what we love or own what we love—but never both."

"Yeah. Irony is one word for it. Are you happy at work? I mean, do you think you'll stay there awhile?"

Jordan leaned back in his chair. "Happy enough? There isn't really anywhere for me to go. It's a small gallery. And my boss has been there forever. They'll have to drag her out in a straitjacket."

"What would you do next?"

Jordan smiled. "No idea. I could go to another gallery. Or try art consulting. Or . . . I don't know."

"Doesn't that scare you?"

Her glass was half-empty now. If they stayed for another round, she would have to rethink her beverage choice. No way could she consume two of these flower bombs.

"It excites me. We're young. We have so much time to try different things."

Lily ran a finger along the stem of her glass. She didn't feel young. She was tired. And out of options. She and Jordan were the same age and he had the positivity of a pre-recession college graduate. He fairly beamed with health. And Lily was like a dried-up puddle next to him. Wherever his optimism came from, she wanted to pay its source a visit.

"I constantly feel like I'm running out of time. Like every decision I have to make needs to happen now."

Jordan added an ice cube to his tequila. He frowned at Lily. "Well, time moves differently for you than it does for me," he said gently, adding, "Even if you don't plan to have children."

"But why should it?" Lily asked as heat rose in her chest. "If I don't, for example. Why should it still affect me?"

"I don't know. It's not fair."

"Yeah." Lily drained the rest of the gin. It coated her tongue in its heavy bouquet. "If you don't have kids or get married, do you think you'll feel like less of a man?"

"I haven't met any guys I'd want to settle down with. I know my parents would like grandchildren." Jordan swallowed the remainder of his tequila.

"You didn't really answer the question."

"I think I'd feel like a disappointment. To my family. But I wouldn't feel like less of a man." Jordan smiled at Lily. "Are you maybe projecting a little? Because you'll feel like less of a woman if you don't have kids?"

"Maybe. A part of me will, yes. And I hate myself for feeling that way. It means I've bought into the messed-up idea that my only worth is my womb."

"Well, you haven't bought into it so much that you're letting it dictate your choices. That has to count for something, doesn't it?"

"I guess. It's not like I could afford children even if I wanted them, not with this job."

"That's what rich spouses are for."

"Do you want to have children? With your future rich spouse, obviously. Like, for yourself, outside of whatever your parents think."

Jordan crossed one ankle over a thigh. "I don't know. I like kids. But I worry that I might want them for the wrong reasons."

"Meaning?"

"I might want them to prove a point. That I belong. And that I deserve to have a family, too."

"You do. And you also deserve to not have one if you don't want one."

"I know. But it's not that simple."

"No. It isn't."

Lily didn't discuss this topic with Marissa. Because she knew that Marissa would almost definitely get married and have children, like all her straight women friends. Any conversation like this would begin from a place of Lily's otherness in relation to convention, a convention that Marissa herself upheld. Lily would be forced to defend her choices in a way that Marissa and her other friends never had to do. Though Jordan didn't experience the same pressure that women of any sexuality did to procreate, his romantic choices, like Lily's, had the added weight of shaping not just the structure of his life, but also the palatability of his sexual identity. If Jordan decided to get married and have kids, he would implicitly be adopting a heteronormative idea of happiness. There was nothing wrong with this, but a part of him might always wonder if his decisions were motivated by some hidden need to assimilate into straight society. Assimilation wasn't categorically wrong, either, but something was often lost in its process. The potential of this loss clouded the waters of his decision-making—and Lily's. The possibility of conformity dangled before Jordan and Lily in a way it hadn't for the generations that came before them. Like so many other rights newly granted to those on the margins, this one came loaded with a complicated calculus.

"Well, whatever you decide, whenever you decide it, I just want you to be happy," Lily said.

"Thanks. And the same goes for you." Jordan eyed Lily's empty coupe. "Another round?"

"Sure. But I'm switching to vodka."

• • •

AFTER DRINKS, LILY and Jordan walked across Central Park South to the west-side subway lines. Jordan headed back down to Chelsea and Lily found a seat on an uptown train. Once safely in her apartment, Lily realized she had never texted B about her earlier interactions at work. She unzipped her dress and hung it in her closet. Surely B would have her own advice to add to Alison's response.

Lily: Our digital editor was a total lech to me today.

Lily: I'd appreciate any coping strategies.

Lily: Besides alcohol after work.

Lily placed a pot of water on the stove. She turned the burner on high and removed a box of pasta from a cabinet along with a bowl. Her stomach craved real food before it would allow her to sleep. Buzz buzz.

B: Are you drunk?

120

Lily: Tipsy.

B: Ah.

B: What happened with your colleague?

Lily: He made a creepy comment about how I look.

Lily: Like, You're hot like these Brazilian women I saw on vacation.

B: Your colleague thinks you're hot?

Lily: It's not what he said. It's how he said it.

Lily: Like leaned in too close. Acted like I should be thanking him.

Steam made a hasty escape from the lid of the pot. Lily dumped the contents of the pasta box into the boiling water and set a timer on her phone. She removed a hunk of Parmesan from her fridge and fetched a Microplane from a drawer. Buzz buzz.

B: You're being dramatic.

Lily: Are you serious?

B: How do you know he wasn't just trying to be nice?

Beep beep. Lily drained the pasta into a colander in the sink; steam basted her face. She transferred the pasta to the bowl.

Lily: Please tell me you're joking.

Lily: I'm thirty-two. I know the difference between a guy giving a harmless compliment and a guy sexualizing you.

Lily: It wasn't like, "Your hair looks nice today." Or: "Those are pretty shoes."

Lily: It was like, "Don't mind me while I undress you with my eyes."

Lily: It made me super uncomfortable.

Lily drizzled olive oil over the pasta and tossed the pasta and oil half-heartedly with her fork. Buzz buzz.

B: Did you tell him that?

Lily: Of course not.

Lily: If I said anything, he'd deny it.

B: If you don't say anything, how is he supposed to know he did something wrong?

Lily: I'm supposed to educate him on how not to be a dick?

B: If you're not going to do anything, what is the point in talking about it?

Lily: It sucks. Now I have to worry about avoiding him and not doing anything that he could mistake as encouragement.

Lily: When I want to go to the office and do my job.

Lily: And he never has to think about it again.

Lily slid the Parmesan across the Microplane until a soft mountain of snowy cheese covered the pasta. Then she mixed the contents and ground some black pepper over it.

Buzz buzz.

B: You have no idea what women before you had to put up with.

B: If you knew, you wouldn't be complaining about something so minor.

B: Things are so much easier for you.

And B had no idea what it was like to be fetishized relentlessly starting in childhood. Lily wanted to ask B how many times grown men had approached her eleven-year-old self on the street like she was a child sex worker while she wore her middle school soccer uniform. How many categories on pornography sites were devoted to her ethnic origins. And how many of her ancestors had been legally banned from immigrating to this country because it was presumed that they were prostitutes. But she knew from past exchanges with other white women, especially those of B's generation, that the mention of fetishization was usually taken as a boast of attractiveness instead of what it really was: an expression of fear at the latent danger that lurked beneath the surface. To hope for compassion or acknowledgment on the topic was to scream into an abyss.

B: You don't realize how much those before you have sacrificed.

B: And continue to.

Lily: Of course I know. I'm not that much younger than you.

The pasta needed more cheese. Lily added another, smaller cloud of shaved Parmesan and tossed it in with her fork.

Buzz buzz.

B: You're eons younger to me.

Lily: It's called a microaggression. In case you're unfamiliar with the term.

Lily stuffed a forkful of hot, cheesy, and peppery pasta into her mouth and chewed it furiously. Buzz buzz.

B: I know the term, thanks.

B: I never had time to worry about microaggressions. I was too busy with real aggressions.

Lily: Shouldn't it be a sign of progress if people who come after you worry about different things?

Lily: Or would you rather I still had to deal with the same shit that you did?

B: No. Of course not.

B: Just be grateful.

Lily: I am.

With her fork, Lily stabbed two pieces of pasta stuck together near the bowl's edge and jammed them into her mouth. So much for her peaceful, drunken dinner. Buzz buzz.

B: You don't sound grateful.

B: This is life as a woman.

B: Deal with it.

Lily: I'm not going to apologize for thinking I deserve better.

Lily: That we all do.

Lily: Including you.

Lily slammed her phone down on her sofa. Fuck B. In the bathroom, she splashed water on her face and brushed her teeth. Then she tumbled into an alcohol-and-pasta-induced coma.

11

· · ·

LILY'S MOUTH WAS dry like sand when she awoke the next morning.
She expected a series of text notifications to dance across her phone.
Surely, in the past seven hours, B had contemplated her actions and crafted
an apology. She had been worked up over something else. Her frustration hadn't been aimed at Lily. She certainly hadn't meant to be so
harsh. She was sorry. But Lily's screen was blank, save for a few emails
and her daily horoscope. Blinking in annoyance, Lily dragged herself to
the kitchen and downed three tall glasses of water. She would give B at
least until noon. Maybe she was the type of person who liked to deal
with these responses the morning after.

By lunchtime, there was still no word from B, no heartfelt apology
or even a generic outreach that ignored the previous night's argument.
And Lily was jittery with discomfort. It was her first fight with B—
uncharted terrain. Lily couldn't recall any major impasses with Marissa
or Jordan. Lily and Alison had also rarely fought in the many years of
their relationship, a blatant affront to the stereotypes about two women
always being at each other's proverbial throats.

It wasn't that Lily was unfamiliar with the fear of damaging a relationship by saying the wrong thing. There had been a time earlier in her

courtship with Alison when Lily had been so giddy with excitement that she had been paralyzed by the assumption that her joy would be short-lived. No one person could be allowed to stay this happy for so long; it defied the natural order. Lily opened her eyes every morning with a clenched jaw and thought, Today will be the day this all ends. I will make a mistake and it will all be over. Back then, Alison was more of an initiator. Alison would text her constantly with suggestions for things they could eat, see, and do. A Japanese-Peruvian restaurant had recently opened in Chelsea. A soft-serve ice cream spot on the Lower East Side was creating confections that looked like pastel animals from a retro children's cartoon show. There was a free screening series of classic eighties movies spread across parks in all five boroughs. Had Lily heard of this dumpling place in Chinatown where one could get eight pot stickers for a dollar? Lily could barely keep up with the rush of date ideas that flooded her phone. The world was a nonstop river of experiences waiting for Lily and Alison to navigate together.

And then somehow, a dam emerged that transformed the gushing river into a trickling stream. It was impossible to pinpoint exactly how or when it happened. Or who put down the first twig. The all-consuming exhilaration of those first seven or eight months settled into a more languid satisfaction. It wasn't the worst thing. There was a different, quieter passion to be had in the simple act of being together for no reason at all. And Lily understood that this type of union was far harder to achieve than the fireworks display of early romance. These days, her jaw was slack when she opened her eyes to the morning light. And it had been some time since that lurking fear had darkened her doorstep.

Until today, under very different circumstances. Lily's body ran cold with the prospect of losing B. She wanted B's approval more than she wanted her apology. Lily's fingers twitched from surreptitiously checking her phone every few minutes. She jumped at every notification and sank even lower with each disappointment.

Lily sought distraction. Fortunately, that was not hard to come by in her magazine's features meeting. The team toiled away on the January issue and was gathered specifically to discuss the well stories. They were a couple of weeks out from the issue's close. There was enough time to commission something new without catastrophe if the current mélange didn't appease the editor in chief. The six-person features department was joined by a market editor delegate from the fashion team, whose job it was to ensure that the conversation accounted for the complicated geopolitics of fashion design brands who took out advertisement pages. The group gathered in a conference room, the back wall of which held printouts of images from each story thumbtacked in a possible page order. The features team stood around and examined each page closely, then stepped back to see things from afar, not unlike collectors in a Chelsea gallery.

"What do we think of the 'Mixed Prints' shoot?" asked Theresa.

The features team should have been focused on the written stories and display copy as opposed to the fashion shoots themselves; the magazine's fashion director and creative director had the real say over the visual elements of the well. Still, Theresa couldn't resist an opportunity to denigrate the fashion director's work, particularly since she was absent from the room. Theresa was above the fashion director on the masthead, but the fashion director reported directly to the editor in chief, just as Theresa did, since they oversaw different departments. This bothered Theresa, that someone beneath her had her same chain of command. These backstabbing moments functioned as petty reparations for Theresa.

"It looks psychotic," said Susan, who believed that relentless negativity was the same thing as incisive commentary. She also despised the fashion director, as she did everyone in the fashion department, and was happy to encourage Theresa's games. "Not good psychotic," she clarified.

"Yes," said Theresa. "And 'Jungle Rumble'?"

"Tropical is very important for resort," piped in the fashion market editor.

"Yes, but does it have to be so sweaty?" said Susan.

"'Asia Minor,' any thoughts?" said Theresa.

I have a few, Lily mused to herself.

"The well is looking a bit ethnic, don't you think?" said Susan.

"Ethnic was everywhere for resort," shot back the fashion market editor. "It's super important that we get it in."

"I think someone needs to choose between the jungle and Asia," said Theresa.

With a quick glance around the conference room, Lily sought a sympathetic pair of eyes. There were none to be found in the surrounding white faces, so she stared down at the floor with an inaudible sigh.

"Those stories have all the advertisers. If we cut either of them, Pat will not be pleased," said the fashion market editor, invoking the name of their imperious and, frankly, terrifying publisher. Nobody wanted an angry call from her.

"Fine," said Theresa, still intent on pretending she had authority over stories outside her domain. "But your team should consider some different options. These are not working."

With that, the meeting ground to an unofficial end, though no actual feature stories had been discussed. As the group filed out of the conference room and back to their respective desks, Susan approached Lily.

"Your story on that new theater district cabaret was nice," she said.

"Thanks," said Lily. Immediately, her internal guard dog was at attention.

"I mean, I don't know how much editing Theresa had to do on it, but it was nice," Susan added with a smirk, then waltzed away before Lily had a chance to reply.

Encounters with her colleagues hadn't always been so demeaning. Years ago, Lily had looked forward to work most days. The environment had been competitive, but healthily so, in a manner that encouraged everyone to step up their game. She couldn't remember a single instance in her first couple of years on the job when an editor had diminished her stories. There had been plenty of constructive criticism on rewriting ledes or streamlining sections or cutting down quotes or digging deeper on crucial points. There had been zero suggestion that she lacked the skills to create good pieces if she buckled down.

These days, Lily had no one she could seek out for advice. An expression of anything that bordered on uncertainty was, to Theresa, Susan, and the rest of the staff, the equivalent of an admission of weakness. Either they would belittle the question or, worse, they would file it away as ammunition to use against her in some to-be-determined scenario in the not-so-distant future. It was like a desert-island dystopian novel but with more expensive clothes and less physical exertion.

Lily understood that this hostile landscape was the product of the greater media world's Darwinian struggle against encroaching digital forces. The prospect of extinction could bring out people's ugliest natures. Her colleagues' verbal slices revealed more of their own insecurities and terror over obsolescence than they did Lily's shortcomings. In response, Lily did the only thing she believed might insulate her, though it couldn't preserve her self-esteem: She opted out. This approach did little to cushion any blows. Instead, it enveloped her in professional paralysis.

• • •

DAYS LATER WITH still no word from B, Lily concluded that the only reasonable thing to do was to go out and numb her anxieties with alcohol. She corralled Marissa into a night of sampling some new mixology places in the East Village, an adult cover for getting tastefully wasted.

"I'm not sure how I feel about Earl Grey in my martini," said Marissa. She considered the cloudy concoction in a long-stemmed glass before her. "I thought it had potential, but it might be too much like drinking at breakfast time."

They were on their first round at their second location, a dimly lit, Southeast Asian–themed lounge one floor up from street level with a reputation for its experimental and sophisticated cocktails. After they had encountered their fifth handlebar mustache at their first bar in the East Village, they had decamped for SoHo's comparatively safer grounds.

"It's like it's trying to be healthy and toxic," said Lily, "but then it ends up being neither. This Vesper is good — citrusy."

"I thought you didn't like gin."

"I don't. But it's okay when mixed with vodka. How's Luke doing?"

"Good. Training for a marathon in January."

"Why would anyone do a marathon in the winter?"

"He says you don't sweat as much. So you're less dehydrated."

"Meanwhile, you're freezing your ass off."

"He's been waking up at four thirty A.M. for long training runs. You couldn't pay me. Opposites very much attract."

Marissa shifted her long, lean legs around on her barstool so that she faced Lily.

"What's Alison up to?"

"She had to work late. But she might meet up with us if she's not too tired when she's done."

"Cool. And how's everything else?"

"Okay."

"You still in touch with that woman?"

"Yes."

"And that's . . . ?"

Lily related her recent showdown with B and the resulting silence.

"Ah. She's the type who has to come out on top. I told you to watch out for her."

"I don't know why I care so much what she thinks of me. But I do."

"Maybe you have feelings for her."

"Definitely not. She's just a professional guide."

"Is she?"

"I barely know her."

"You seem to be pretty wrung out over someone you don't really know."

Marissa was right, of course. Her lawyerly reasoning cut to the heart of the matter. Lily had no reason to be this upset. B had gifted her a few months of free career advice. Lily had earned a well-story assignment and some nice boosts of confidence as a result. If this was all their interactions amounted to, that wasn't so bad.

And here she sat, a jittery mess, worried that in B's mind, Lily would forever be a silly, insipid girl on whom B had wasted her precious time. Lily knew she wasn't devoid of potential. She could feel it prickling at her fingertips as she typed at her desk or clutched a metal subway pole or diced some garlic for dinner. These electric sensations brought with them a peek at who she might become if she cast aside her old habits and manifested a new self. These pinpricks felt a lot like the buzz buzz of her phone. Lily had become convinced they were the same thing. When the buzz buzz of her phone ceased, her potential might disappear with it.

"I feel like I'm on the brink of a breakthrough. At work. And I guess in life," said Lily. "And for whatever reason, it's linked to her."

"You need her to get to this next stage."

"Yeah. And I worry this is my only chance to figure out who I could be."

"Right. I get that. But whoever you're meant to be should already exist. I mean, she shouldn't change you."

Maybe B already had. When Lily didn't bask in her adrenaline over-load, she was a parched desert, drained of her usual reserves. On mul-tiple occasions, Alison had asked her where she was, where she had gone. "I'm right here," Lily always replied. But she wasn't. This was the sleepwalking life B had accused her of leading. What a sick joke that was. Lily had had a life, a real and full one, before B crashed her way in. That's where B wanted her. Codependent and desperate. This was not who Lily was. She was no one's charity case.

"I think I need to stop texting with her," she said.

"It's worth considering."

"I'm so tired."

"And what about Alison?" Marissa took a reluctant sip of her Earl Grey concoction.

"What about her?"

"How does Alison figure into all of this?"

"This isn't real. It's a bunch of stupid text messages about work with someone I don't even know." Lily rubbed her fingers together.

"That's not the point. The issue is that this mentorship or whatever is totally consuming you. Where you can't focus on anyone else. Includ-ing Alison."

"So, once you're in a relationship, your career plays second string?"

"Of course not. But is this really only about work?"

"Yes!" Lily said in exasperation. "It's not even a friendship. An actual friend wouldn't behave like this."

"Exactly. Then why are you putting up with this shit from someone you barely know?"

"I told you. It feels like this is my only shot to make my life better."

"And while you're busy trying to make your life better, you're forget-ting there are parts of your life that are already great. People who are great."

"Yeah, I know."

"And they may not be there forever. Just saying."

The women finished their drinks and parted ways outside the bar. They turned off toward their respective subways. Lily walked in the direction of the Houston Street station. Every bar Lily passed teemed with patrons; they laughed and imbibed their way into the weekend's easy leisure. Restaurants steeled themselves for their final hour of operation. Servers pushed through their last rounds of entrées and desserts before the Fernet-Branca shots that would send them home. At the intersection of Houston and Varick Streets, Lily descended to the subway's depths. She had just missed a train. She checked to see if Alison had texted her. The station was in a no-service bubble.

Eventually, another train arrived and Lily lucked upon a seat. The car was more than half-full, a patchwork of riders of all shapes, ages, genders, and races seated on the plastic benches or leaned up against the glass doors, in defiance of the signage instructing them to do otherwise. In contrast to the other spheres through which Lily moved, the subway was a system where whiteness was not a default strain. A cluster of twenty-something friends huddled in one corner and rehashed their exploits from earlier in the evening. A man in a shirt and suit pants, his tie loosened, his jacket folded neatly in his lap, bulky headphones glued to his ears, destressed from his punishing Wall Street job, or so Lily imagined based on his attire and demeanor. A young woman, possibly the same age as Lily, was seated across the center aisle, her face blocked by the cover of her novel. At one point, the subway slowed to a crawl and the young woman lowered her book's cover and glanced up at the digital signage to check the time and next stop.

The young woman was mixed-race and Asian—Lily determined these facts instantly with a practiced expertise that she could never have broken down precisely for another person. It wasn't the young woman's features or coloring, though naturally those factored into Lily's quick conviction. It was a recognition of familiarity that resonated somewhere deep in Lily's chest, mainly because it was a feeling she experienced with such acute infrequency. The young woman held her book in her lap now and leaned forward to continue her reading. Her hair, a medium chestnut brown that was lighter than Lily's, was in a long ponytail that was flung casually across one of her shoulders. A cloth tote bag was on the bench beside her. A beeping noise resounded from inside the bag. The young woman reached into the tote, extracted a phone, and without fully training her gaze on its screen, silenced the device and jammed it back into her bag. She continued to read.

Lily could be like this young woman. Six months ago, Lily had been this young woman, someone whose priority was the book or person in front of her, not the buzz buzz of her phone. Minutes had passed and this young woman didn't seem to care who or what had prompted the ringing on her device. The young woman's hands didn't shake. She didn't tap tap tap her feet on the subway's floor in impatience for a reply. She was so centered, so in the moment of her own action, she hadn't even noticed Lily's curious gaze lingering on her hunched-over figure. It was as though Lily watched a miracle play out before her. No, it wasn't a miracle she saw; it was an alternate version of who she could be if she finally abandoned B for good.

When Lily arrived home, she would tell Alison she wanted to go away with her for the upcoming holidays. Somewhere cozy and removed, where they could focus on each other. She would finally pitch those feature story ideas she had saved up, worried that her colleagues would shoot them down and claim they needed her attention on other things. Or worse, that they would steal her ideas and assign them to someone else with more "experience." Lily was ready. She had been ready for so long. The woman she had always hoped to become was ready to emerge, too. Enough waiting. More doing. And screw what anyone else thought.

LILY'S SUBWAY REVELATION tickled her brain at work the following morning. Tonight, over dinner, she would make plans with Alison for a proper vacation in some off-the-grid locale beyond the reach of a cellular network. She would delete B's contact info from her phone, or better yet, she would block her. Lily could taste the full sweetness of imminent freedom on her tongue. She was so close to self-actualization. Just a few more hours of daydreaming about the possibility, and then she would make it real.

The phone on Lily's desk rang with a call from Theresa, who asked her to swing by. Lily knocked on her glass door, and when Theresa looked up and waved her in, Lily lowered herself into one of the chairs that faced her.

Theresa cleared her throat.

"As you know, we've been amping up our digital-only offerings. We announced those two new hires last week, in video and social."

Lily nodded.

"But it isn't just about adding staffers. We also need current staffers to pitch in more."

Theresa paused. Her eyes expected Lily to speak. When she didn't, Theresa continued.

"We'd like for you to write two long-form digital-only stories a week."

"Instead of what I'm doing for print? You want me to move over to digital only?"

"No, no—of course not! That's not what this is. Those digital stories will be in addition to what you're producing for print."

"I see."

"It's all hands on deck, Lily. We all have to pitch in."

Lily's jaw tensed. "Everyone else in the features department is also being asked to produce two long-form stories every week for digital?"

Theresa crossed her thin, white arms over her chest. "This isn't about other people, Lily. It's not a competition. It's about you. And what you have to offer us. You've asked to write more well stories. We gave you that Antonio Russo piece for December. Here's your chance to keep writing longer pieces for us."

Except this wasn't an offer to write more well stories that telegraphed one's status and abilities as a writer worthy of tackling lengthier narratives. This was a request to write eight extra, long-form stories a month for a website that paid its freelance writers 15 percent of what the print magazine offered for the equivalent-length piece. Essentially, Theresa had informed Lily that the market rate of her future work had plummeted precipitously.

"See this as the opportunity that it is," Theresa pressed. "You can write all those actor and actress profiles that we never have space for in the magazine. And with your work ethic, I'm sure you won't have any problem fitting these extra pieces in."

Say no, Lily thought to herself, just say no. There was nothing Theresa could do if Lily said no. But Lily didn't utter a word. The only sounds in Theresa's office were the humming of her desktop computer and the quiet whoosh of air from the vent in the ceiling.

"And look, I know it's extra work," she said, relenting in response to Lily's icy silence, "but you don't have to kill yourself with these pieces. This is really a numbers game at the end of the day. Nobody's going to read your stories anyway; online, people only look at headlines and pictures. Don't overexert yourself." Theresa paused. She pursed her thin lips. "Okay, that's all I've got. Let me know if you have any questions. You can send your pitches and stories directly to Marc."

Lily nodded. She stood up from her chair and left Theresa's office. Back at her desk, she gripped the plastic arms of her own chair with a force that might unlock a secret eject button that would propel her out of this office and into another dimension where such meetings didn't occur. Theresa wanted her to do more work, with a lower street value than her current load, but it wasn't going to be stressful because, surprise, no one would ever read it. What a relief! Oh, and she could look forward to more conversations with Marc. Lily snatched her phone from its spot beside her keyboard.

Lily: How's your day?

Lily: Mine isn't going so great.

On her desk computer, Lily opened a new browser window to research an upcoming interview with a former magazine editor and passionate animal lover who had launched an organic dog treats line. A slew of onetime editors had quit their media jobs to embark on tactile, solid businesses like gluten-free baked goods companies and organic mushroom skin care lines. Buzz buzz.

Alison: Not bad.

Alison: Just led a good team meeting.

Alison: We're cracking this case.

Lily: How are those two new hires?

Alison: Lazy. They complain if I ask them to stay past six.

Alison: This younger generation.

Lily: The worst.

Alison: Seriously.

Alison: What's going on there?

Lily: They're asking me to write eight extra stories a month.

Lily: For the website.

Alison: For more money?

Lily: What do you think?

Lily: The best part is Theresa told me no one would read any of the stories I wrote for digital.

Lily: So I don't have to put too much effort into them!

Alison: Jesus. Some salesperson she is.

Lily: What am I going to do? This is only the beginning of more.

Lily: The sad thing is, the digital stories might be fun.

Lily: But nobody values them.

Lily: They give them away for free.

The former editor's dog treats were as beautiful as one would expect from someone who forged a career from her impeccable taste. Instead of generic bone cutouts, the biscuits were shaped like shoes, handbags, and dresses, a nod to the former editor's past life and perhaps to the many accessories her own pets had chewed beyond recognition. Buzz buzz.

Alison: It makes no sense.

Alison: Implicitly devalues the work of the creators involved.

Alison: And doesn't monetize the built-in audience.

Lily: I might have to give up on this whole writing thing.

Lily: I've made it as far as I ever will.

Alison: Sorry, babe. I have to hop on a call. Promise we'll talk later.

The tie-dyed treats floated before Lily. If only she could manifest her version of this former editor's plan B.

Speaking of, she had promised herself she wouldn't text B. She was done with B's twisted version of career coaching. Alison would advise her later that evening. Together, they would brainstorm a game plan. Except Alison didn't know much about the media world. The companies for whom she consulted were Fortune 500 titans, like health care brands or mass retailers or oil and energy corporations. And this was serious, far more serious than a PR person strong-arming her interview or a story assignment predicated on tokenism: This was Lily's current and future value as an employee. It didn't get more serious than this. She couldn't navigate this entirely on her own. B would know exactly what to do.

It was one more text exchange. One more question. And then she would be done. This was a desperate situation and Lily needed that dose of self-assertion that only B could extend.

Lily: I'm slowly being forced to move over to digital at work.

Lily: Even though my manager is pretending otherwise.

Lily: Which means my work will have implicitly less financial worth.

Lily: And I could really use your advice.

She had sent her appeal. B would reply. And then Lily could walk away for good.

12

. . .

THE TWO WEEKS after the New Year's holiday settled on the city like a wet wool blanket. All the joy, all the merriment, all the sparkling lights and clinking glasses faded like a dream of another world. In their place came the drudgery of salt-stained boots trudging through gray slush, past the brown corpses of dry trees stacked haphazardly on street corners. People roamed the city with dazed expressions. Websites and magazines churned out self-improvement tips—"How to Lose That Holiday Weight!" "37 Ways to Stop Drinking!" "28 Recipes for a Healthy New Lifestyle!" Gyms were packed with sweaty, out-of-shape bodies that ran on treadmills, shuffled on elliptical machines, climbed stairs to nowhere fast. Most of those bodies would be gone in a month's time, relegated to lumpy sofas with beers and bags of chips as accessories. Life in January was one collective failure at atonement.

Lily hadn't overindulged too heavily during the holiday season. There had been a handful of cocktail parties, including one for the magazine's staff at a basement-level speakeasy in a trendy hotel. Aspiring male models who moonlit as catering waiters passed out pigs in blankets, miniature grilled cheese sandwiches, and smoked salmon canapés to fashion editors. Coupes of $300-a-bottle champagne filled tray after silver tray. A friend of Jordan's from college hosted an impromptu New Year's Eve get-together in her tiny SoHo apartment, where Lily and Alison sipped deceptively strong punch from porcelain teacups and then passed out at Alison's place a couple of minutes after midnight.

Now it was a Saturday afternoon in January and all Lily could think about was work. She had a panel discussion that she had agreed to attend later that evening. The event was to take place in the library of a private members' club downtown, one of a new generation of elitist institutions that enticed young socially connected types to pay $3,000 a year for the privilege of rubbing shoulders with other socially connected types in the club's various public spaces. The panel in question was entitled "Wellness and Social Media: A Happy Marriage." Its promotion was overseen by a PR woman, Rebecca, with whom Lily was tangentially friendly and who had suggested that Lily might sit in, not for coverage, but purely for edification.

Offhandedly, Lily had confided to Rebecca, in a clandestine corner of an autism gala a year ago, that she was concerned, in general, about the state of her chosen industry. It was hardly a bracing revelation and Lily figured she was safe to put forward such a benign feeler. One would be hard-pressed to find a magazine writer or editor who wasn't terrified of the future; to choose this profession was to commit to life in the perpetual grip of fear that one was just a scary meeting away from complete extinction. Rebecca had promised to let Lily know if she stumbled on any leads. When Rebecca emailed her about the wellness panel, Lily understood that the event was likely more about Rebecca's promotion of her client, the private members' club, than Lily's career. But she figured there was no harm if she attended with an open mind. The panel was at five P.M. Lily planned to meet Alison for dinner afterward.

On this snowy afternoon, Lily sat on her sofa at home and typed away on her computer. At first, following her demoralizing meeting with Theresa, she had sunk into a depressed morass, convinced that writing had no part in her future. As Theresa had made abundantly clear, what Lily wrote had no worth, monetarily or spiritually, to a potential reader. Lily certainly hadn't operated under the gross misconception that what she did was of immense importance. The planet would revolve, contentedly, without another profile of a beautiful twenty-five-to-thirty-year-old actress on the verge of mega-stardom or a satirical piece on the silent auction offerings of New York City galas.

Lily had entered into this whole magazine-writing mess not because she considered it necessary work or a ticket to renown. Rather, magazines embodied a professional version of one of her greatest passions: the creation, exchange, and discussion of stories. In her magazine work, she could discover something interesting, interview someone about it, and dissect the narrative threads that hid in their words and that made the topic come alive for others. Each conversation she had with an interview subject, and there had been hundreds over the past decade, left her a bit more knowledgeable about and connected to the world around her. These conversations fed her ongoing growth; they reminded her that other people's stories and perspectives were crucial pieces in understanding the puzzles of our own existence.

And the construction of these stories mimicked the internal synthesis that Lily experienced in the interviews. To spin research fragments and observations into a coherent whole constituted a form of alchemy. Storytelling was the closest Lily would ever get to magic. She was not possessed of superhuman athleticism or a prodigious musical talent. She would never be the smartest or most impressive person in a room. Through writing she was able to leave her tiny mark on this planet.

Theresa and the world at large had voided that one little thing that made her feel capable. It was now meaningless. And she was, too. So yes,

Lily was depressed for a week or two. And then she grew angry. If no one was going to read anything she wrote for the magazine's website, then fine, she wouldn't drive herself into the ground. She still wanted her pieces to be better than legible, though, for the three people who might deign to skim them, despite Theresa's exhortation. Lily wouldn't submit crap on a stick because the higher-ups had collectively decided that anything in a digital state had to be dumbed down, as if literacy were somehow at odds with basic internet access and smartphone ownership.

And Lily would not give up on writing, nor the magic embedded in its process that allowed her to make sense of the people and things she experienced. That part was hers forever and no one could tear it away from her. The problem, she realized, wasn't the writing itself; it was that Lily had let the magazine enjoy full ownership of her ability to do it. Once Lily's anger at Theresa and the corporate world lessened, she arrived at a solution, which was to make writing her own. She needed to differentiate what her writing might look like outside the dictates of her magazine. This led Lily to her experimentations with fiction.

Lily typed away on her personal computer in the mornings before work, in the evenings, and during the weekend hours whenever she and Alison were apart. Her literary meanderings were compressed, vignettes with random characters, short scenes, isolated snippets of dialogue, and made little sense. Unlike her stories for work, they didn't have to adhere to other people's expectations or her own. There was no end goal beyond flexing her imagination. Eventually, she hoped her musings would crystallize into a form of clarity. For now, their very existence planted in her a seed of hope.

At four P.M., Lily closed her laptop. The sidewalks along Broadway were unevenly shoveled. Patches were covered in icy slush that rendered navigation treacherous. Once in the subway station, Lily was fishing her subway card out of her bag to swipe it through the turnstile when her phone vibrated.

B: Hi there.

B: Staying warm and cozy with your girlfriend tonight?

Quite the opposite. Lily proceeded through the turnstile and found an empty spot on the subway platform. Her promise to herself that she would abandon B after extracting one final piece of advice had lasted the length of time it took B to respond to Lily's professional SOS. After her urgent messages regarding the Theresa digital meeting a couple of months back, B had issued Lily her version of a pep talk, more an open-handed slap to the face than an encouraging shoulder squeeze.

B: You need to see this as an opportunity.

B: Build your name online.

B: That's where the future is.

B: Use the digital platform these stories will give you.

B: Stop pretending digital is going away.

Fury had flooded Lily's veins. This wasn't an opportunity; it was exploitation. Perhaps B had been out of the trenches for too long to recognize the difference. In fact, B's advice sounded suspiciously similar to Theresa's defense of the extra workload. All corporate managers must study the same rhetorical playbook on how to suck their direct reports dry under the guise of upward mobility. Once Lily inhaled a few deep breaths and threw down some laps around Central Park, she realized that regardless of whether B was right, in principle, her suggestion was the only way Lily could emerge from this intact. She needed to reframe this story. If she behaved like a mule, people would treat her like a mule. If she approached this like an opportunity for expanding her byline, then her byline would expand and more opportunities would come as a result. Her fate was in her hands, and thanks to B, she knew what the situation required.

She wrote those extra stories, the ones no one would read, the ones with zero value. And she didn't abandon the idea of a life built on fantasies and writing. She simply shifted those fantasies and that writing to a different part of her brain.

As for B, she and Lily were back where they had begun: the iconic powerhouse and her ever-devoted mentee. Lily had experienced a momentary flash of shame at abandoning so quickly her resolve to cut ties with B. But she was wiser now. She was better equipped to filter out the utility of B's wisdom from the strong-arming of her messaging. Lily didn't have specific evidence to back up this conviction, yet she knew, without the requirement of proof, that she was correct. The reignition of this texting with B wasn't a sign of her weakness; it was an expression of her pragmatism. With the hypnotic spin of a scammer, Lily told herself that she was using B, not the other way around. Forget cave painting—self-deception is the oldest art form there is.

The station was a tunnel of freezing air. Lily tugged a glove off momentarily and typed out a response.

Lily: Not exactly.

Lily: I am going to a talk downtown.

Lily: About the rise of influencers.

Lily: Aren't you proud?

A faint metallic rumbling and a shift in the air signaled the train's imminent arrival. Lily stuffed her phone back into her coat pocket. The car was nearly full. A messy snowstorm was no deterrent to the Saturday evening plans of the city's inhabitants. The car doors closed and the train careened out of the station. Lily pulled a book from her bag, an old used copy of a nineteenth-century British novel of manners from her high school days. Buzz buzz.

Alison: There's a cute-sounding bistro a few blocks from the club.

Alison: Want to go there for dinner?

Lily removed a glove to type a reply.

Lily: Sure!

Lily: The talk's supposed to be over at 6:30.

Lily: Why don't we meet there at 7 to be safe.

A man and a woman a quarter of the train car away from Lily spoke in heated tones about the woman's sister, younger it seemed, who had a crush on the man's best friend from college. The sister wanted the couple's permission to pursue a relationship with him. Lily closed her book.

"This seems like a terrible idea," said the man.

"Why?" said the woman. "She's not good enough for Jim?"

"Of course she is. She's too good for him."

"Isn't that up to Kaley to decide?"

Buzz buzz.

B: Well, aren't you the A student.

B: But all work and no play might make Lily a dull girl.

B: We wouldn't want that.

Lily unlocked her phone to respond, but the car was between stations and she had no service. She turned back to her book. The couple was still at it and Lily's concentration dissolved into their words.

"Look, we're already fighting and they haven't started dating. What's going to happen if they break up?" said the man.

"You're assuming their relationship will fail!" the woman growled.

"No, I'm not. But come on, Kaley doesn't have the best track record with guys."

"And Jim is such a beacon of romantic success?"

The train ground to a violent halt. A voice came over the loudspeaker.

"This is your conductor. We are experiencing delays due to train traffic ahead of us. We'll be moving shortly. We apologize for the inconvenience."

"Now we're going to be late to meet Kaley."

"She's coming to dinner with us? Jeanne, what the hell?"

"You never had a problem with her joining us before."

"But she's going to bring up Jim, and what are we going to say?"

The train lurched forward. Buzz buzz.

B: Let me know how the panel is.

B: A full review.

B: Some Saturday night entertainment.

Lily unlocked her phone.

Lily: I didn't realize I was a source of entertainment.

Lily: I'll do my best.

Lily: Hope I don't get performance anxiety.

The messages started to send, then paused partway through. Lily had no service again. She shoved the novel in her bag. So much for her new or old undistracted self.

"We are not walking into that restaurant until we agree on what to tell Kaley," said the woman.

"Fine by me. I can sit on this subway all night!"

The train doors whooshed open. They were at Fourteenth Street. Lily squeezed out the doors past the incoming passengers. She would never learn the fate of Kaley and Jim, not to mention Jeanne and her boyfriend, whose partnership appeared increasingly fraught. So much of Lily's experience of New York was a trailer reel, full of tantalizing tidbits but no actual plot or resolution. Buzz buzz.

B: You seem like a high performer in all areas.

B: Don't let me down.

At the private club's discreet glass-doored entrance, Lily gave her name to the stark woman seated at a desk in the lobby. The woman checked Lily's name against a list on her tablet and then motioned to the nearby elevators.

"Fifth-floor library," she said.

Once on the designated level, Lily located the library room, which was covered in a wallpaper that featured a trompe l'oeil print of multi-colored leather-bound books instead of shelves of actual books. It was as though Lily had stepped into an artfully constructed metaphor. She selected a chair near the back in case the panel proved so insufferable that she was forced to flee. Across the "library," near the makeshift stage that had been cordoned off, was a tall, slender woman in a pencil skirt, oversized gray cardigan, and low-heeled pumps. In the slushy aftermath of a snowstorm, Rebecca appeared immaculate. Lily glanced down at her cozy Fair Isle sweater and black jeans tucked into vintage combat boots. Her outfit had seemed both weather- and setting-appropriate when she had left her apartment, but now it read as ironically scruffy at best. Rebecca waved at Lily, then stood up from her front-row seat and walked over to hug Lily in greeting.

"So glad you came," she said as her porcelain cheek brushed against Lily's. "The program should be starting soon. Hope you enjoy it."

Rebecca returned to her spot, and Lily observed the three people seated in the stage area, their chairs angled toward a separate chair designated for the moderator. According to the press release Rebecca had emailed earlier that week, the moderator was a male journalist, Frank Jackson, who had started out in media five years after Lily had. Frank had quickly ascended the ranks from assistant to features editor through an assiduous campaign of late-night partying with celebrities and top fashion editors, during which time he became a go-to confidant for a slew of bold-faced women. Frank was sleek and darkly handsome in the manner of a fifties film star, and he was possessed of a mischievous charm that tricked women into unloading their juiciest gossip. Once he had extracted enough secrets to last him through retirement, Frank became untouchable; the sheer prospect that he might one day resort to blackmail scared everyone into giving him exactly what he desired. Two years ago, Frank had decided that what he really wanted was to transition out of the slowly dying magazine world and into the social media realm, where his one true talent, amassing popularity, had quantitative support, in the form of hundreds of thousands of followers. Frank now worked for a photo-sharing app as a "consulting curator of culture," one of those Kafkaesque digital titles that gave no indication of what a person really did to earn their keep.

Thanks to his current position, Frank had assembled a panel comprised of three top influencers, one of whom Lily had profiled in the magazine a few years prior. All three women ranged from twenty-four to twenty-eight years old and had the sort of inoffensive, pale-skinned prettiness that was typical of their chosen calling. The influencers were uniformly thin in a manner that suggested that they followed vegan, gluten-free diets, not out of deep concern for the planet or for their internal inflammation levels, rather as a clever cover for their dysfunctional eating. Those croissants in their feeds from Paris fashion week had never crossed the thresholds of their aggressively glossed lips.

Frank was on the stage now, and seated closest to him was Alyssa (@Nature4Eva), who per the bio on her profile page was a "natural beauty and cosmetics advocate, clean stuff only, margarita aficionado." Next was Penelope (@FoodNotShame), a healthy-eating "activist"—her term—who encouraged her followers to make colorful, plant-based meals with ingredient lists that often numbered well into the teens. And finally, Ceci (@LaDolceVitaaa) was an Italian transplant to California who devoted her feed to sustainable fashion. This endeavor usually produced countless selfies in various luxury fashion looks, made of recycled cashmere and organic cotton, that she borrowed directly from different labels for the purposes of the photo shoots. When Lily had interviewed Ceci four years ago, she'd had around fifty thousand followers; Ceci now boasted 1.2 million and counting.

Frank introduced each woman briefly, then read his first question off an old-school index card from a stack on a side table next to his chair.

Digital people liked to ostentatiously display their affinity for analog items such as no. 2 pencils, vinyl records, and stickers, as if to say, *Look, we're not the devil! We appreciate tactile stuff, too.* His first question went to Alyssa.

"What inspired you to start Nature 4 Eva in the social media beauty space?"

Alyssa tossed her toasted-almond hair. "I kept getting these breakouts from all the chemicals in standard beauty products. And I thought, I can do better! I did a deep dive into the clean brands that were out there, but no one was paying attention. And I was like, if I can bring attention to them, I can save my skin and the planet. At the same time. And help others, too."

Technically, so-called natural ingredients like tea tree oil and honey were still chemicals. But okay, Lily would try to give Alyssa the benefit of the doubt.

"And what about you, Penelope, what inspired you?"

"Like Alyssa, I was feeling sickened and overwhelmed by all the hormones and chemicals I was ingesting, through the food I was eating. My skin was terrible. I was bloated and sluggish all the time. And I believed that I deserved better. I embraced a vegan, gluten-free diet. But I wanted to eliminate the deprivation that's usually associated with that way of eating by making it fun, colorful, and accessible."

"That's great, Penelope. And what about you, Ceci?"

"I have always loved fashion. With a passion. But it felt like my love was bad for the planet. I wanted to reclaim fashion as a manifestation of health, personally and ecologically. Looking good should do good, too! That's my motto."

"I couldn't agree more! And what does wellness mean to all of you? Maybe we could start with you, Alyssa."

Lily shifted in her seat. She uncrossed and recrossed her legs.

Alyssa delivered a spiel about how happiness with the way one looked and felt in their own skin was known, thanks to a slew of non-specific studies she failed to cite, to have a positive impact on one's psyche; this, in turn, made beauty a crucial facet of wellness. And Penelope droned on about how health starts in the gut. Beautiful and conscious consumption was the heart of a well body and mind.

Ceci smiled brightly at Frank and then the audience. She strutted into her answer.

"I have loved fashion for as long as I can remember. As a little kid, I was obsessed with picking outfits and getting dressed. I'm old enough that fashion magazines were still an important place for learning about style when I was growing up."

Lily was not a fan of Ceci's prominent usage of the past tense, not to mention her answer ignored the original question.

"But today, they are a dead medium. No one cares what they have to say anymore. The reason is because they are the opposite of wellness. They promote an endless cycle of consumption, encouraging people to buy new clothes all the time to stay trendy, therefore creating more waste."

Sure, ignore the fact that social media promoted an endless cycle of consumption whose byproduct was the waste of everyone's time, and further, the deterioration of our collective psychological well-being.

"With social media, we all have the means to self-actualize. We can be whoever we want to be. We don't have to follow some magazine's ideas of what's cool and interesting. We decide what that is through the content we produce. In my case, I use my platform to promote sustainability in style. For example, last month, in honor of the holiday season, I wore the same dress every day and posted one daily selfie styling that dress differently. I called it 'Thirty-One Days of Dress.' In doing that, I dismantled the harmful idea that we can't be seen wearing the same thing twice. That's something a magazine would never do."

Lily's head pounded so hard, she could barely focus on another word that Ceci uttered. Thankfully, the panel wound down and Frank delivered some final remarks that Lily didn't bother to process. There was applause around her and a swell of noise and movement as people stood up from their seats. Lily hurried out of the library. She pressed the button for the elevator. As she waited, she unlocked her phone and texted Alison.

Lily: Leaving panel now.

Lily: I may get to the restaurant before seven, but don't worry or rush.

The elevator doors opened. Lily was relieved to find the mirrored box empty of other passengers. Finally, she could be alone with her thoughts.

To start, there was Ceci's outright dismissal of the current weight that magazines held. Lily's article about Ceci had given her a validity that no amount of digital-only promotion could achieve. If Ceci didn't believe that magazines still held sway over popular opinion, she shouldn't have bothered to appear in one.

It was impossible to contest, though, that the status of magazines had waned; the panel's mere existence implied as much. More upsetting to Lily was these influencers' stance that what they did was a version of altruism. If they wanted to make a living by posting selfies, then go for it. Models made a living off their beauty, too. Arguably, so did some actresses. Beauty had its advantages. Lily could understand why someone blessed with beauty would cash in on its rewards while they could. It was the need to justify it as activism that ate at Lily's patience. Perhaps if these influencers were not white and tall and thin and conventionally attractive, they might have stronger grounds for that defense.

Ceci's posts of the same dress every day for a month did not make her a digital Joan of Arc. Not to mention, no one besides Ceci knew if she had, in fact, worn that same dress every day or if her photos had simply made it appear that way. Her feed, like every feed on social media, was a highly curated performance. Which made it not that different from the aspirational stories embedded in magazines, save for one key distinction: fashion magazines didn't pretend to depict unvarnished reality, though they were unquestionably misleading about the extent of the varnishing in question. These influencers had profiles built on personal authenticity. In this respect, their social media fantasies were even more insidious than the ones in magazines because theirs claimed not to be fantasies at all. They claimed to be the truth.

And Lily had helped elevate Ceci and all her contemporaries and their performances of authenticity to their current primacy in popular culture. Lily's casual endorsement of them in her stories as people worth knowing continued to feed their significance. The increasing dominance of these influencers in turn diminished the weight that magazines carried because they all competed for the same capricious attention of advertising dollars. Which meant that Lily's coverage of Ceci and her ilk contributed, in essence, to her own professional obsolescence.

Lily could insist, as she tried to in this moment, that she had covered the trend of social media, not helped create it. That's what journalists did, not that she was a journalist: They reported on things; they were detached from any action or change. The more carefully Lily examined this assertion, the more it lost its shape of certainty. It began to resemble a deferral of responsibility. Wherever she landed in this chicken versus egg circularity, the reality was she could not suddenly ignore influencers. They had become both the subject of the story and the preferred medium itself. To pretend they didn't exist was to risk utter irrelevance. It was a shortcut to extinction.

13

• • •

OUTSIDE THE PRIVATE club, Lily eyed her wrist. It was 6:21 P.M. The restaurant likely wouldn't seat her so far before her scheduled reservation. It was too cold to stroll around outside until then, so Lily headed to a queer bar a few blocks away. After the panel's onslaught, she needed a comforting space. Hopefully, there wouldn't be any aggressively snap-happy influencers there. The clunking of cars on the cobblestone streets reverberated in the frozen night air as Lily crossed the ambivalent divide between the Meatpacking District's oversized tackiness and the West Village's quaint elegance. It was like walking from Las Vegas to Paris in a few minutes.

The bar was situated at an enviable intersection between two pictur-esque streets, dotted with nineteenth-century town houses that likely cost upwards of $20 million; this duality encapsulated the patina of history and the brashness of new money that defined so much of Man-hattan's current identity. An unassuming green storefront masked a profusion of maximalist delight within: an outpouring of colorful tchotchkes, ornaments, lanterns, parasols, Christmas lights, chande-liers, kites, tinsel, snowflakes, dolphins, and other imaginative creations hung from the ceiling in a dense cluster that imparted the feeling of a psychedelic phantasmagoria slowly encroaching on a person from above.

Lily approached the security woman bundled in a down parka and knitted cap at the bar's entrance. The woman checked the date on Lily's ID and nodded her in. It was still early, so the bar's stools were only half-occupied. Lily hoisted herself onto a seat close to the entrance and draped her coat across the stool's high back. A Swedish singer's champagne-fizz voice popped steadily from a set of speakers. The tart scent of citrus, from the lemon-twist garnishes piled in a glass behind the bar, sliced through the room's coziness. Finally, there was a minute for Lily to catch her breath and erase the nausea of the panel.

The bartender wore faded black jeans and a muscle tee that revealed the delicate calligraphy across her arms, a bold affront to the wintry draft that rushed in every time the door opened. Lily's bourbon order arrived in a plastic cup. She plucked her phone out of her bag to text B.

Lily: Panel was a nightmare. Influencers acting like they're changing the world by posting selfies.

Lily: Can't believe this is the present and future of media.

A fortifying sip of three-year-old sour mash dulled the painfulness of this observation. Buzz buzz.

B: Beat them at their own game.

B: It shouldn't be hard.

B: Plenty of people would want to see photos of you.

Lily: Thanks, but that's not my MO.

Lily: I couldn't do what they do.

B: Someone sounds very self-righteous.

B: And envious.

Lily: Envious? Please.

B: Yes, you are.

B: There's nothing wrong with taking advantage of beauty.

Lily: I didn't say there was.

B: You're judging them for it.

Lily: I'm judging them for pretending it's a form of activism.

B: You wish you could do the same.

The bourbon's low burn coated Lily's throat. She didn't want to be like Ceci and her crew. All that pressure to embody a physical ideal every day seemed soul sucking, not to mention futile. Time would come for them like it came for every woman, and all the value they had collected through followers would disintegrate into thin air. B had a point, though. Lily's frustration with Ceci et al. didn't emanate from a position of womanly solidarity; its source was something darker. She didn't want to be a Ceci or Katrina. Still, she envied their audacity. They harbored zero concern over building a livelihood on their beauty. They saw their physical attractiveness as a purely positive force. In that respect, they were not so different from Antonio Russo. Except that they were—they were fearless. He didn't have to worry about personal consequences for his self-presentation choices. These women did. And they stared those potential downsides straight in the eye and told them to go to hell. They might combust years from now thanks to their reliance on beauty, but at least in this moment, these women were in charge. They were unafraid to take a risk.

Lily: Maybe I do. But not for the reasons you're implying.

B: Those influencers are no different than you.

B: They're using whatever resources they can access.

B: You have a built-in platform. They don't.

B: You gotta play the game if you want to stay alive.

Lily: I wouldn't even know where to begin.

A fellow patron, in a beat-up motorcycle jacket, her dark hair streaked with violet chunks, feline flicks of liquid liner at the corners of her eyes, paused mid-step on her way to the restroom and sized Lily up.

"Do you know where you are?" the woman asked Lily. Confusion and animosity found harmony in her squinted eyes.

All the whiskey's cozy heat evaporated in an instant. It left Lily's skin chilled beneath her sweater.

"I do, thanks so much for your concern," Lily replied. She forced her lips into a semblance of a grin.

Unconvinced, the rock-star-cool woman aimed another look at Lily's long, dark hair and folksy sweater, then rolled her eyes and continued on her intended path. Lily asked the bartender for the check. She drained the bourbon from her plastic cup. Lily slipped her coat back on, checked her watch again; there were still nineteen minutes until dinner. Jaw tight, she exited the bar and went back out onto the frosty sidewalks. Better the actual cold than the icicles of intragroup rejection.

Lily understood the source of the woman's rancor. These spots were supposed to be safe spaces, hard-earned and barely maintained, not bars to be colonized by straight people. Lily's ability to pass, to be freer from homophobia's omnipresent ugliness, was more of an affront than heterosexuality itself. Her sexual fluidity, not that the woman had asked, only worsened matters. But Lily's conventional femininity was not a falsehood she had slipped on as a disguise to protect herself from bigotry. It was as much a part of who she was as her attraction to women; to dispose of it would have meant rejecting part of her identity, something she refused to do.

• • •

THE FRENCH BISTRO was cacophonous when Lily arrived there a few minutes before seven. The host led her to a table near the bar, and Lily removed her coat, patchy with moisture from the melting snow that dripped from the surrounding buildings. A server came by, and she ordered a glass of pinot noir.

Alison materialized beside the table in a flurry some ten minutes later, her eyes narrowed pinpricks of heat. She plopped her coat and bag onto an available chair, sat down, and pushed her sweater sleeves up past her elbows. Her breathing was slightly labored.

"I almost wiped out on the snow outside," she said.

"I'm so sorry. Are you okay? You didn't have to rush. Let's get you a drink." Lily scanned the room for the server.

"It's so cold out. And my bag is so heavy. From the stuff I need for tomorrow." Alison planned to stay at Lily's that night.

"I'm so sorry."

"And then I realized on the subway here that I left a sweater at home. The one I was going to wear tomorrow."

"You can borrow one of mine."

This was not the snowy, romantic post-panel dinner Lily had envisioned.

"I'm sick of lugging this stuff around!"

"You can always leave whatever you want at my place." Lily was about ready to grab an unattended wine bottle from a nearby table and place it in front of Alison.

"But then I forget things at your place! I don't have duplicates of everything I need."

"Okay. Well, you can always borrow something from me, whenever you need it."

"I don't want to have to borrow. I want to have my things when I need them."

"We won't be doing this forever. This is just for now."

"Is it?"

"What can I get you?"

The server stood next to their table with two menus. Alison asked for a scotch neat. And then the women sat there unspeaking.

"I'm going home after dinner," Alison said. "We can share a cab uptown."

"Okay," said Lily. Her forehead felt warm. There was a heavy pressure slowly building at her temples.

"I'm exhausted."

"I get it. I'm sorry."

The warmth of Lily's head blunted the edges of her thoughts. But she was sorry. Not just for this moment of annoyance, but for all of it. She was sorry for the walls that she erected and the distance she put between herself and everyone around her, especially the people she loved. She was sorry that she was so beaten down by the world's pettiness that she had resigned herself to a range of half-fulfilled identities, at the expense of whole personhood. And most of all, she was sorry that this resignation caused such frustration for the one person who wanted to push Lily toward a fully dimensional existence, in which she couldn't run and hide every time she felt unseen.

"I know. And I'm not blaming only you. I agreed to this setup, too. Let's just have a nice dinner."

The two women scanned the menus and decided to split the frisée aux lardons and a coq au vin entrée.

"Is this reminding you of Paris?" Lily asked.

Alison smiled. "Definitely."

She and Lily had traveled to Paris on vacation six months into their relationship, with help from Alison's abundant airline miles and hotel points, collected over her many consulting cases. It had been their inaugural international trip together and Alison's first time in the French city. Lily had bubbled over with excitement to show Alison a place that she knew from multiple visits. But she had also been seized by nerves. A visit to a foreign place with its own culture and set of rules was something she craved because she knew how it felt to be treated like a foreigner even on her home turf. Travel reaffirmed for her that foreignness need not be a source of alienation, that it could serve instead as the basis for discovery and understanding. The separateness she experienced in travel was of her own volition, unlike the exoticizing to which she was subjected in her native city.

Alison, however, did not know the same sense of daily dislocation that Lily had considered an unhappy bedfellow her whole life. Lily worried that Alison might see the strangeness of Paris not as a source of enlightenment but as an unfortunate departure from the ease of home. How pleased Lily was, then, when Alison embraced their trip in all its explorative possibilities. Alison delighted in wandering down unknown streets, with no specific destination in mind. She loved the sidewalk café seating, where one could relax for hours over a succession of caffeinated beverages and observe the city's stylish denizens. And she gamely tasted any culinary adventure Lily presented her: escargots, frogs' legs, liver pâté, delicacies that both she and Lily knew she would never eat again. As she observed Alison take joy in unfamiliarity, Lily fell more deeply in love with this person who was secure enough with who she was that she could derive pleasure from venturing into uncharted terrain.

On their last night in Paris, Lily and Alison dined at a bistro in the sixth arrondissement, where they split an order of coq au vin. If the chicken they ordered tonight was half that delicious, they had a good meal ahead of them. Buzz buzz.

B: Yes you would.

"Who was that?"

"Billie. She wanted to know how the panel was."

"She's texting you on a Saturday night?"

"She's home."

"Right. How was the panel?"

Lily gulped cold water from a glass. "Pretty terrible. This fashion influencer Ceci, who I did a story about a few years back and, you know, helped publicize, was all like, 'Magazines are dinosaurs and totally irrelevant. Social media is the only thing that matters.' Meanwhile, my story probably helped get her thousands of followers. And she had a one-page piece in last month's *Vogue*."

"Gross."

"Anyway, all three of them were so high on themselves. Like they're changing people's lives or something by posting selfies. I wish they would just say, 'Yeah, I'm hot and I make a living from it.' Supermodels don't apologize for being gorgeous. Nor should they."

Lily drained the rest of her water glass. Her brain was a gray fog that seemed to hover outside of her skull.

"Well, you cover them, though, right?"

"Yes. I write about them because I feel like I have to because that's what readers want. And then I give the influencers more influence, making the situation worse." Buzz buzz.

B: And I should add, I'd be happy to vet some options.

"Was that Billie again?"

"Yeah. Sorry, I'll put my phone away."

"Why don't you ask her what she thinks you should do?"

"I did."

A server settled the frisée aux lardons on the table between Lily and Alison.

"Thank you," Lily said to the server, then turned back to Alison. "She thinks I should become an influencer, too."

"Tell me you're joking."

Lily stabbed a crispy lardon with the tines of her fork and crunched on it hesitantly. "Maybe she's right. It's not like what I'm doing now is working."

Alison frowned at Lily. "You can't be seriously considering becoming an influencer after everything you just said."

"Why? It works for other people. Why not me?"

"Come on. You barely use social media as it is."

"So? I can learn. I can change. And I could build a bunch of followers and then use them to do something else. There are magazine editors who have half as many followers as the publications they work for."

Alison swallowed some of her wine. "That isn't you, Lily. Like, I can't even imagine that happening."

Lily's head pounded more steadily. "And what if it becomes me—you won't be with me anymore? I'll be too basic for you to date?"

"Jesus, Lily. No. I want you to be happy. As yourself. And I don't think that is you." Alison stared hard at Lily. "That doesn't sound like you. It sounds like her."

"Billie?"

"Yes."

"How do you know what she sounds like?"

Their coq au vin arrived and interrupted their argument. Lily's face was on fire. A small, spiky animal was trying to bulldoze its way out of her frontal lobe. The chicken was one-quarter as good as its cousin that she and Alison had consumed in Paris, which made it perfectly passable by New York standards, though Lily was in no state to judge food in this moment.

"I don't feel so great," she said.

Alison reached over and caressed Lily's forehead. "You feel a little bit warm. Let's get you home."

The women shared a taxi uptown, and Alison dropped Lily off in front of her building. By the time she stumbled upstairs to her apartment, Lily ached all over. Her forehead and upper lip were slick with sweat and her head was a flaming mass, her own personal heating system. Her stomach clenched as her key hit her lock. She rushed inside, threw her coat and bag into the hallway as she dove for the toilet. Sour bile and the inelegant souvenirs of her French repast gushed forth. Lily scooped her hair back with one hand as she flipped up the toilet seat with the other. When her retching was complete, she shakily made her way to the kitchen for some water, only to be seized by another urgent movement in her throat that sent her running back to the bathroom. She repeated this sequence, the flushing, the washing, the hoping that there was nothing left to expel, one more time before she resigned herself to the virus's arc. Lily curled up on the bathroom's cool tiled floor in the fetal position.

A few hours later, with no further retching, Lily dragged herself upright. Her legs wobbled, her head spun. She splashed some water on her face, swirled some mouthwash, and slowly made her way to bed. There, she collapsed in a shivering, throbbing heap.

●　●　●

IT WAS PAST noon the next day when Lily awoke to a series of notifications on her phone. One was a text from Alison to see how she was doing. The others were from B. Lily tried to walk to the bathroom, but her body, wrung dry of any hydration or sustenance, was not up to the task. She texted Alison.

Lily: I am really sick. Was throwing up all night. Can barely get out of bed. I think I have a stomach flu.

Then she lay back down, the cotton pillowcase cool against her neck. She needed electrolytes. Water wouldn't do. She would ask Alison to bring her a sports drink when she texted her back. Her phone vibrated.

Alison: Yikes, so sorry! Rest up. Will text you later. Thank god I didn't get it, too.

That was it. No offer to bring her anything. Just an effective "good luck with that and talk to you later." Lily could text her back, ask for help. But after their disagreement the previous night, she was wary of any request that bordered on neediness.

She wished that Alison implicitly understood that Lily wanted someone to take care of her. That she wanted Alison to take care of her. That although she had chosen a life that left ample room for solitude, Lily wasn't capable of survival without the ministrations of those she loved. No amount of emotional armor and physical sequestering could change the fact that she needed other people. It was a painful realization to arrive in the midst of a stomach bug, but here it was: She could not do this alone, "this" being making it in this world as a whole and fulfilled person.

It was selfish, though, for her to seek comfort in Alison when she continued to deny Alison the comfort of cohabitation. Lily didn't deserve Alison's support—or anyone else's, for that matter. Lily had chosen self-reliance as her personal philosophy. These were the rules of the game. What she needed was to make good on this choice, to drag herself out of this bed, stumble to the nearest drugstore for supplies, then turn around and haul herself back home.

After she successfully completed her travails, Lily summoned the energy to read B's texts.

B: Hey there.

B: You left our conversation last night so abruptly.

B: Too busy filling your future grid?

B: Or did your girlfriend distract you?

Fantastic, two women had texted her, neither of whom would come over and play nurse for the day. She could only imagine if B showed up. She would walk in on Lily vomiting and then turn in the opposite direction and bolt. Lily was supposed to be a picture of youthful energy, not a sick lump crying on the bathroom floor between bouts of puke.

Lily: Hi, sorry. I'm sick.

Lily: Was throwing up all night.

Lily twisted the cap of the sports drink bottle and swallowed a few tentative fake-citrus swigs. Buzz buzz.

B: Too bad.

B: Are you okay?

Sports drink bottle in hand, Lily shuffled over to her bed and eased herself beneath the covers.

Lily: I will be.

Her phone rested on the bed next to her. She lay back against the pillow. Her eyes were closed. Buzz buzz.

B: You getting help?

Typical B. Outsource her concern.

Lily: No. There's nothing anyone can do for a stomach bug.

Lily: I just need to rest.

Her eyes would barely stay open. Texting B required a spark she didn't currently possess. Buzz buzz.

B: But someone is taking care of you?

B: Your girlfriend?

Lily: No.

Lily: I'm taking care of myself.

Down went Lily's phone. B's silence revealed all. Alison should have been there. Sickness should transcend the pettiness of a protracted argument. After all, Alison would strengthen her cohabitation case if she could provide evidence of its tangible benefits. And Lily shouldn't have to telegraph her desire to be nurtured. She changed her mind and texted Alison.

Lily: Do you think you could bring me some Gatorade?

Eyes closed, Lily leaned back against the pillow. Buzz buzz.

Alison: I just ordered some for you.

Alison: It should be there in twenty minutes.

Alison: I have a huge week at work. I can't afford to get sick.

Through the filter of B's disapproval, Alison's response no longer seemed like exactly what Lily deserved, the product of her militant self-sufficiency. It sounded like a cold rebuff. Clearly, Alison was mad about their conversation last night. And B wanted Lily to be mad at Alison for not taking care of her. And Lily wanted—well, Lily didn't know what Lily wanted beyond the obvious, for this stomach virus to dissipate and for the hole in the ground that she had systematically dug to magically fill itself. Lily powered off her phone. Her forehead began to burn again. Her eyes watered, with frustration or illness, she couldn't say. She curled up into a ball in her bed. First, she would sleep herself back to health. Then she would figure out what was next.

14

• • •

MARISSA HAD SOME news. She had texted Lily as much the evening prior. When Lily texted her back, Marissa replied that she wanted to share it in person. And so tonight, after work, they were to meet at a Japanese whiskey place in SoHo to toast Marissa's news. Lily guessed that Marissa had earned a promotion at work. That she had been made one of the youngest partners at her firm. Or she had nabbed a new, partner-track job at another firm, one that would acknowledge her talents instead of treating her like a token woman whose photo they could plaster over any front-facing materials. *Look how evolved we are, we have a* woman *as a partner!* Whatever it was, Lily was ready to celebrate.

A little after seven, Lily arrived at the lounge, off the main drag of Houston Street, populated with red-sauce joints and subterranean sushi-meets-Thai-food outposts. Unlike its more convoluted fusion neighbors, which appealed to tourists and downtown university students alike, this spot telegraphed its authenticity, and therefore its interest in a more discerning patron, through its attention to detail. The whiskies on offer were exclusively Japanese, not a bottle of Jack Daniel's in sight. The food menu, a range of snacks and appetizer-sized sharing plates, was indistinguishable from what one would find at an izakaya in Tokyo. And the ice for the beverages was hand-cut to order with a stainless-steel saw by the bartender, a trim dark-haired man in a fitted white shirt with a taut black vest over it. On his hands were black rubber gloves that gave him the air of a serial killer with a penchant for Savile Row. He slid a menu wordlessly across the bar to Lily and poured her a tumbler of ice water.

Marissa entered the bar a few minutes later. She folded Lily in a hug and settled on the stool beside her.

"What's your news?" asked Lily. "Or are you going to make me work for it?"

Marissa placed her left hand on the bar in front of Lily. On her ring finger sparkled an emerald-cut diamond nestled between two small baguettes.

"Oh, wow," said Lily. "That's amazing news, congratulations!" She sipped her water.

"Luke asked me last night."

"That's so great! How did he do it?" Lily motioned to the bartender for more water. Her throat was suddenly dry.

"I came home from work late. And the lights in the apartment were dim. It smelled amazing. He had grilled these incredible steaks and roasted some potatoes. There were candles on the table. And I walked in and he took my coat and handed me a glass of champagne. And I said, 'What's going on?' And then he said, 'I want you to know how much I appreciate you.' Then he got down on one knee and proposed. He still had a gingham apron on."

"That's so sweet. Were you surprised?"

"Yes and no? I mean, I hoped it was coming. We've obviously talked about kids and the rest of our lives. But there never seemed to be a rush, so . . ."

"Well, I'm so happy for you guys. And the ring is gorgeous. Let's order so we can toast."

Lily should have seen this coming. Marissa and Luke had dated for almost four years and had known each other for longer. They lived together. And they were in their early thirties. She and Marissa didn't discuss their lives as possible wives and mothers. Their conversations were always about professional ladder climbing, new books they had read, college friends that they no longer saw. Marissa had never expressed an abiding yearning for marriage or motherhood and Lily had never inquired. She had assumed that Marissa would pair off into conventional domesticity like everyone else in her life had, but it felt as inevitable as the sinking of Venice, a reality too far off in the future to be worth contemplation in the present. Apparently, the future was now.

And Lily was happy for Marissa, really she was. Luke was easy to like, four thirty A.M. marathon training aside. Lily could easily visualize herself at their apartment for drinks or dinner. The three of them would chat as though part of a unit. She could see Marissa receive a work call in the middle of their meal. She would peel off to a separate corner of the apartment while Lily and Luke continued to converse, no awkward pauses to be found. She hadn't lost Marissa; she had gained access to another side of her.

None of this could account for the gaping hole in her stomach, her tight throat, her clenched jaw. Marissa sat there in front of her, vibrant with happiness. And a cold lasso of dread coiled tighter and tighter around Lily. It dragged her down toward the ground, further away from the people she loved. Eventually, she would be so far gone, so deep beneath the earth's surface, that when she looked up at the land above her, she would barely recognize the places and faces that she had once called home. The world would move on without her. Her friends would have children and second homes and graduation parties and weddings and grandchildren, and she would be stuck in the primordial past, where she looked on helplessly, reaching for the outstretched hand that would never come.

Every wedding and baby shower Lily attended spurred on a new round of dread. She would sit at a table. She would stare across floral centerpieces and artfully composed platters of grilled vegetables and poached salmon at the newly married bride or expectant mother and her chest would seize up in preparation for that tightly coiled lasso. It was not envy that instigated this fear, or at least not in its standard form. She didn't want to be the bride or the mother. Lily wanted to want to be them. She was, in fact, envious of those other envious women, the ones who glowered at the brides and expectant mothers and wondered why they weren't in the white gown or the elasticized maternity jeans. At least those women were committed enough in their goals to hate someone else for having arrived there first. Even Lily's envy seemed to float at an icy and diluted remove.

Marissa and Lily chatted their way through two rounds of Japanese whiskey old-fashioneds and a plate of panko-crusted prawns. After the announcement of her marital news, Marissa retreated to the safe topics of workplace politics and literary consumption.

"Did you read that new novel *The Lightening*?" Marissa asked. She regularly sought out books with characters of all ethnicities, sexualities, and backgrounds, not for the sake of appearances, or worse, out of a sense of white duty, but from a place of genuine interest. Marissa was equal parts corporate lawyer and English major. She loved to win, but she also yearned to explore. In their severely limited spare time, her office mates clung to the nonfiction bestseller lists to collect tidbits for competitive use at cocktail parties and work lunches. Marissa preferred to go on adventures—alone. And then talk about them with Lily after the fact.

The Lightening was a work of speculative fiction in which, due to unknown forces, everyone in the United States was suddenly white, even the people who previously were not. The unknown forces that erased nonwhite skin tones did not, simultaneously, erase people's memories of them. Someone invented an antidote that restored racial diversity, except some people didn't want to relinquish their newly acquired whiteness. By the end of the book, the white population was more numerous than it had been at the start, and the nonwhite population comprised a much smaller percentage than it had previously.

"I did," said Lily, and wrinkled her nose.

"Yeah. It was . . ."

"Speculative, but I wondered the whole time if it was actually fantasy fiction."

"Oh god."

"Like, the author thought: 'What is my fantasy of the world?' And this is what he came up with."

"Totally. Like, this is the future bible of creationism for the right."

"Alternate title: *And Then There Were Almost None*."

Lily imagined herself wandering the earth, wan and translucent, drained of all her so-called color. She saw dense blue-green veins poking out beneath her melanin-deprived skin. She looked like a ghost of herself. Shudders reverberated up Lily's spine and she reached for her tumbler of whiskey.

· · ·

ONCE HOME, LILY texted Alison about Marissa's engagement.

Lily: Marissa's getting married!

Lily: Wedding is this November.

Lily: She's not doing bridesmaids, thank god.

Lily picked up the novel she was currently reading, *Cold Heart*. The book was set in eighteenth-century New England. It followed two women who were trapped in a cave during an epic snowstorm. Over the course of their terrifying confinement, they managed to fall hopelessly in love. Each woman was married, naturally, and knew that her husband would look for her once the storm was over. The two women risked life and limb—literally; frostbite was a serious concern—to prolong their heady but doomed romance past the storm's end. They foraged for animal carcasses and timber to eat and burn. They drank melted snow from cups they fashioned out of woven maple leaves. Basically, they did everything in their power to avoid the return to their sad but warmer married lives. The novel featured the typical queer mise en place, with an Emersonian twist. And yes, someone died at the end. But Lily had read in a review that it featured well-honed dialogue and scene-setting.

Buzz buzz.

The two women had just kissed for the first time. They now slept together beneath a ratty shawl. Their bodies shivered in near unison. Lily paused her reading.

B: I'm just leaving the office now.

B: Keep me entertained on the ride home.

B: I can't look at another email.

Lily: Okay.

Buzz buzz.

Alison: Great news.

Alison: On both counts.

Alison: And that's a short engagement.

Alison: Guess they're not afraid of commitment.

Alison's zinger hung in the air. No words of reply would mitigate her obvious anger, so Lily opened the pages of her book instead.

It was daylight in *Cold Heart*. The storm was finally over. The women had realized in the span of forty-eight hours that they were madly in love and needed to spend the rest of their lives together. That's what being trapped in a cave in 1792 will do to a girl. But they were hungry because they hadn't eaten anything for two days. Even by period standards, that was still a long time without sustenance. The women ventured out into the forest, in search of edible plants and animals who hadn't survived the storm and whose carcasses they could tear apart. One woman stumbled across a dead deer. It was too large for the malnourished women to drag back to the cave on their own. They found some sharp rocks and spent the next few hours hacking away at it. They cut off a small enough piece that they were able to carry it back. The rest of the deer carcass they covered with snow in the hopes that it would keep and that they could return for more the next day.

Buzz buzz.

B: Great job you're doing so far.

Lily: Sorry. I'm distracted.

Lily: My best friend got engaged tonight.

Lily: And I'm happy for her.

Lily: But it's tough being the only person who isn't headed to an altar.

The women were back in the cave. They roasted the deer over a fire they had started. One woman fed the other woman from a twig skewer.

Buzz buzz.

B: You don't know that you'll never get married.

B: Do you?

Lily: It would be easier if I did.

Lily: But chances are slim. I've never even lived with anyone else.

Lily: Did you ever want to get married?

"Dinner" was over and the fire had dwindled, too. It was time for the inevitable sex scene.

Buzz buzz.

B: Never.

B: I've never lived with someone else either.

B: If anyone ever pressured me to, I'd send them packing.

The sting of Alison's zinger returned. This time, instead of feeling guilt, Lily smarted with defiance.

Lily: How's work going anyway?

One woman took the initiative.

Buzz buzz.

B: I'm starting a new thing.

B: That's why I was there so late.

Lily: A new thing?

Lily: Like a new makeup line?

But wouldn't you know it, the fire went out just as the women removed their clothes. They were now in the dark.

Lily closed her novel. In the bathroom, she wet her face and massaged a cleanser into her skin until it foamed lightly. Her phone, on the sink beside her, buzz-buzzed.

B: Skin care.

B: Though you can't tell ANYONE.

Lily patted her face and hands dry.

Lily: Skin care. Wow. How cool.

Lily: And lips are sealed.

Back down went her phone. She squeezed toothpaste onto her brush.

Buzz buzz.

B: Yes.

B: Super exciting.

B: Okay. I'm home now.

B: I should go.

B: Night.

Lily: Night.

Nestled beneath the covers of her bed, Lily allowed her mind to unfurl. Marriage wasn't everything. Life existed without it. Look at B. She'd never married. And she was free to stay all night at work, to expand into a new market area, without concern for mouths to feed or partners to placate when she returned home late from the office. Lily visualized B in her corner suite, her suit jacket on the back of her chair, the cuffs of her button-down shirt loose and rolled up, a take-out container of half-eaten dinner and sketches of moisturizers and serums on the desk in front of her. Those products would eventually be bestsellers; they would revolutionize the skin care industry. And B would be a brighter star than she already was. She would receive a promotion at her company. She would move to the very top spot.

A blaze of shimmering heat rushed across the length of Lily's body. She could be a person of value, the type of person a company saw as irreplaceable. She could dream up ideas and watch them materialize into reality. If she stuck close to B's example, if she maintained her position in B's phone, one day, Lily could be like B. And then all her concerns would disappear, and finally, she would be at peace.

• • •

AN ALARM BLARED from Lily's nightstand. Her hand rushed to her phone. She had slept the heavy, dreamless sleep of cerebral release. There was a string of notifications on her phone, probably more texts from Alison, enthusing about Marissa's news. One notification had a thumbnail of a photo; it was of something elongated and bright pink, like a chubby tentacle. Lily peered closer. Was that—? No. She unlocked her phone and pulled up the image. It was a photo of a fluorescent pink dildo encircled by a strappy black harness with silver studs; the accessory sat on what appeared to be the black leather surface of a car seat or a chair. And below it was a string of texts.

B: I'm finally home.

B: Ready for you.

B: To make me cum.

B: Fuck. Wrong person!

B: Delete ASAP.

The messages were time-stamped 11:32 P.M. the previous evening, a few minutes after Lily and B had said good night. Jesus. B must have been texting someone else at the same time as Lily, while also— Lily reread her text exchange with B. Their messages were mere minutes apart. For a modern beauty executive, that was still an impressive feat of multi-tasking. B had been in the back of a car for most of their conversation— or so she had claimed. Some car service arrangement she had. And B had waited for Lily to respond, in some form, for the past seven hours.

Lily: You sure keep yourself busy.

Lily slipped on a pair of leggings for her morning run.

Buzz buzz.

B: Ha.

B: I guess so.

Lily: Way to multitask.

Lily twisted her earphones in and donned a baseball cap to shade her face from the increasingly sunny March mornings. She stuck her phone in the pocket of her windbreaker.

Buzz buzz.

B: Yep.

B: I'm on the way to work.

B: Early meeting.

A twinge of jealousy plucked at Lily's chest. She entered the park and began her run. She wasn't as special as she had hoped, not worth a few minutes of B's uninterrupted focus. And not worthy of an illicit photo from B. The fact was, Lily wanted to be the photo's recipient because of what it would signify: that she was desirable enough to pique the libidinal interest of someone as discerning as B. She wanted B to respect her brain and consider her fuckable, too. It was disgusting. Lily was disgusting.

Then there was the photo. Yes, Lily looked again when she returned home from her run, in the privacy of her apartment, before she obeyed B's directive and deleted the image. The dildo was smooth and shiny. It had a metallic sheen. It was gently curved, too, though shorter than Lily would have expected, not that she had devoted any time to imagining what length dildo B would prefer. The hot pink was a surprise, too. B didn't strike Lily as a hot-pink woman. A tasteful silver or a somber black or even a muted lavender: These were the colors Lily would have selected for B's phallus, had someone presented her with a paint-chip-style array of options. Hot pink seemed too conventionally feminine. Too girlish. It was for someone who liked bubble baths and champagne and hearts dotting their i's, not a chief creative officer known for her pantsuits and corporate bravado.

Lily reread the messages that accompanied the photo. *Ready for you. To make me cum.* To make B come. Someone—some mystery woman—was going to make B come. Not the other way around. No shock there, that B's texts would center her orgasm, instead of the desire of this other woman. There was that word *make*. This other woman was going to *make* B come. She was going to make B do something. B was not going to be in control. B was not going to be on top, for once in her elevated life. The strap-on was not for B to wear. It was for her to receive.

The situation called for reinforcements. Lily texted Marissa immediately.

Lily: Congrats again on your amazing news!! Had a weird rest of the night.

A few minutes later, Marissa called Lily.

"What happened?"

Lily explained the events of the previous night and the morning.

"Can you believe she's not an exclusive top?"

"You're missing the point here. That photo was for you."

"No. It seems pretty clear that it was for someone else."

"How do you accidentally send someone a photo like that? Think about the way a phone's camera and text functions work. It's not easy."

"She was obviously texting me and some other woman at the same time. We've all accidentally texted a message to the wrong person."

"I haven't."

"You're a lawyer."

"Fine. But taking a photo, that kind of photo, and sending it is very different. It sounds like she was pretending to cover it up. Listen, I've gotta run to work, but remember what I said from the start about women like her: careful. What a mindfuck."

Marissa ended the call with Lily. The suggestion that B had sent the photo to her on purpose crackled, teasingly, on Lily's skin. It would mean that B found Lily attractive. That Lily was someone capable of making a woman like B come. That Lily was capable of topping a woman like B. The sensation quickly morphed into discomfort as her mind drifted to Alison. Technically, Lily hadn't done anything. She hadn't sent a photo; she had merely wished that it was for her. At a certain point, though, passivity becomes its own form of action.

And there was a more unsettling truth that Lily was loath to explore: She wasn't entirely sure that she deserved better than B's digital half-attention, professionally or otherwise. There would always be a part of Lily that believed that she would never be as appealing in real life as she seemed on paper—or in this case, on the liquid crystal of her phone's screen. She was a writer, after all; she would always be most comfortable in the shadowed crevices between words, those that belonged to others as much as the ones that belonged to her.

• • •

THAT AFTERNOON AT her desk, Lily transcribed an interview with a famous director's twenty-two-year-old daughter who had parlayed her privileged Hollywood upbringing and hundreds of thousands of followers into a career as a health food caterer in Los Angeles. A slew of luxury brands had already signed on to use her services for their events. The daughter had a limited menu for now; it included organic lettuce wraps stuffed with sautéed kale and corn, and sprouted wheat tortillas with grilled tempeh sprinkled with nutritional yeast, a vegan iteration of the ubiquitous mini grilled cheese sandwiches at cocktail parties. Every few minutes, Lily had to pause her recording to search online for the various ingredients, including ashwagandha and colloidal silver, that the daughter name-checked, to have some inkling of what she had described.

"Hey there."

It was Marc. He leaned over her cubicle wall per usual, his navy vest partially unzipped, its collar flopping against his white neck. Lily had managed to avoid him in person for the past couple of weeks, knowing that her luck would run out eventually. She paused her recording but kept her headphones on.

"Hey," she muttered.

"I was going through press releases for new bar openings next month," he went on. At least he spared Lily the cubicle walk-around. He brushed a lock of hair off his face. "I'd like you to do a roundup story for the site. My SEO insights suggest we need to do something on cocktail bars."

Lily clenched her jaw. She couldn't believe she was in a position where Marc now assigned her stories. And based on search engine keywords.

"Okay."

"I want all your stories to have a serious ROI." Marc had never met an acronym he couldn't use in place of actual insight.

"Right."

"There's a killer-sounding tiki place that just opened on the Upper West Side."

"Okay. I'll make sure it's on there."

"We could get drinks there after work one night. As research for the story. You live in the area, don't you?"

Lily tried to recall when she had, in a rare unguarded moment, told Marc that she lived on the Upper West Side. She knew that he lived on the Lower East Side, since he offered up personal details like take-out menu flyers. And the Upper West Side was nowhere near either work or his neighborhood.

"I'm really busy for the next few weeks," said Lily, who motioned toward her digital recorder, "and I need to finish this transcript."

"Fine. Get me that story by next week. And I'll hit you up another time."

Please, god, don't, Lily thought as she pressed play and watched him saunter away. She considered texting Alison to vent. As if her phone were clairvoyant, it buzz-buzzed.

Alison: What was that random selfie you posted two days ago?

Alison: I just saw it in my feed today.

Lily: Which one?

Alison: The one where you're wearing lipstick.

Alison: Since when do you wear red lipstick voluntarily?

Two nights ago, Lily had been home alone while Alison was still at the office. Lily had swiped through her social media feed. She had tapped over to her profile page. Her grid had looked sad and empty. She had scrolled down to a picture of herself from three years ago. She was at a cousin's wedding in Massachusetts; she had worn a lavender dress and espadrille platforms, and a friend of her cousin's had taken a picture of her as the sun began to set. The friend of her cousin's had posted the photo to her feed, so Lily had reposted it to her own grid. There, the photo had earned more likes than any of the other photos, of books and museum shows and restaurant interiors, that she occasionally posted. This was what people wanted to see, Lily thought as she examined the image.

On a whim, she had grabbed one of the tubes of red lipstick left over from her magazine story months prior and applied it to her lips. Then she had snapped a selfie in her bathroom mirror, like she had seen so many other women do, and posted it to her feed with the caption, "All painted up with nowhere to go." Thus far, the red-lipstick selfie had garnered a hundred likes, which was 10 percent of Lily's minuscule follower count.

Lily had been aware that this selfie was exactly the kind of photo Theresa had wanted to run as art for her red-lipstick story, the type of photo that Lily had vetoed. In taking the photo herself and posting it to her own feed, Lily convinced herself that she had subverted the unease that Theresa's dissemination of a similar photo would have created. It was self-appropriation, which was practically the same thing as empowerment. The content of the image didn't matter; the source and the means of production were the only significant factors. That was how this was supposed to work.

Lily: I thought people might like it. And they did.

Alison: Why would you tell Theresa not to run a photo of you in a magazine and then post the same thing as a selfie?

Alison: It makes no sense.

Alison: Anyway, I don't know that I can come to your place tonight.

Alison: I left a prescription I need at home. And I really don't have the energy to go back to get it and then come to you.

Alison: I'm so over this.

Lily: Why don't I come to you?

Lily: I just have to leave for my run before you wake up.

Lily pressed play on her recording. She typed some lines about adaptogens.

Buzz buzz.

Alison: I don't know what time I'm going to be done at the office.

Alison: And I don't want you to wake me up early with your alarm.

If they shared a home, they would presumably share a bed, and so the timing of her alarm would be an issue regardless; Lily had to restrain herself from pointing this out.

Lily: Okay, no problem.

Alison: You're just going to spend the whole night on your phone anyway.

That was enough digital drama for one day. Lily powered off her phone and shoved it deep in her bag. Alison didn't know about B's strap-on photo, and somehow, as if by osmosis from the digital trash bin, it had leaked its disruptive energy into Lily's exchange with Alison. B's hot-pink phallus should have come wrapped in red sirens and yellow caution tape for the danger it posed even in a figurative state.

Something throbbed in Lily's chest; some amalgam of guilt and fear washed over her. She and Alison had never argued to this degree. These fights about their living circumstances were becoming a repetitive chorus instead of an occasional, isolated lyric. Soon, they would comprise the entire song of their relationship itself. And yet, this percussive fear only inspired stasis instead of proactivity. She couldn't lose Alison. The mere possibility was intolerable. Alison was the most stunningly real human Lily had ever met. It had been this way from the very start. Whatever impasse they currently faced, Lily knew it was entirely her fault. She wished she could flick some hidden, internal switch to set them back on the correct path forward.

15

· · ·

LILY AND ALISON'S first date, three-plus years ago, had been drinks
at a Spanish wine bar Alison suggested in the Flatiron District. Lily
asked that they meet at nine P.M. It was a Tuesday night. In retrospect
this could have implied she hoped to convert their rendezvous into a
hookup. But in truth, she had a work cocktail event she had to stop by
on the way there. For the two hours before their date, Lily maneuvered
around the fifth-floor restaurant of a tony department store in Midtown, the site of a party fêting a new handbag design from a heritage
Italian fashion label.

Lily wove her way through the packed restaurant, around bony socialites and imperious fashion stylists. She needed a quote for her story
from the Italian label's creative director. Lily spotted her, a petite
woman whose midcalf-length skirt and thick cardigan suggested the
presence of a philosophy graduate student more than a style arbiter — at
least to unpracticed eyes. The skirt was finely pleated silk and the cardigan was decadent five-ply cashmere. The creative director was huddled in a corner, a glass of water clutched in her hand. Everything about

her seemed calculated to attract as little attention as possible, including her hunched posture, as though she wished the restaurant's walls would swallow her up and transport her back to Italy.

"Excuse me, I'm sorry to bother you," Lily said. She approached the creative director delicately, like one would a skittish animal. "Could I ask you some questions about your handbag design for my story?"

"Yes, of course," came the soft reply.

And so, Lily queried her about the choice of napa leather, the boxy trapezoid shape, and the studded gold metal hardware. Duties complete, Lily decamped for her own corner near the bar, where she lingered over a glass of prosecco.

After they matched on an online dating site, Lily and Alison had quickly exchanged cell phone numbers. Lily interpreted this as an auspicious sign; she preferred to remove their correspondence from the third-party site as quickly as possible. In the days prior to their planned date, they sent casual messages about their weekend activities, television shows they watched, and meals they prepared. It was less the content of their texts than the rapidity of their volleying that struck Lily. Alison responded to most of her messages within minutes, and so she did the same. No one performed the cool detachment of leaving a few hours between replies. Their interest in each other was free of games. For most of her twenties, Lily had tiptoed around the fragile egos and nonchalant posturing of guys too scared of rejection to admit that they cared. She breathed a sigh of relief that she could finally show that she did.

The peak of the handbag cocktails dissipated, so Lily rode an elevator down to the lobby. A stroll through an empty department store at night, its gleaming shelves of purses and glass jewelry displays unattended, always felt unnervingly discordant. Public spaces, stores, restaurants, coffee shops, etc., were built for people. And while there was subversive pleasure in such private access to a normally fought-over arena, in the realm of retail, the lack of customers equated with a dearth of desire.

Lily walked to a nearby subway station and boarded a downtown-bound train. A few stops later, she located the Spanish wine bar Alison had chosen. Per Alison's dating profile photo, she was a blonde with gray-green eyes and a big, wide smile. The space was narrow and lively. Votive lights flickered on the tops of a few small tables. Alison was seated in a corner nook by the window. She stood up and smiled when Lily walked in; she wrapped Lily in a hug.

"It's so great to finally meet," she said.

"Yes," Lily said, pleasantly taken aback by this unabashed physical display. "It is."

They each ordered a glass of albariño, which a server brought them, along with a bowl of Marcona almonds.

Lily reached straight for the nuts. "Sorry, I'm famished," she said. "There wasn't much to eat at that event."

"How was it?"

"Oh, you know, fashion designer, handbags, bubbly, starving women. The same old."

"That's not really normal for anyone in my field, except for maybe the bubbly."

"Right, of course."

Ten minutes in and already Lily sounded like a total asshole. This girl was gorgeous and friendly and suspiciously free of neuroses. Maybe try not to screw this up. Fortunately, once the albariño revived the flagging prosecco in her veins, Lily's tensed jaw slackened and her shoulders dropped a couple of inches. She leaned back in her chair and smiled at Alison across the table.

"Have you always wanted to work in magazines?" Alison asked. Her lashes were thick and glossy and she had expertly applied smudges of charcoal liner around her eyes. She wore a heather-gray sweater and black wool trousers, her work uniform of choice.

"Yes, since high school. I was obsessed with fashion. And reading and books. Writing for a magazine made sense."

"What about books? Did you ever think of doing that instead?"

"No, never. I love books, but magazines were always the goal."

Lily had never dated anyone, man or woman, with Alison's level of steadiness. Her consultancy work was secure, unlike Lily's choice of career. Alison's personal interests, according to her online profile—exploring New York's dining scene, trying out new cookbook recipes, watching movies—were wholesome and unobjectionable. Her demeanor in person, the way she managed to sit upright and still appear relaxed, the calm that shimmered on her skin, it looked like peace. Alison was peace. She exuded faith in herself, in who she was and who she would be in the future. And anyone who was lucky enough to be by her side could experience some of that peace and faith, too.

"What about you? You're a consultant?"

"Yes. Technically, a management consultant."

"Sorry, what does that mean? Full disclosure: I looked up your firm. It's super well-known, but I don't really understand anything on its website."

"That's okay. I barely understand what I do."

"You're joking."

"Yes. Companies hire us to come in, temporarily, and help them figure out how to create new revenue streams, operate more efficiently, ramp up profitability. That kind of thing."

"You give companies feedback on what they're doing wrong."

"Essentially. And then we help them fix those problems. We offer solutions. Or at least that's the party line." Alison sipped from her glass of wine.

"You have a different opinion than the party line?"

"Most of the people I work with are pretty high on what we do. They act like we're saving the world or something by fixing these companies' problems. But really, all we're doing is telling them how to make more money. And there's nothing wrong with that, so long as our suggestions are legal and ethical. But I hate this posturing where people insist on the goodness of what we do. We're not good; we're profitable."

"Did you always want to be a consultant?"

"Nobody always wants to be a consultant."

"Why do it?"

Alison smiled like she couldn't believe Lily had asked such a silly question but she would humor her. "Security. And it's a job. Your job doesn't have to define you."

"But you work crazy hours?"

"Yes," Alison acknowledged. "But time consumption and identity are not the same thing."

Alison made the separation between work and existence sound entirely natural. They were the same age and had gone to similarly rigorous liberal arts colleges. Somehow, Lily had graduated with the idea that she was supposed to love her job, that her profession would be the source of her life's intellectual and spiritual meaning, and anything less than that was ingratitude for her education. And Alison had entered adulthood believing that a job was a means to an end, that end being fiscal safety. Lily had never seen herself as independent of her work. Alison, who toiled far longer and harder hours than Lily ever had, took her existential separation as the basis for her occupational choice. Lily wondered if Alison possessed some secret to fulfillment that Lily had failed to learn.

"How would you describe your identity, then?" Lily asked.

"Outside of gender and sexuality?"

"Yes."

"I want comfort. I want my life to be comfortable, in every sense of the word. I don't think anything should be difficult for the sake of it. What about you?"

"I think I'm still figuring it out."

"Do you still love what you do?"

"I'm not sure. Do you?"

"I don't know that I ever did. That wasn't really the goal."

"Would you ever do something else?"

"I've never told anyone this—"

"No pressure."

"It's going to sound crazy. Because it's sort of the opposite of what I do now. But at some point, it would be awesome to work in the nonprofit sector. Like to use the analysis and managing skills I'm building now and apply them to nonprofits instead of to corporate America. So, I could split the difference between goodness and profitability."

"That would be really cool."

Lily considered Alison across the table, now cluttered with the remnants of their drinks and Lily's nibbling. For all her talk of security and comfort, Alison harbored a dissatisfaction with the status quo, too. Maybe she wasn't quite as divergent from Lily in her goals as she had first appeared. Alison sought meaning from her job; god knew, she burned through enough hours at the office that she deserved it. Her route to this meaning was more conventional, more socially approved, than any path Lily might traverse. But the end point was the same: Alison, like Lily, needed to believe her efforts had value. That she had value, too. Lily realized that she and Alison were on related quests, and already, she could sense that she wanted them to succeed at their individual but equal aims together.

"We should probably get the check," said Alison. "I have an early-morning meeting tomorrow."

"Yes, let's," said Lily. "We can share a cab back uptown."

16

· · ·

AS SHE RODE up to the penthouse apartment in a steel-walled, industrial lift, Lily fidgeted with the straps of her camisole. She smoothed the front placket of her jeans. She undid her hair from its messy ponytail and raked her fingers through the ends to separate the strands. A chill cut a brisk path up her spine. The elevator arrived at its destination and the door opened to the expansive loft apartment. Lily edged into a vestibule crowned with an aged gilt mirror and turned a tight corner into a living area. B reclined, legs stretched out in front of her, on a pale mint sofa. She wore a wrinkled white T-shirt and loose pajama bottoms; her gray-streaked hair was in a haphazard half loop at the nape of her neck. B didn't utter a word. She stood up and strolled to the nearby open kitchen. Her casually upright stride signaled that Lily should follow her.

Four barstools were tucked beneath the kitchen's granite island. Lily pulled one out and eased her weight onto its cushioned seat. B removed two handblown glass tumblers from the cabinet overhead. She opened one of the doors of her massive refrigerator and extracted a bottle of gin from a freezer drawer. She didn't ask Lily's beverage preference. Instead, she dropped an oversized ice cube into each glass and topped them with an inch and a half of gin. She placed the gin bottle back in the freezer and removed a lime from the refrigerator side. A cutting board and knife rested on a drying rack adjacent to the sink. She sliced the lime and squeezed one half into each glass, then used the tip of the knife to stir the juice into the frosty gin. Her mixology complete, she slid one tumbler across the counter to Lily and sipped from hers. B leaned forward, one arm rested on the granite island.

Lily brought the glass to her lips. The icy, acid-spiked liquid slid across her tongue and down her throat. It left a fiery, fortifying burn in its wake. Lips slightly parted, her brown eyes sharp, B observed Lily thoughtfully, like she was a piece of art on which she wasn't sure she wanted to bid. B sipped from her glass again, this time with more urgency. Tumbler in hand, she looped around the end of the island and strode back toward her living area. Lily slid off the barstool and followed behind B. The two women settled on the sofa, an arm's length of cushioned seating between them.

B smiled her wry smile, a look that said, *I know you find me interesting* and *I find you intriguing* and *but maybe not for the reasons you might wish.* She reached out a hand and tucked some of Lily's hair behind her ear.

A percussion filled Lily's chest. B slid closer and moved her hand to the back of Lily's head, to steady it as she closed the gap between their faces. She pressed her lips gently to Lily's. B's lips were more temperate than Lily had expected and more slippery, too, as they glided up and down and back and forth in an improvised dance. Two minutes passed, maybe ten, who could say.

B's mouth separated from Lily's for a minute. Her eyes traced the planes of Lily's face until they connected with Lily's eyes. B's gaze softened. One of the straps of Lily's camisole had meandered toward the edge of her shoulder, set on its course by the vigor of her movements. B reached for the strap, as if to correct it back to its rightful place, but instead gave it a helping hand in its loosening trajectory and urged the other strap to join the downward slide. Lily's top settled at her waist.

A small noise escaped B's throat, like a choked cough, and she kissed Lily again, once, twice, on the lips, then across her chin and down her throat, to the hollow at its base and across the shelf of her left clavicle and then down beneath the bone, further down to the top of her chest muscle, and then inward to her sternum. She hovered there, her nose and mouth pressed against it in equal intervals.

This was really happening. All the months of banter had coalesced into this gauzy rapture without a word of discussion.

B knelt now, topless, on the living area's carpeted floor. She had removed her T-shirt. The rosy nipples of her softly drooping breasts were pointy from the air-conditioning. She unbuttoned and unzipped the constraints of Lily's jeans. B's fingers kneaded the shallow upper valley of Lily's inner thigh. They moved upward and plucked at the edge of Lily's underwear.

Lily was on her back on a beach, velvety soft sand beneath her. Salty waves lapped at her toes, her calves, her thighs, and so on. The sun's rays bleached out the sky. They touched her skin. Fingers of heat reached down and wrapped around her limbs and torso. They embraced her in a radiant light that tunneled through her body, firing up every atom and cell until she thought she might combust.

An eruption and a gasp and Lily brought a hand to her chest, as if to slow her frenetic heartbeat. When she looked down at her hand, it was pale and pinkish, with manicured red nails. Her breasts were pale, too, and larger than they had ever been. Her nipples were a rosy pink. Lily's jeans had somehow disappeared. She was completely naked. Except for the black leather straps that wrapped around her hips and butt. And the hot-pink appendage that protruded from her groin. This was B's dildo.

These were B's breasts. This was B's hand. This was B's pale, pinkish skin. What was Lily doing in B's skin? How was Lily ever going to escape?

Another gasp and she opened her eyes. Now Lily was on her bed. She was back in her own skin. The early-dawn light trickled through her windows. It glinted off the laptop screen she had left open from the previous night's writing session. Her breathing was lightly labored, slowly returning to its regular cadence.

This was the third time Lily had awoken in a similar state since B's allegedly accidental photo landed in their text exchange. Lily left her bed. She walked to the kitchen. She took a glass out of a cabinet and filled it with water. Lily drowned her thirst in water. She refilled the glass and drank some more. If only she could rinse this dream away, too.

• • •

THERE WAS AN editorial meeting at the office for the upcoming September issue. Years ago, Lily had found it disorienting to design a future of rust-colored leaves and camel coats when, outside the tower's chilly pedestal, restaurants set up sidewalk seating, and bare legs and open-toed sandals had begun to replace denim and ankle boots. The features staff was gathered around a long rectangular table in one of the office's conference rooms. In mismatched chairs, some permanent companions of the conference table, others visitors from nearby desks, the team sat and dissected the various merits of a group of young actresses whose ranks they needed to shave down for a fall up-and-comers package.

"She's a bit old," said Theresa, who glanced at a sheet of paper, copies of which each staff member had in front of them.

The woman in question was twenty-seven.

Lily reached for her phone to text B, then retracted her hand, as though repelled. Fragments of her dream flashed before her. B had never acknowledged the strap-on photo again since their first and only conversation about it. She clearly expected Lily to do the same, which was to say, forget that it had happened. Lily couldn't fathom how B might react to her recurring soft-core reverie.

"Her last project was beyond lame." That was Susan.

"Okay, we can lose her. How about this one? She's had some good buzz on the festival circuit."

"Too dykey." Susan again.

With that, Lily's text hesitation evaporated.

Lily: Tips for dealing with homophobic colleagues without coming across as a "bitch"?

Lily stared at Susan and imagined sticking her bony white body in a confined room with an empty bucket and the bare minimum amount of food and water to keep her alive, then locking the door for ten or fifteen years. How might Susan's opinions change if she was forced to spend considerable time alone with her feelings in a literal closet? And how might the disappearance of a Susan, of all the Susans and their relentless nastiness, benefit Lily's professional trajectory? This image of Susan in solitary confinement hardened in Lily's mind and she shook her head to clear it away. No, this wasn't who she was; she wasn't someone who looked at her colleagues, even Susan, as obstacles to be eliminated. Besides, if things progressed in their current direction, the inevitable collapse of the print magazine world would eradicate all the Susans and Theresas—and Lily right along with them. There was no need for Lily to fantasize about targeted extermination. Evolution would do that work for her.

"But her girlfriend is a famous director. If we do her, we might have a chance at her girlfriend's next project. I'm keeping her in the mix. And this one has three films coming out next year. Apparently, she was discovered at a taco stand."

"What a cliché," snorted Marc, who now attended these meetings in the continued forced marriage of print and digital.

Buzz buzz.

B: I don't have homophobic colleagues.

B: Because I do all the hiring.

Lily: Not helpful.

B: Tell them to fuck off.

Lily: Also not helpful.

"Her boobs are too big," said James, the editor in chief's assistant, who wrote occasional stories. "The fashion department will lose it if they have to pull looks for her."

Buzz buzz.

B: Then ignore them.

Lily: Says the woman in power.

B: Ha.

Lily: Do you think things will ever get better?

"Yes—I don't think couture comes in triple D," cut in Susan.

"Fair point," said Theresa. "Remember that other actress we did a few months ago? Lily, what was her name? The chubby one?"

Lily's phone, burning with the energy of her texts, lay facedown in her lap.

"I don't think we've ever done a chubby actress."

"Yes. We did. She was so curvy. Emma, was it?"

"She was a size four."

Buzz buzz.

B: You're going to have to be more specific.

Lily: For women.

Lily: Physical standards. Social standards. Sexual standards. All of it.

B: I think I'm doing fine.

Lily: You're not a normal case study.

"Yes. Anyway, we don't need to give the fashion department any more tough cases," said Theresa. She scanned their list of potentials.

Lily could sit alone at her desk for hours and not utter a single word and somehow feel less lonely than she did in a roomful of living and breathing humans.

"How about this one?" asked Theresa.

Buzz buzz.

B: True.

Lily: Like, how do you reconcile selling beauty products that exploit women feeling unattractive?

B: I wasn't aware that's what I was selling.

Lily: If women liked the way they looked inherently, they wouldn't need to buy makeup.

"She's very dot-com," said Susan. Her tone implied that the magazine's website held lower standards than its older print sibling did. On that point, she was correct. The website gave its content away for free; there was no reason to insist on standards if no one was paying for it.

Marc glared at Susan and Susan smirked back.

Buzz buzz.

B: Makeup is enhancement.

B: Like putting on a dress.

B: Women don't buy dresses because they feel unattractive. They buy them to feel more attractive.

Lily: Dresses and makeup are not equivalent.

Lily: People have to get dressed. It's illegal to go outside naked.

Lily: No one has to wear makeup.

The team finished their evaluation of the remaining candidates. They had whittled the final list down to a mere ten slim, interchangeably pretty, pale-skinned actresses between the ages of seventeen and twenty-five. The meeting adjourned. Per usual in the aftermath of such gatherings, Lily emerged from the conference room with a renewed sense of her declining physical appeal to men and women alike. And her silence on such superficial matters hardly elevated her above the team's catty pronouncements. There were no innocent bystanders on the playing field of gendered debasement. One was either offense or defense — the benches had been removed.

Buzz buzz.

B: Well, you don't.

B: I bet you'd look good without it.

Lily's face flushed from the compliment and her dream rushed back. She needed to change the subject.

Lily: I really meant to ask if you feel like your work has to share your personal values.

Lily: Or are they ever in conflict.

Back at her desk, Lily had fifty unread emails in her inbox since the actresses meeting. Buzz buzz.

B: My work has to embody my company's values.

B: Which are linked to my customer's values.

B: That's how we sell things.

Lily: Have you ever sold anything you weren't a hundred percent behind?

B: No comment.

Lily: Ha.

Once the quick and easy deletions were finished, Lily skimmed the first couple of sentences of the remaining emails. She flagged those that she determined required a timely response.

Buzz buzz.

B: You can't be so idealistic.

Lily: Or have ideals, period.

B: That's not what I said.

B: But idealism will get you in trouble.

Lily: So will amorality.

A PR person had a new, young client who had a part in a streaming series about alien operatives and was also slated to play the lead in a radical off-Broadway Greek tragedy.

Buzz buzz.

B: I feel like you want clarity.

Lily: Maybe.

B: It's not something I can give.

B: You should never trust clarity anyway.

• • •

MEMORIAL DAY WEEKEND rolled into New York on a lazy wave of suffocating heat and high humidity more akin to a July sauna than the unofficial kickoff to summer. Subways crawled through rush hour. Their meat locker interiors offered an icy blast of relief to the passengers who boarded the cars from the searing platforms at each stop. Avenues across town were deliciously empty of bumper-to-bumper traffic. Their asphalt stretched uninterrupted seemingly to the horizon. Even the buzziest restaurants had vacancies at prime hours. Their servers moved at an unhurried pace and extended ninety-minute meals well past the two-hour mark. The entire city and its millions of residents, at least those too financially challenged or lazy to retreat somewhere else for the holiday, relaxed into a leisurely bubble of uncaring idleness.

Lily wasn't in the mood for laziness, so she convinced Alison to ride a train from the Metro-North Harlem station up to the botanical gardens in the Bronx. It was a short trip, but in the unexpectedly soupy May heat, their bare legs fused to the train's plastic seats within minutes of sitting down.

"Remind me why we're hauling up to the Bronx to see a tropical garden when we can experience the tropics anywhere in the city right now?" asked Alison. She fanned her face and pushed a damp strand of blond hair behind her ear.

"Because if we're going to be in the tropics anyway, we may as well look at something floral and pretty," said Lily.

"You know, if we had a house in the suburbs, we'd have nature right outside our door. No need to travel."

"You said it sounded fun."

"That was before I saw the weather forecast and sat on this train."

"Well, we're here now. You want to turn around when we get there and head back home?"

"No, of course not. Jesus."

The women sat in sweltering silence for the rest of the ride. They swiped aimlessly through their phones. At the designated botanical gardens stop in the Bronx, they disembarked onto a wide boulevard across from the gardens. The museum was exhibiting a well-reviewed, blowout show in celebration of a famous Brazilian landscape designer. An undulating concrete path of black and white, like an abstract zebra print, cut across the gardens' verdant landscape. It snaked toward the conservatory building, with its ornate metal and glass dome. There were mini palm trees and bromeliads, spiky, pointy plants in a fiery array, that seemed painted by a trail of molten lava. Starbursts of bromeliads filled planters, and larger varieties sprung fronds the size of a domestic pet. Birds of paradise shocked with their florid effusions.

A central fountain's carved concrete façade had the feel of street graffiti crossed with mythological symbolism. The women strolled along its perimeter. One could easily forget one was in New York, a phrase New Yorkers liked to toss around as the highest compliment to a site's immersive qualities, as though their main objective in living in a city they claimed was superior to all others was to pretend that they were in fact somewhere else.

"Isn't this idyllic?" Lily asked. With the back of her hand, she blotted sweat from her upper lip and forehead.

"I can't tell if you're serious," said Alison, who picked up the hem of her striped T-shirt and waved it as a makeshift fan for her stomach. "I mean, it's beautiful, don't get me wrong. But we're both melting here."

"You really don't want to be here, do you?"

"No, of course I do. But come on—aren't you dying?"

Lily was, but she was loath to admit it now that they had staked out their respective territories: pro—escaping New York while staying in New York; anti—going anywhere that didn't involve air-conditioning. Normally, she would have been on board with a dark and cool afternoon at a superhero blockbuster, a small box of questionably fresh popcorn on the armrest between them. Or some aimless day-drinking in the ventilated window seat of a West Village watering hole, as women in sundresses and men in cutoff shorts glided by. Certainly, her cotton T-shirt would have appreciated that choice over the current one. It now clung to her sticky back, like a wet Band-Aid that wished to be freed from its duties.

An admission to all these facts felt like a confession of something deeper-seated than a failure to pick an appropriate leisure activity for a sweltering weekend. Lily longed to be a woman who pushed past undesirable circumstances, who prioritized exploration over creature comforts. She wanted to do and see and grow, not sit and rest and stagnate. She wanted to accomplish things and travel the world and read every book she could get her hands on and let all those innumerable experiences mold her into the sophisticated woman she thought she could become. And she wanted Alison to want to do all those things with her, no prompting necessary. They had to start right now and never look back.

"Why don't we get something to drink and then we can get out of here? Do you want to check when the next train is?" Lily steered them to a nearby concession stand.

"Okay. Sorry. I didn't mean we had to leave right now. We can stay longer if you want."

"It's fine," said Lily. She paid for a bottle of sparkling water that was already dappled in sweat. "I don't need to see anything more. Let's drink this and go."

"Okay, sure. I'm sorry. I didn't mean to upset you."

"I'm not upset."

"You're clearly mad at me."

"I'm fine. Here, take a sip."

With her phone Lily snapped some photos of the gardens. She walked back toward the central fountain, and reluctantly, Alison followed her. Lily blotted some of the sweat from her face. Then she handed Alison her phone.

"Can you take a photo of me in front of the fountain?"

Alison looked at Lily in perplexity. "Why?"

"So I can post it to my feed."

"No offense, but heatstroke isn't the most flattering look."

Lily stood closer to the fountain and turned to face Alison. "I'll filter it. You won't be able to see any of the sweat."

Alison clicked two shots.

"Can you take a few more? So I have options?"

Alison snapped a series of images.

"Why are you suddenly interested in posting?" she asked as she handed Lily back her phone. "This wouldn't have anything to do with Billie saying you should become an influencer?"

"No, of course not. But this is a good opportunity. To post."

"Is this opportunity accidental? Or is it the reason you dragged us up here?"

Lily didn't answer. And Alison strode away, in the direction of the gardens' exit.

• • •

AFTER THEY RETURNED to the Harlem Metro-North station, Lily and Alison walked to a small Italian restaurant on Lexington Avenue. It was a pizza parlor that also served antipasti, pastas, and meat dishes. For reasons Lily couldn't explain, she and Alison had never ordered a pizza there, despite its being the dining spot's main selling point. The restaurant was the sort of neighborhood place that would not appear on a hot spot guide, as it lacked the showiness and overt atmosphere that people normally associate with a New York eatery.

The women chose an indoor perch close to the air conditioner, whose efforts were aided by a ceiling fan but diminished by a pair of glass doors open to the steaming street.

"Should we try a pizza this time? The primavera one sounds good," said Alison with a glance over the laminated menu.

"Why tempt fate?" said Lily.

They ordered marinated artichokes, a caprese salad, and rigatoni all'Amatriciana to share. The waiter brought them a bottle of rosé.

"It's a bit sweet," said Alison after she sipped from her glass. "Don't you think?"

"Then ask for another," said Lily. Her glass remained untouched.

"Can you taste it?"

Lily sipped the pale pink wine. "I think it's fine."

"Okay. Maybe it will mellow out as it breathes."

"Why don't you ask for another bottle?"

"This one's already open. I feel bad. It's fine."

The women sat simmering. They swallowed their too-sweet wine. The whoosh of the fan stood in for conversational chatter. Their years of intimacy made impossible the polite small talk that would generally relieve such awkwardness.

Outside the restaurant's window, at one of the sidewalk tables, a couple enjoyed what was clearly, without hearing their exchange, a second or third date. Lily and Alison used to eavesdrop on other couples near them at restaurants. They would guess based on their interactions how early in the courtship the couples were and what might be their chances for long-term success. The woman in this couple laughed at something her male companion said. Her hand grazed his arm as an extension of her release. From the bright orbs of his eyes it was clear that he was totally smitten by her.

Lily and Alison had little problem polishing off the bottle of wine; its sweetness waned a touch, but not enough. The pasta all'Amatriciana, though, proved too much. Brown paper bag of leftover pasta in hand, Lily and Alison strolled west and then south toward Lily's apartment. The dark sky took the edge off the pummeling heat. The avenues were pleasantly busy with other couples who enjoyed postdinner strolls. Teenagers congregated on corners to map out their next moves in their nocturnal quest for illegal libations. Solo men and women took their dogs for one last amble before they tucked in for the night. The possibility of languor hung in the air.

The women arrived at Lily's building and climbed the stairs. Once inside her apartment, Lily poured them each an inch of scotch into a cut-crystal tumbler. They settled on her sofa to sip their beverages to the soundtrack of the vibrating air conditioner unit.

"Are you mad at me?" Alison asked.

"No, of course not. Why would I be mad at you?"

"It feels like you've been angry at me all day. Longer than that. And I don't know what I did wrong."

"You didn't do anything wrong." Lily's eyes burned and her nose began to run. "I don't know what's wrong with me."

She didn't understand what was happening. Maybe it was the wine, that stupid wine. The whiskey likely didn't help. Her body was suddenly seized with a sob. Alison had done nothing to deserve her ire. And yet every time she looked at her, Lily's body hardened and her jaw clenched. Whatever lightness percolated within her was quashed. She was a trained sentinel, ready to defend the sanctity of her self-determination. And Alison was somehow, against all supportable reasoning, the enemy. The exact nature of Alison's so-called threat escaped her; all Lily knew was that this person, whom she loved and wanted to protect with every atom in her body, had somehow become incompatible with her mutating thoughts and needs.

"Something is different about you, Lily."

"What do you mean?"

"I don't know what it is. But you're always somewhere else—"

"That's not true. I'm right here."

"—and when you're here, it's like you wish you were somewhere else. Or someone else."

"I'm not. I don't."

"I don't know who you are anymore."

"I don't know, either."

Both women cried now, Alison in small, continuous trickles, her pale face reddening as though windburned, Lily in choking gasps, her left hand pressed to her mouth and nose like a mask. With her right hand, Lily clutched one of Alison's hands. What a monster Lily was, to withhold herself from the person she loved most. And worse, she knew that Alison was right. Something about Lily had changed, and she was worried it wasn't for the better. The obsessive draw to the buzz buzz of her phone. The stupid social media posts. The dreams about Billie. Lily had become someone who was so scared of living, she buried herself in the digital ether instead. If she couldn't handle the pain of real life, she didn't deserve to enjoy its pleasures, either.

"Maybe I need to take a break for a bit," said Lily.

"Okay."

"Just a break."

The women were quiet a moment, the only sound their labored sniffles.

"I should go."

"You don't have to."

"I think I do."

Lily walked Alison to her door.

"I love you so much," said Lily.

"I love you, too."

They kissed, a deep, prolonged embrace. Tears mixed with the wetness of their lips. Their tongues merged into one connected being; neither wanted to separate. Then they pulled away from each other.

"I'll talk to you," said Lily.

"Yes."

"Let me know when you're home."

"Okay."

"I love you."

"I love you, too."

And then Alison was gone. Lily was alone in her apartment. She was alone everywhere and in every way. She was going to be alone forever. Lily was too drained dry to sob, too stunned to fall apart. She couldn't process how a day of minor annoyances had escalated into a break. She was overcome with a compulsion to grab her keys and rush out the door, get in a cab and go to Alison's apartment, bang on the door, beg her to take her back. She couldn't even make it ten minutes without her. She must have been insane to think she needed a break. But she knew that the desperation of her corrective would defeat its very purpose. The only fix here was time: hours and days and weeks to marinate in the convoluted landfill that her life had become. She shouldn't trust clarity, she reminded herself as she turned off the lights and crawled into bed. And then she prayed to a god she wasn't sure existed and asked for clarity, nonetheless.

17

. . .

A GREAT GUST of wind thrust Lily backward as she walked south along Eleventh Avenue. The blocks had little foot traffic, save for tourists who ogled a copper sculpture shaped like a dystopian tornado. The buildings were chilly and arrogant, their architecture spiritually soulless and at odds with the inherent messiness of their human residents. The closest subway was brand-new, and its multiple escalators were so infinite, they seemed to transport a person to and from the afterworld. Despite this new MTA outpost, the neighborhood felt defiantly set apart from the convenience that is the hallmark of New York City living. It existed on the perimeter, as if it hoped to retain the benefits of urban development without getting its hands too dirty.

Annabelle and Jonathan's city apartment occupied three floors in one of the Hudson Yards area's skyscrapers. The building was, modestly, less than forty stories, comprised of a glass curtain wall. The apartments featured towering ceilings and massive windows that overlooked the Hudson River and New Jersey on its other shore. And there were enough amenities, including a luxury gym, a bowling alley, a regulation-sized basketball court, a full pool, a library, to eliminate the temptation to venture through the bronze-clad lobby and out into the greater city. Jonathan had committed to the apartment before he and Annabelle were married. And while she would have chosen something more central on the island, a converted loft in SoHo, say, or a prewar place on Fifth Avenue that she could fill with provocative contemporary art for the sake of contrast, she had come to terms with her West Side Highway fate. The lighting was unbeatable, the sunsets performed extremely well on her social media accounts, and the apartment's distance from all her engagements proved a powerful bargaining chip in her insistence that Jonathan keep a car and driver on retainer, a fight she likely would have lost had they been a few avenues over.

It was only mid-September, but the last remnants of the summer had disintegrated, at least temporarily, in a recent string of sixty-degree days, replaced by the brisk, biting weather of undeniable fall. The city was a bed of papery rusts and caramels and cranberries and marigolds. The colors floated down from the trees and fluttered across sidewalks. Fall was the season of bounty and demise, of peaking and then sliding downhill. Its beauty was in its knowing wistfulness. The change of the leaves brought a yearning for the time that had just passed, a recognition that the height of this spectacular showing signaled an inevitable decline. To walk through the city on a crisp autumn day, the air like a spoonful of tart sorbet, the crackle of foliage beneath one's feet, was to feel nostalgia for the very moment one was in, even as one experienced it for the first time. The premonition of death was everywhere. It was beautiful.

This was Lily's third visit to Annabelle's place in the last two weeks, and she dreaded the trek from the subway each time. Lily would arrive at Annabelle's door breathless. It felt less like a typical city commute through a neighborhood than the crossing of time zones. Annabelle would eye Lily's winded face with perplexity. Subways were a foreign concept to Annabelle. They existed in a far-off land, alongside fast-food establishments and discount clothing emporiums: okay for the occasional, wry photo-sharing post, but otherwise unnecessary. Lily was at a loss to explain to her that for most people, proximity to public transportation was a selling point for real estate locations, not to mention romantic partners, professional gigs, and secondary friends. It hardly mattered since her trips to Annabelle's were not social occasions.

Annabelle had hired Lily to write the copy for a new website she was designing. Since Annabelle wanted the voice to sound personal, as though she was addressing her customers directly, Lily had thought it best that they have a few in-person meetings so she could better emulate Annabelle's inflections. The time spent on this website had outpaced its freelance financial benefits, however. Particularly since Lily struggled to funnel all her nonwork waking hours into her nascent fiction writing.

In the past few months, Lily had experienced something akin to a breakthrough on that front. Suddenly, her random fiction musings had coalesced into a veritable entity. The exact shape and size of the story she wrote was fuzzy, but her early-morning, post-work, and weekend stints at the helm of her laptop had uncovered a sense of cohesion—or at least the beginnings of thematic echoes. Each session she spent focused on the expanding document chipped away at the story's opacity, and she thrilled at the sparks these tiny revelations bequeathed her. Lily had grown particularly protective of her free time. She was resentful of anything and anyone that impinged on her ability to unload onto her laptop's keyboard.

It was a Saturday afternoon. Annabelle answered the door in what was, for her, an appropriately casual outfit of eight-hundred-dollar jeans and a four-figure sweater. The women cheek-kissed twice—Annabelle was from Oklahoma, but her greetings were always continental—and sat at the long dining table that Annabelle used as a desk. Lily retrieved her laptop from her shoulder bag and powered it on, while Annabelle went to the nearby open kitchen.

"Would you like something to drink? Tea? A Diet Coke?"

"Just some water is fine, thanks."

She returned to the table with a paper-thin glass tumbler, which she placed atop a woven coaster, and a tall bottle of French mineral water. Lily sipped from the glass, which she held tentatively, for fear it would shatter if she gripped it too firmly.

"Do you want to work on the brand statement for your home page?"

"Yes. What do you think of these dresses?"

Annabelle had opened a browser window on her large monitor screen for the website of an emerging London-based fashion designer. She scrolled through his runway show from a month ago. A recent graduate of the city's famed arts and design college, he had populated his collection with cocktail dresses and evening gowns encrusted with heavy layers of pearls, paillettes, glass beads, and seashells. He had rubbed them with salt water and bleach and sand, to give them the effect of lost treasures that had spent centuries underwater, only to wash up on the shore of a sun-drenched beach.

"They're beautiful. Are you thinking of using them as inspiration for a new bag?"

"No, the dialysis benefit is next week and I was going to ask him if I could borrow one for the night." Wearing a dress practically off the runway, and from a hot young talent, no less, was a foolproof way to announce one's aesthetic superiority.

"Isn't that a seated dinner? How will you sit in that dress? It looked like the models could barely walk in them."

"I could wear it during arrivals and cocktails and then change into something simpler for dinner and dancing."

"That seems needlessly complicated. It's not the Met Gala."

"I suppose you're right."

"Want to get started on this brand statement? What would you say are the most important traits represented in your handbag designs?"

"Luxury, for sure. Chic. Maybe European flair, too? What do you think of these?"

Annabelle flipped her thick, flaming mane. She had now trotted over to the website of a famous shoe designer, where she had zeroed in on a pair of his stilettos fashioned from champagne silk sateen embroidered with ostrich feathers, grosgrain ribbon, and crystal rhinestones.

"They're pretty, though not the most practical."

"When has anyone ever accused me of being practical?"

"Right. Do any other traits come to mind besides the ones you gave? Maybe something more specific?"

An hour and a half later, Annabelle had worked her way through six more e-commerce sites. Lily had managed to extract approximately four pieces of useful information for Annabelle's company's bio. Lily had become accustomed to this ratio of aimless fashion detours to actual productivity. Annabelle was like that friend in high school who always wanted to study together but would spend most of that time flipping through magazines instead of textbooks. On the one hand, it was infuriating; on the other, there was a certain charm in her devoted defiance of life's necessary tedium. And the thing was, she pulled it off, which caused a person to wonder what they had done wrong that their life didn't resemble hers.

All those gowns and accessories had eaten into Annabelle's caffeination levels. She fetched a Diet Coke refill from the kitchen. Lily picked up her phone, which she had kept on silent mode so as not to interfere with their labors. There was nothing from B, whom she had texted days ago.

This was a more regular occurrence, these lengthy lapses between responses from B. Ever since she had informed B of her "break," not "breakup," to be clear, in her relationship with Alison, B had become increasingly withdrawn. Over the past few months, she had been less likely to initiate texts with Lily and slower to respond. It was confounding. If anything, Lily had envisioned their communication amping up in response to her announcement. Lily no longer had the distraction of a personal life. Her entire focus could be on her career, like B's was, save for the occasional phallic text. She had assumed that B would congratulate her on her emotional sacrifice, on her willingness to whittle her time down to only its most necessary elements, as though love and affection were gratuitous flourishes.

There was an uglier explanation that Lily couldn't help but consider: that the existence of Alison had given B motivational fuel. Without Alison, Lily's life was a soundless chamber, save for work; there was less noise for B to cut through to capture Lily's attention. B thrived on competition. She didn't know how to function otherwise. Though she had never explicitly said as much, it was possible that all along, B had considered Alison a de facto foe in the battle for Lily's loyalty. Alison was no longer in the picture, so B had no reason to show up for work on time. Part of her job here was done.

Annabelle returned to the table with her Diet Coke can.

"By the way, your ears must have been burning the other day. I was talking about you with someone."

"Oh really?" Lily folded her laptop screen down. It was a good thing for Annabelle that she wasn't paid by the hour.

"Yes. It was at that dinner for that new candle. No, wait, it was over text."

"Who were you texting?"

"Billie Aston. You sat next to her at the Alzheimer's gala, right?"

"Yes." Nausea churned in Lily's stomach.

"I can't remember what we were texting about. Or how your name came up. Maybe I said you were helping me write my new site. Anyway, she texted me something strange."

"What did she say?"

"She called you a 'clever girl.'"

"I hate the word *clever*. It's so patronizing. It's what you call someone when you don't want to admit that they're smart."

"It sounded like a compliment to me. Have you two become friends?"

After a year and a half of correspondence with B, Lily had no answer to this question. They were people who texted, decently regularly, present circumstances notwithstanding. They shared some interests and worldviews, though not on topics like harassment and exploitation in the workplace. Sure, they were friends, though apparently, B viewed Lily more as a cute plaything than as a fully developed human being.

"I guess. We text occasionally. She's been offering me some work tips. I can't believe she called me a 'clever girl.'"

"I'm sure she meant it affectionately."

Please. Affection wouldn't know how to find purchase on B's frosty surface. The woman was a one-person iceberg. In many ways, Lily envied B her coolness. It was the very quality that had so drawn Lily to B's aura; that chilly detachment saved B the considerable overthinking and emotional whiplash that Lily counted as her modus operandi.

"Whatever," Lily told Annabelle. "It's good to know she thinks of me in such youthful terms."

"You can never be too young or too beautiful," said Annabelle.

"We all long to return to a fetal state."

"Exactly. Should we get back to work?"

*   *   *

TO ADD FURTHER intrigue to all of this, Lily's temporary break with Alison had extended her the very thing Lily had yearned for and that B had refused to impart: clarity. In the weeks that followed their post-botanical conference, Lily had been sideswiped by her overwhelming grief. Every restaurant she dined in, every television show she watched, every meal she cooked, they all carried the scent of her recent loss, like a lover's shirt a few weeks after she last wore it. Once the shuddering sobs had run their course in the days after their break, Lily settled into a stultified emptiness. Her workweeks provided a distraction, but she dreaded the weekends, with their forty-eight hours of unstructured time that even writing couldn't fill completely.

She tried to schedule away her grief. She committed to dinners and drinks that she might otherwise have declined in favor of a restorative evening at home with a good novel. No matter the vivacity of the company, she couldn't stave off the penetrating loneliness that would eventually creep up on her from behind. A part of her was missing. Lily would be forever incomplete without her.

It was Lily who sent the first text a month after the start of their break. She was out to dinner with Jordan, at a Greek restaurant in the West Village. He had gone to the bathroom. In his absence, Lily was scrolling through photos on her phone when she came across an image of her with Alison from their trip to Long Island. They wore T-shirts and jeans. Rows of grapevines rolled out behind them. They both smiled widely. Lily's eyes began to tear, and before she could reconsider the wisdom of her action, she typed out a quick message for Alison.

Lily: Hi. At that Greek place we kept wanting to try. The food is really good. Jordan and I split a lamb burger and the branzino.

Jordan returned from the bathroom.

"Should we get dessert?" he asked.

"Definitely."

"Let's ask for a menu."

Buzz buzz.

Alison: Hi. Yum. Glad to hear it's good and you finally got there.

Alison: I went to that Korean gastropub after work with some colleagues the other night.

Alison: The fried chicken was insane.

A smile broke across Lily's face.

"Who was that?" asked Jordan.

"It was Alison."

Once the dam was opened, Lily's text conversations with Alison grew progressively elongated. Each subject detoured into another in rambling, overlapping sequences. At her desk, Lily often had to silence her phone for portions of the day simply to finish her stories, though she rarely lasted more than an hour without manually checking the notifications anyway. One afternoon, it took her nearly six hours to finish the transcription of a forty-minute interview. By her slower typing standards, this was nonetheless an achievement.

Lily: I really should get back to this transcript.

Alison: Who's it with?

Alison: No, wait. Let me guess!

Alison: She's under thirty.

Alison: White.

Alison: Size 0-2.

Alison: Has at least one famous parent.

Alison: Is independently wealthy and still makes more money than any of us ever will because she has half a million or more followers.

Alison: Did I nail it?

Lily: You think you're so funny.

Alison: You didn't answer my question.

Lily: Yes. You nailed it.

Lily's nights were just as deliciously distracted. Sometimes, she and Alison would go out separately and alone to different bars they had previously frequented as a couple or had planned to audition for a regular spot. And they would sit there, Lily on the banged-up chair of a SoHo dive, and Alison at a cozy side table in a midcentury modern den in Chelsea, and compare the menus at their respective establishments.

They would decide on their orders together. Then they would sit in their individual locations, two or three miles apart, and sip their drinks and text each other the whole time, as if no one around them existed.

Those moments were like fun house mirror reflections of Lily's early interactions with B. Unlike with B, these texting bouts with Alison flooded Lily with a soothing familiarity. She knew what Alison looked like when she sipped from a glass, how she tended to lean toward the vessel, her long blond hair falling over her shoulders, instead of pulling the glass closer to her. They were a few subway stops away, but they may as well have been seated beside each other, because Lily could visualize with startling clarity how Alison looked through the entirety of their chats. Their phones were not the basis of their relationship; they were conduits for a preexisting connection, a love that would bloom and flourish with or without this digital interface.

A week ago, while on one of these separate-but-apart dates, Lily had broached the possibility of an in-person dinner, a suggestion to which Alison had agreed. Their meal was planned for two weeks from now. They had concretely resolved very little in the three and a half months of their voluntary parting. But then what had been the matter in the first place, Lily reasoned. They had different timelines for cohabitation; Lily's was, admittedly, as far off as a flight plan to Pluto. And their approaches to how they spent their leisure hours were sometimes at odds. Well, Lily's current writing stints would occupy those windows quite neatly. Alison would have plenty of space for her necessary sofa and streaming sessions. And yes, then there was B.

Naturally, Lily declined to share with B her revived proximity with Alison. B had hardly seemed interested in her break; there was no reason she should be kept abreast of a possible reconciliation. When B had retreated during Lily's mourning period, Lily had followed suit. Once she had moved past her anger over this perceived abandonment, she had blocked out B from her mind with surprising ease, focused as she was on processing her loss of Alison. The closer she crept to her dinner with Alison, the more Lily felt compelled to reinstate a normal rhythm with B. And the more frustrated Lily became with her inability to do so. She needed to prove to herself that she was capable of juggling these two entities in order to sever any possible tie-in between the rise of one and the demise of the other. There was a belief, too, that the peaceful coexistence of both relationships could exculpate her for any past emotional transgression. After all, innocence is rarely about the presence of good intentions but rather the absence of malicious ones.

Where this left her, Lily couldn't say. Fortunately, she had a surprise all-hands editorial meeting to keep her mind busy. The editor in chief was in Europe for the latest fashion shows. Only two delegates from the fashion department had joined him, as the magazine operated on an increasingly tight budget that put a damper on group travel. In her second-in-command position, Theresa gathered the thirty-strong editorial staff, including the digital team, in the office's largest conference room, on whose massive monitor she would videoconference in the editor in chief. Once everyone sat at the table or leaned against the walls and cabinetry, Theresa commenced the call. Timothy Jacobs's elegant, lined face loomed on the room's oversized screen.

"Hello, everyone. I'm sorry I can't be there with you today. I have some news to share."

This was it, the moment that every writer and editor awaited, the guillotine that hung quietly above their necks as they diligently went about the anachronistic task of producing a monthly magazine. They were all going to be fired, and by videoconference, no less, as fitting a means as any. They couldn't have written a more appropriate deletion of their jobs.

"I'm afraid it is mixed news."

That's what they called paltry severance these days, mixed, like a snack medley in some sad airport bar. *I'm sorry that your position is no longer available, but on the upside, you can wait two weeks until you experience the full despondency of unemployment.*

"We are going down to eight issues a year."

Okay. Not a full bleed-out; a prolonged and painful demise instead.

"On the upside, everyone will now contribute to digital daily. We want nonstop stories. Everything you wish you could do for the magazine, you'll now do for the website."

Death by poison, then. A strangled choking on foul venom until one's organs and airways gave up their struggle.

"I hope you're all as excited about the future as I am! I'll let Theresa take it from here. Thanks, everyone."

O true apothecary! Thy drugs are quick. Thus with a kiss I die. Theresa made no effort to disguise her displeasure as she took over the proceedings. For her, the only upside to the digital media revolution was the opportunity to work from home.

"I know this is probably a bit of a surprise, though, hopefully, not too much of one. I think we should take solace in the fact that they haven't eliminated us completely, and instead, they're giving us the chance to flex our digital muscles."

Theresa was not the woman to talk a person out of jumping from a bridge.

"We'll roll this out at the beginning of next week," Theresa continued. "I'd like a list of pitches from each of you, stories you want to see online, things you've been itching to cover. After we approve them, we'll hand out deadlines. Thanks, all."

The magazine's staff filed out dutifully. They branched off into small clusters once past the conference room's glass borders. Lily meandered back to her desk alone. She had no interest in a play-by-play analysis of the editor in chief's announcement. Her fate had been sealed since the invention of the first smartphone and the creation of the first blog. Her livelihood was a hostage with an explosive device wrapped around its chest and a countdown clock visible only to those with a high enough perch.

Not for the first time, Lily wished she could rewind or fast-forward her date of birth. Even eight extra years of age would have given her a little more time to enjoy the sunset before the industry went dark; if she had been younger, she would have avoided this moment altogether and woken up to a newly reconfigured landscape where her next move would be self-evident. But no, here she stood in this increasingly dank purgatory, trapped between the golden past and the invisible future, with no clue as to when she would emerge into the eventual dawn.

Lily could barely recall the shimmering moments that had brought her to this inevitable crossroads. When she had started her career, the initial appeal of a fashion magazine had morphed into something more layered. It was no longer only about the presentation of an aspirational lifestyle, but also about participation in an endlessly thrilling conversation. She and her colleagues gathered a finely tuned assemblage of people and places and ideas that they felt their readers had to know. It was true that this array had been deeply white, even more so than it was today. The past was not as golden as Lily's burst of indulgent nostalgia would have her believe. Still, those first few years of her career had been dizzying; it was like sitting at a dinner party, surrounded by the most interesting guests, each of whom had their own tales to share. The courses of food kept arriving and the wine flowed endlessly. Until they didn't.

There was no specific instance when the end started. There were small shifts in the atmosphere that escalated into a larger storm. The discourse was not as enthralling. In fact, it was a version of a conversation that other people were having and had already had, at some earlier date and at some other table. Everyone seemed to be talking about the same thing, and purposely so. The magazines no longer introduced readers to the things they needed to know, through a specific lens honed by perspective and experience. That happened on digital channels, often sans perspective and experience, where ideas broke at a speed that a monthly magazine couldn't possibly capture. The magazines didn't initiate a different conversation. They tried to interject and collect whatever loose discursive threads they could spin into their own pages. Eventually, everyone talked over everyone else and the content didn't matter so much as who said it first or loudest and how many people were there to hear it. A bound book of paper required money, time, and labor. No matter how beautiful the finished product, it could never win at a game predicated on speed and popularity.

Lily's first impulse was to text Alison. They were still a week out from their reconciliatory dinner, though, and she was wary of imposing her work concerns before their reunion. It was preferable to keep her interactions with Alison to their light and playful digital dates. Instead, Lily turned to B. A professional cri de coeur might finally elicit the response that could restore equilibrium to Lily's conscience.

Lily: They lowered our issue count. And they're amping up our digital story load. Again. The end is near.

The magazine sold slices of intricately decorated cake, while the website handed out complimentary candy corn. The competition had been a joke from the start.

"Tough meeting, right?"

It was Marc, who leaned over Lily's cubicle barrier.

"I guess," said Lily, though what she wanted to say was, *Not for you— you must be thrilled. You'll probably get a promotion out of this.* She turned to her computer screen to signal that she was too busy to talk.

Marc walked to the edge of Lily's desk and, once again, sat on its surface. Lily scooted her desk chair back.

"This means we'll probably be working together more," he said. Marc crossed a faded denim shin over his thigh, flashing a sliver of pasty ankle. Today, his zip-up vest was black, as though he had predicted the meeting and had worn it in solidarity with—or in celebration of—the ongoing funeral for print media. Lily imagined a different funeral. One where Marc's intermittent-fasted figure was the body in the coffin. It would be an open-casket proceeding, so all the attendees could see how young Marc was when he met his untimely end. His tombstone would read, "He loved algorithms and SEO keywords." His obituary would report exactly how many unique views his funeral had amassed and the average number of minutes its attendees had spent gazing at his corpse.

"I guess."

"Good—because we really need more people like you."

"What kind of people is that?"

"Hard workers," said Marc. "You're like a machine."

Was that supposed to be a compliment? Because last she had checked, Lily was human. "Marc, I'm really overwhelmed with work right now."

"Let's have lunch today. To talk about upcoming stories."

"I eat lunch at my desk. Because as I mentioned, I have a lot to do."

"I'll swing by when I'm going to the cafeteria. In case you free up."

"I really can't today."

"Tomorrow, then."

Lily stood up from her chair. This conversation needed to end. "I'm going to the bathroom."

Marc remained seated on Lily's desk. "Okay, see you later." He paused. His eyes grazed the lines of Lily's denim legs. "Those jeans look really good on you. Who makes them?"

"They're vintage," Lily said. She hated herself for answering his question.

"You'll have to give me the name of the store. So my wife can get a pair."

Lily sped away, in the direction of the bathroom.

• • •

LATER THAT EVENING, Lily picked at some leftover salmon and veg-etables from the meal she had cooked the previous night. She cleaned up after her dinner and sat on her sofa. Her open laptop screen stared at her judgmentally. For months, her fictional words had danced from her fingertips to the increasingly lengthy document on her computer. But lately, she confronted a standstill, unsure of how to proceed. No amount of soul-searching managed to dislodge whatever blockage prevented her forward momentum.

Buzz buzz.

B: Bit dramatic, don't you think?

Lily: No. Once you go down, you never go up again.

Lily: It's a distinct trend.

Lily broke off a square of dark chocolate from a bar beside her computer. Surely a rush of sugar and natural caffeine would nudge things along.

Buzz buzz.

B: So double down on digital.

B: Since that's the future.

B: Like I've been telling you for months.

Lily: The digital team doesn't have the same creative concerns. All they're focused on is numbers and speed.

Lily: At that rate, I may as well just become an influencer.

Her fingers slid back and forth across the keyboard's surface. She didn't press down hard enough to type, but she hoped that mimicry of the act of writing would bring it forth through the power of muscle memory.

Buzz buzz.

B: Well.

B: Then you have your answer.

If Lily knew the answer to her own question, she wouldn't have texted B in the first place. *Come on, play your part, B. I'm the insecure ingénue; you're the omniscient icon. Don't make me do your work for you.*

Lily: Is that what you would do?

The pads of Lily's fingertips rested on the keyboard in anticipation of that first typed letter. She would not move them until some writing happened. She would sleep on this keyboard if that was what it took.

Buzz buzz.

B: We are in very different places in our lives.

Lily: If you were in my shoes.

B: I've always believed in doing what you love.

Lily: What if that isn't possible?

Lily: And what you love ceases to exist?

What Lily experienced was a form of anticipatory mourning. It wasn't in honor of a human being, but that didn't make it less painful. Instead of jumping into planning-for-the-future mode, Lily was paralyzed by the numbness of occupational grief. Everything good comes to an end. She hadn't expected this aphorism to collect on its wisdom so soon into her career. This stasis wasn't laziness. It was a symptom of her broken heart.

Buzz buzz.

B: Then you find something else to love.

B: Try something new.

B: You'll fuck up.

B: Move on to something else.

B: Eventually, you'll find another thing that you love.

Lily: I'm worried that I'll never love like that again.

Lily: That this was my one shot. And it was short. And now it's gone.

Lily: And everything else will just be a job from now on.

Maybe that wasn't the worst thing. It was childish to believe that

one's work was supposed to provide happiness as well as financial security, if it even did that. A job was a thing a person did to fund the life
they wanted to have. There was no reason it needed to transcend this
basic utility. And things would be easier that way, without the messiness
of emotional attachment to something that should function purely on
the level of pragmatism. Lily needed to grow the heck up, that was the
real challenge at hand.

Buzz buzz.

B: You will find something.

B: Or it will find you.

B: Either way, it will work out.

B: Have faith.

Lily: Why should I?

Just type. Lily pressed down firmly on one of the keys. Who cared
what it said. Put something down on that page. She could always go
back and revise it. At least in this realm, nothing she did was permanent. No mistakes were beyond repair.

Buzz buzz.

B: Because I told you to.

18

· · ·

A VISITOR TO Lily's apartment could be forgiven for assuming they had stumbled upon an undiscovered literary black hole. Books were stacked everywhere. They crowded in spindly piles beside the sofa and chairs and table. They leaked from shelves and made appearances in unusual locations, such as the bathroom sink, the entryway, the side of the stove. Their surfaces did hybrid duty as drinks platters and serving stations; their spines filled the apartment with a ticker tape of colorful titles. They were portals to the past and ladders to the future. The thinness of their papery DNA belied their indelible weight in Lily's life.

The weekend hours strolled by in leisurely expanses as Lily buried herself in the pages of her books. She splayed across her sofa—or on Alison's blue sectional now that they were back together. Over the past few months, Lily's love of reading had developed into a creative awakening. Whereas fiction had been, in childhood, a sanctuary from a world in which she often felt lost and alone, she realized it could also make this same world feel more tolerable. The fictional narratives in her writing experiments had generated a new sense of purpose for Lily that transformed her daily reality into a joy.

Up until recently, Lily had felt satisfied with her magazine work. The range of people she had interviewed seemed, for a time, excitingly varied, so long as she ignored any desire for real diversity. And the privilege of listening to and telling their stories was fulfilling. The hungry buzz she experienced while writing a magazine piece on someone or something she cared about would never fade. But as social media had grown, the magazine industry had shrunk, and with it, that sweep of interview opportunities. Each print piece had to be a hit online, to justify its expensive real estate. Pithy sound bites, fragmented roundups, and clever — not smart — lists took precedence over less neatly packaged narratives. Headlines mattered more than the stories themselves. Compression in every form became the goal.

Though hardly a contrarian, Lily craved expansion. Her fiction expanded her word count, the amount of time she devoted to her writing, and, crucially, her creativity. In a magazine piece, Lily had to decide exactly what a story was, speedily and concisely, based on limited facts, no matter how complex the subject, for the sake of an arbitrary deadline. In fiction, she could return to the same idea over and over again, for months and, she hoped, maybe years, and relish the deeper layers she unpeeled with each successive visitation. Slowly, word by word, Lily could replace the aspirational fantasies that had first seduced her to magazines and that had held her there, in their thrall, with something arguably more powerful: her imagination. Lily's mind contained all the inspiration she needed to build her version of life.

Still, Lily couldn't live exclusively in her books or her fiction writing, as much as she might wish for this possibility. The outside world beckoned. And these days, it had some joy of its own to offer. Lily and Alison were together again and back in their same pre-break entwined-but-apart configuration. They had chosen as the location of their first date the very restaurant where they had dined before their break, the up-town pizza parlor whose eponymous dish they had never sampled. The thinking had been reclamation for Lily, who had suggested the venue. She and Alison needed to revise their story, and that required confronting the site of their last supper and the food item they had refused to try.

"We need to order one," said Lily as she sat across the table from Alison and flipped the laminated menu over to its selection of pizza pies.

"I don't know," said Alison. "What if we hate it? Then we'll never want to come back. This place will be ruined for us."

Lily's fingers trembled with nerves. She tucked her hands into her lap to hide them from Alison. Her question could just as easily have pointed to the stakes of their very meal. If this dinner went poorly, it might seal their fate for the worse. Lily tried to focus on Alison's pointed use of *us*, a word she wouldn't have thrown out casually had dissolution been on her brain.

"I think we'll manage either way," said Lily. "I have faith that we can overcome that obstacle."

Alison's wide smile enveloped her face. "Are you still talking about pizza?"

"Sure. I mean, other things, too. If that's okay?"

Alison reached her hand beneath the table and clasped one of Lily's shaky hands in hers. "It's definitely okay. And I think we should get the margherita."

The pizza was perfectly good, though the women preferred the restaurant's pastas. Per Lily's faith, they survived. On the surface, it would seem they had simply reverted to a comfortable, flawed pattern, the very structure that had enabled their cooling of ardor and its accompanying temporary dispersal. It was possible that Lily fooled herself with the belief that this time things would be different. She had been lulled into a delusional state that tricks lovers into repeating their romantic mistakes.

But the air between the two women was lighter. The thick fog of their acrimony had blown away in the months of their break and in the weeks since that reconciliatory meal. In its place was a clear view to the surrounding country. What lay on the horizon was anyone's guess, but the journey there appeared less rife with turbulence. Having laid out their respective concerns, Lily and Alison accommodated each other's eccentricities and, crucially, avoided apologizing for their individual needs. Alone time was granted. Hyperactivity was humored, within reason. Previously, their partnership had been amateur and clunky; now it had the makings of a well-rehearsed performance. Or perhaps that was simply a pipe dream.

· · ·

THE SMOOTHNESS OF her reunion with Alison was in marked contrast to the plodding difficulty of Lily's job. The magazine staff toiled away on the January issue, though outside the glass tower, October had barely taken hold. Lily had been assigned a feature story comprised of eight individual profiles of actors and actresses to watch for in the coming year. The subjects ranged from a twenty-two-year-old man having his film festival debut to a twenty-six-year-old woman who had made an early career out of playing the smart-aleck best friend to a range of leading women. At last, she had received her own starring turn. It was a challenge in and of itself to wrangle eight interviews, through eight separate, but equally aggressive, publicists, in ten days. There had been no small number of cancellations and reschedules. Lily's work calendar was like a pockmarked city street in the midst of repaving. Somehow, Lily had prevailed and submitted her text, all eight smaller stories, on time. Her copy cycled through the regular editing channels. And the art department flowed it into their working layout.

One day, she stood by the office printer and waited for her transcript to emerge; the research editor needed it to check her text. The completed layout of her up-and-coming actors and actresses story whooshed out. The photos were vivid and Lily's textual industry was apparent. As she flipped through the pages, she noticed that instead of a typical byline alongside the photographer's and stylist's names on the first spread of the story, her credit had been relegated to a mere tagline buried at the bottom of the last page, where no one would ever see it. The magazine had run similar packages of multiple, smaller profiles in the past. In those cases, James, the editor in chief's assistant, who also wrote stories and had been assigned previous iterations, had been given a full byline. Precedent was on her side.

Lily carried the printouts back to her desk and retrieved her phone from her bag.

Lily: Can I ask your advice on something quickly?

She plucked two back issues of the magazine from the stacks she had piled on her desk and flipped through them to find the previous examples of similar pieces. There it was in each instance, James's byline, in big bold letters on the first spread of the story.

Buzz buzz.

B: Sure.

B: Shoot.

Lily: I've been working hard on this package of young Hollywood profiles. I saw the layout and they gave me a tagline instead of a proper byline.

Lily: We've done these packages before. In all the other cases, the writer got a proper byline.

The space where Lily's byline should have been mocked her. It must have been a mistake. In which case, she would simply have caught an error. No one could fault her for that. Theresa would shrug her shoulders and correct it. No harm done.

Buzz buzz.

B: You have to say something.

B: You deserve credit.

B: Be calm about it.

B: Don't get angry or emotional.

B: Mention the other examples.

B: Ask for the same thing.

Why did Lily have to ask for something that her junior colleague was handed by default?

Lily: Okay, will do. Thanks!

She stood up from her desk chair, smoothed her hair, and walked across the hall, more shakily than she cared to admit. Theresa was alone at her desk, reading emails on her computer. She motioned Lily in. Reluctant to take a seat, Lily hovered in front of her desk. Hopefully, this would be a quick conversation.

Theresa looked at her expectantly.

"There was a copy of the 'Young Hollywood' layout at the printer. It looks great," Lily began. "I noticed that I had a tagline instead of a byline. I wasn't sure if that was the final version?"

"It is, yes."

Theresa leaned back in her chair. She crossed her bony arms over her chest.

"With 'Young Hollywood' packages we've done in the past, the writer has always received a byline. I had hoped this time would be the same."

"The writers in those instances were more known."

"The last two were written by James. And he is still an assistant."

Theresa's white face remained stoic. "What you saw is the final version."

Don't get angry or emotional. Lily clenched her hand into a fist behind her back.

"I'd really appreciate it if you would consider changing it."

Theresa's eyes registered surprise. She had expected Lily to walk away.

"In the past few months, I have taken on the additional work of weekly digital stories," Lily continued. "Without extra pay. Or a title change."

Theresa opened her mouth to interject and Lily's gaze stopped her.

"And that was before the rest of the print staff was asked to do the same."

Theresa's mouth closed.

"I recognize that digital work is part of the job now. For everyone. But so is print. And I'm not asking for something extra; I'm asking you to show me that you value my work for the magazine. The same way you valued the work when James did it."

Before Theresa could answer, Lily turned and closed Theresa's glass door gently behind her. Eyes stinging, she walked back to her desk. She wanted to rip her computer's cords out of their sockets and throw the machine out the window, send it hurtling down to the gray city below. Seated in her desk chair, she willed her heart rate to settle down and the tears forming in her eyes to disappear.

She had been too emotional. Lily knew Theresa would reject her request. It had been absurd to think that she could stride in there and ask for what she deserved and somehow receive it. She wasn't a man. Or B. She was Lily. The quiet, well-behaved girl who took her workload like a champ, who spat out stories so that somebody upstairs could say, *Yes, our numbers are exactly where they need to be.* She wasn't a human. She was a machine. Or worse—she was an obedient child. B had essentially said as much to Annabelle.

Lily picked up her phone.

Lily: That went well.

She dug in her handbag for a tissue. Unable to locate one, she stormed to the office's kitchen, where she grabbed a few paper napkins. Back at her desk, she dabbed her face. Forget it, just forget it. She had tried;

there was nothing more she could do. Lily scrolled through the unread emails on her computer.

Buzz buzz.

B: Good.

B: Or wait.

B: Was that sarcasm?

Lily: Yes.

Lily: She said that was the final version.

Lily: I pushed back, but doubt it did anything.

B: That's disappointing.

B: You deserve better.

The thing was, Lily hadn't asked for better. She had asked for exactly the same thing that others had received. She wasn't a revolutionary. Somehow, the higher she climbed on the editorial masthead, not that she was in any danger of ever bumping her head on its ceiling, the more fruitless Lily's struggles became. The gap between the value Lily knew she possessed and the role the magazine insisted she play grew larger and larger. At some point, the former would outpace the latter to such a degree that Lily would no longer be able to tolerate it. In this moment, that eventuality seemed particularly imminent.

Straight out of college, Lily had worked as an assistant to a powerful, well-respected magazine editor. It was a dream position that proffered entry to every facet of the publication via the editor's authority. Plus, the editor was known to hire aspiring writers, eager to sculpt them into future staffers of the features department's ranks. Of course, the job of assisting someone of the editor's ilk did not limit itself to writerly endeavors. There was the expected iced latte fetching, even in the dead of winter; the lunch grabbing; the FedExing of sometimes sizable and not remotely job-relevant packages; the delivery of items to her doorman; the pickup of personal possessions accidentally left at previous appointments all the way across town; etc., etc. None of this should have been outside the realm of anyone's expectations for this assistant job and it certainly wasn't at odds with Lily's presumptions. The editor was an absurdly busy person who needed all the help she could get.

The surprise lay not in the minutiae of her daily tasks or the occasional ask that went well beyond her occupation. Lily was amazed by how easily she sidelined her own needs in favor of someone else's. Evening plans with friends, workout classes, sleep: Lily jettisoned all of these with no hesitation if the editor required her aid. In fact, Lily took pleasure in their abandonment. It made her happy to cancel a dinner she had looked forward to for a month because the editor needed her to stay late to proofread a last-minute story shipping the next day. She loved waking up at six thirty A.M. on a Sunday to arrange for a car service for the editor to and from a photo shoot upstate. None of this was an exaggeration. Lily felt competent and needed in a way that many recent college graduates probably didn't.

The editor said *please* and *thank you*. She didn't throw food and phones at Lily, as other, similar editors were rumored to do with their assistants. The editor was polite, mostly grateful, and generous with positive and constructive feedback. She relied on Lily, trusted Lily with her life. Just ask her where her wallet was. Ask her to find her keys. What was the password for her voicemail? When was her next appointment? What time was her interview with that very important fashion designer? The editor's basic ability to function was determined by Lily.

It was thrilling to be the secret ingredient in someone else's power. Everyone else sought fame and public pats on the back. Lily wanted to be the generator running steadily in the basement corner, unnoticed until something goes wrong. And her assistantship to the editor offered a temporary reprieve from the muddle Lily was certain to make of her own career, as evidenced by her current state a decade later. Lily wondered if she would have been better off as a lifetime executive assistant, a person who never had to worry about advocating for herself, and failing at it, as Lily was sure she had, because her entire existence revolved around the betterment of another person. Maybe her assistantship had been not a stepping stone but a premonition of the only life she knew how to build. Except, if that was true, if that was the type of work that would satisfy her, then she wouldn't have spent the past nineteen months trying to forge something different for herself, under B's tutelage.

Buzz buzz.

B: Would you ever leave magazines?

Lily: Sure. If the right opportunity came along.

B: I might have something.

B: I'm looking to hire someone for a new position.

Warmth spread across Lily's face. It sounded like B was offering her a job.

Lily: That would be amazing.

B: I haven't told you what it is.

Lily: It's working for you, right?

B: Yes.

"Lily, do you have a second?"

It was Theresa, who had approached Lily's desk.

"Sure."

"I was a bit harsh earlier. I was dealing with some upsetting news about our digital numbers."

"It's no problem."

"I'll make sure you get a real byline."

"Thanks, I appreciate it."

It demanded all of Lily's restraint not to tell Theresa exactly where she could shove that missing byline. B was a woman far superior to Theresa and she had chosen Lily as a future employee. Lily practically salivated in anticipation of that future day when she would waltz into

Theresa's office and inform her that two weeks from now, her servitude would be over. She couldn't wait to watch Theresa squirm in her chair while she failed to maintain a stoic response to Lily's news. In her biggest dreams, Lily would choose to give her notice when she had the largest possible story count on her plate, stories that she would be incapable of finishing in the final two weeks of her job. The promise of this dream was almost more succulent than its reality could ever be. Lily was on the move. Nothing could slow her momentum. She would soon become the woman she was supposed to be.

19

· · ·

THAT WEEKEND, LILY and Alison emerged from their Sunday leth-
argy and ventured out for lunch. Technically, it was a late brunch, but
brunch was a meal better reserved for recent college graduates who
needed $15 avocado toast and bottomless mimosas to feel fulfilled. The
women chose a farm-to-table restaurant a couple of blocks north of
Union Square. The restaurant's arrangement of individual tables, in
long, parallel rows, gave the room the feel of a clubby cafeteria, wherein
everyone was on equal footing. One could rub literal shoulders with a
celebrity or media mogul as the restaurant was popular with the magazine and publishing industries. But they would also sit in the same min-
imalist, uncomfortable model of chair and struggle with the same issue
of how to squeeze all their various plates, glasses, and condiments onto
a square table better suited for hands of Solitaire. The restaurant embodied the rare form of elitism that ends up leveling the social playing
field.

The cramped seating also meant that eavesdropping during one's
meal wasn't so much a sport as it was a default setting. As Lily and Alison chewed their way through a shrimp salad with produce from the

farmer's market and a charred spinach, dill, and goat cheese pizza, they were easily privy to the chatter on either side of them. The key was to maintain a quietly conspiratorial level for one's own conversations to maximize one's overheard content and minimize the amount one shared.

Two women in their twenties seated to Lily's left finished up what appeared to be a rather boozy brunch. They were on their third round of mimosas since she and Alison had sat down. Who knew how many they had consumed prior to Lily and Alison's arrival.

"Did you see who she left with last night?"

"You mean Chris? I give that two weeks. Tops."

"Why can't I ever find someone?"

"You will."

"You know what I really want?"

"What?"

"An older, really fat guy, preferably Japanese or Korean."

"I feel like you're fetishizing fat Asians."

"That doesn't make my desire any less genuine."

Lily tried to catch Alison's eye so she could alert her to their neighbor's highly specific fetish. But Alison was focused on the quartet to Lily's right. Three men and one woman, a few years north of their liberal arts bachelor degrees, leaned over the remnants of soft scrambled eggs and ricotta pancakes. The sharp acidity of spiked tomato juice drifted up from their half-empty glasses.

"Anderson James is supposedly stepping down this spring."

"Voluntarily?"

"What do you think?"

"About time. He's been EIC for, what, twenty years?"

"Since he had hair on his head."

"Burn."

"I hear Stacy Jones is one bad cover away from the chopping block."

"You're a few days late on that tidbit. I've been working on a story about it all week. Off the record."

"Did she comment?"

"Of course not. That woman loves an air of mystique."

The members of the quartet were media reporters who covered the magazine beat. They were second only to gossip columnists in the fear and exasperation they inspired in the rest of the industry. While their colleagues strove to build careers based on their own stories and reputations, media reporters bolstered their professional standings through critiquing other people's stories and reputations. It was a brilliant vocation, no arguments there: a low-stakes investment with a high-power quotient return. Every so often, a talented media reporter would break a genuinely important story about a top editor or publisher who had committed gross negligence, abused their office, harassed their staff, etc., etc. This one story would then justify a whole slew of ass-kissing puff pieces and needlessly aggressive deep dives until the next genuinely important story emerged to take its place.

The vulturous quartet had moved on from foretelling the demise of various editors in chief to a dissection of the recent November-issue covers, which had just hit the five or so physical newsstands that still existed in Manhattan.

"Did you see *Vogue*?"

"What was that lighting?"

"Tragic."

"And *Elle*."

"I didn't mind that one."

"That's setting a high bar for achievement."

"Well, better than what Timothy Jacobs did."

"That was a disaster."

"And what were those cover lines?"

"I hear they're going down to six issues."

"Eight."

"Same thing. They may as well give up."

"Who's buying advertising these days?"

"No one. They're down twenty pages this month over last year."

"The whole industry's going to hell."

"Gives us something to write about."

Alison frowned at Lily. "Aren't they talking about your latest issue? Timothy Jacobs is your editor in chief, right?" she asked.

"Yup."

"Are you worried?"

"Always. But what can I do?"

The women finished their meal and merged with the pedestrians outside. The unseasonable warmth persisted. It was looking to be a balmy Halloween. Despite the eeriness, it made for good strolling weather, so they walked down lower Fifth Avenue. Large chain stores gaped with a dearth of customers, and women in leggings, oversized hoodies, and colorful sneakers filed out of various fitness studios. As the two women meandered below Fourteenth Street, the retail locations gave way to university centers, redbrick churches, and stately apartment buildings manned by doormen in crisp uniforms. Soon, the women were at Washington Square with its Roman marble arch standing majestic sentinel over Greenwich Village. Skateboarders swooped lackadaisical loops around the park's fountain. Older couples lounged contentedly on the surrounding benches and soaked up the unexpected sun.

This was what Lily loved most about New York. It was like reading a book side by side with a friend or lover who was absorbed in their own, different novel. Everyone was engaged in their separate reveries, and yet they did it together. They were cerebrally apart but physically close. New York forced that sharedness on a person, whether they wanted it or not. The crush of bodies in a rush-hour subway car, faces in strangers' armpits, shopping bags pressed into anonymous backs. The aggressive sideswipe on a pavement strip as a fellow pedestrian informed someone of their lagging walking speed. The lines and the crowds and, dear god, the traffic. It all served to prevent a person's arrival at the false conclusion that they were entirely alone, even if that was the very scenario they craved. And yes, it could be far too much most of the time. There was the frustration and rage at the lack of personal space; the inability to breathe and the impossibility of serenity. But embedded in that swirling chaos was the beating heart of human truth: Connectedness wasn't a Silicon Valley buzzword or a clever marketing tool; it was our evolutionary fate, and the sooner we acknowledged it, the better off we would all be.

Of course, this constant reminder of her interrelatedness to others was exactly why Lily sought the refuge of solitary living. It was possible to appreciate the delicate threads that tied us together and still thirst for a small patch of concrete that was entirely hers. Aloneness and loneliness were so often conflated, but for Lily, their relationship was far more nuanced. One did not necessitate the other. Aloneness was physical solitude. It was a cabin in the woods, a bench all to oneself in the park, a run down an empty street. Loneliness was an emotional chasm. It was the space between who a person was and how others saw them. Loneliness was other people. And other people were our shared fate. Better to bathe in this fluid contradiction than pretend it didn't exist.

Lily and Alison selected a bench on one of the less trafficked paths in Washington Square that wound off the main fountain. The trees were partially bare. Faint clouds speckled the gray-blue expanse of sky.

"Billie offered me a job," Lily said.

"Okay."

"I mean, not formally, but she said they're adding a new position. And asked if I was interested."

"Do you know what it is?"

"No, not yet. I assume any job under her would be a great opportunity."

Alison frowned. "It could be. But maybe wait to hear more."

"She gave me more work advice the other day. She knows how discouraged I am."

"You definitely need to go somewhere else. Make sure whatever is next is what you really want."

Lily reached for Alison's hand and cupped it in her own. She had almost lost Alison to her obsession with B. Somehow, they had made it back to each other. Alison was the one person in her life whose merit never wavered; Lily wouldn't risk such a precious gift again. If she struggled to keep B from devouring her when they only interacted digitally, Lily couldn't imagine how she would maintain her bearings when B became part of her in-person experience.

"I don't know that I'm ready to give up on writing."

"Who says you have to? You can do whatever you want. Write your own rules. Isn't that what writers do?"

Lily wouldn't know. Her entire career had been devoted to the narration of other people's stories and achievements. She was a professional listener, a cataloger of pithy quotes and flippant asides. She watched others perform their lives or their characters' lives on screens and stages, at parties and galleries, in the bland rooms of Midtown hotels where press junket interviews always happened. Then she described their actions, their incomparable talent, their incandescent beauty, their effervescent personalities, and spun it all together into a neatly packaged two-hundred-to-eight-hundred-word spiel for her readers' entertainment. Lily was made to be an empty vessel, carefully shaped to hold another person's outpourings. Once those had reached the vessel's top level, she poured them out so she could be replenished with someone else.

Lily had devoted so many of her adult years to this perpetual emptying that she had come to mistake it for actively living. The very skill that made her so adept in her public role had somehow stagnated her personal growth. Or it was the reverse. She had found a way to recast her detachment from daily existence as professional sustenance. Her career as a magazine writer was, in fact, her most adroitly woven yarn of all.

This emptying was so imprinted on her muscles that Lily worried her newer fictional creation would prove just as consuming as her magazine work. And the result might be far worse. Currently, Lily had steady employment, with all the protection that conferred. There was zero promise that her fiction would ever grant her stability. More likely, she would end up destitute, with only vestiges of her dreams to keep her warm at night. A job with B was exactly that: a job, with a paycheck, benefits, and some measure of security. There was the implication of a trajectory, too. It would lead somewhere. B would make sure of that. Lily could build a career that granted her future independence, like B had, while she wrote her fiction on the side. Once she grasped that eventual autonomy, however many years from now, she could focus exclusively on her writing, without risk. B and her fiction were better than compatible — they were mutually beneficial.

Lily located her phone and texted B.

Lily: What's the deal with this new position?

. . .

LATER, UPTOWN, LILY stood in her tiny kitchen and diced some shallots for dinner. Alison, in gray sweatpants and a T-shirt bearing the insignia of her undergraduate college, searched for something to watch on one of the streaming services. She clicked on a film, convinced that she had unearthed some unknown gem in the queer category.

"It's called *Deep in the Valley*," Alison informed Lily, who barely glanced at the television, to avoid slicing one of her fingers.

"No."

"It has five stars and a bunch of glowing reviews—I can't believe I've never heard of it."

"There's probably a reason for that."

"Stop being so pessimistic. At least let me watch it until dinner is ready."

Buzz buzz.

With a dish towel, Lily wiped her hands. She reached for her phone.

B: We're hiring in the next month or two.

B: It's related to that skin care line I mentioned.

Lily: Cool.

Lily: Can you give me any hint about the job?

Lily drizzled some olive oil into a pan, turned the burner on, and set it at medium-high heat.

"I haven't seen you here before . . ."

"It's my first time."

"Oh, is it . . . well, I'm happy to be your guide."

"I'm not even looking at the screen and I can tell this movie is awful."

"Maybe it will get better!"

Buzz buzz.

B: What kind of a hint?

Lily: Area of expertise?

Lily: Who it reports to?

When the pan was sizzling, she placed two chicken thighs skin-down in the hot oil. She eyed the television, where an older blonde appeared to be fulfilling her role as guide to a younger brunette woman.

"Which woman in the movie do you think is going to die?" Lily asked.

"Definitely the brunette. It's more tragic if it's the younger one," said Alison. "Plus, she's the one with the husband and kid at home, so she is more deserving of punishment."

The chicken skin was brown and crispy. Lily flipped the two thighs over to cook the other sides, briefly. She minced some garlic and zested a lemon, then cut the lemon in half and squeezed its juice into a glass.

Buzz buzz.

B: It reports to me.

Lily: Cool.

B: It's an editorial position. We're building a new site for the line.

B: And there will be a blog on the site, with fashion and culture stories that are symbiotic with the line's messaging.

Lily: I see.

Lily removed the chicken from the pan. She lowered the heat on the burner and sautéed the shallots.

Buzz buzz.

B: Okay, twist my arm.

B: It's an editorial director position.

B: This person will be responsible for all editorial content decisions for the site.

B: Carte blanche.

Lily: Very interesting.

The shallots were glossy and translucent. Lily added the garlic and sautéed it for a couple of minutes. She poured in chicken broth, vermouth, and the lemon juice and brought the mixture to a simmer. Lily nestled the chicken thighs skin-side-up into the bubbling liquid, covered the pan with a lid, and turned the heat down to medium low.

"I don't think I can ever go back to the way things were."

"You don't have to."

"But I can't just leave my husband and son."

"She'll go back to her husband instead of dying?"

"It's looking that way, but I'm still holding out for death in the remaining forty-five minutes. It's what hetero society really wants."

Buzz buzz.

B: I know you've been resistant to digital.

B: But don't rule this out.

B: This is the equivalent of being a beauty magazine editor in chief.

B: I wouldn't come to you with something I didn't think was a good fit.

B: I need someone with serious editorial chops to give this thing credibility.

Lily: No, I get it.

Lily: I'm not ruling it out.

Lily: At all.

Lily: I appreciate that.

Dinner was ready. Lily turned the burner off. A sprinkling of lemon zest and some cracks of black pepper finished the dish.

Buzz buzz.

B: You have so much potential.

B: I know how to shape potential.

Lily: I have no doubt.

Lily scooped some rice from a cooker onto each dish and placed the two plates of chicken on the coffee table. She left her phone on the kitchen counter and settled next to Alison on the sofa.

"Do you mind if I finish this while we eat?" asked Alison. "I kind of want to know what happens."

"Sure. I wouldn't want you to miss that death scene."

Director. Lily let the word linger on the tip of her tongue. It tasted sweet and potent—like triumph. She couldn't wait until her colleagues found out she was leaving the magazine for a title bump and an industry upgrade. Beauty was a land of astronomical growth. The desire for skin care and makeup had no ceiling, and unlike fashion, it was priced at a level of partial accessibility. It embodied a dazzling contradiction: attainable aspiration. Theresa and Susan would explode with envy. The very prospect made Lily dizzy with excitement.

This position with B would offer new challenges and a fresh start. Lily could construct a narrative, for herself and for this editorial vertical, from scratch. She would have control over what stories made the cut. She would develop editing skills and give other writers opportunities to build their own portfolios, because, surely, she would not write all these stories on her own. Lily would possess creative power for the first time in her career. And Lily's power would be bolstered by the foundational power of B.

It was true, Lily had reservations around anything digital. After all, the so-called digital revolution was the reason she was in search of a new job. Briefly, Lily wondered if this position was too much of a spiritual compromise. If she became a part of the movement that had destroyed her original dream occupation, that might be the equivalent of surrender — or collaboration with the enemy. Lily dismissed this pang of confusion with a quick shake of her head. Compromise wasn't selling out; it was inevitable, as inevitable as evolution. The opposite of evolution was far too dire to contemplate. And Lily was ready to thrive.

20

. . .

THE PRECURSOR TO a headache throbbed between Lily's temples.
Her mouth was rough and sour. She had a vague recollection of a Jell-O
shot consumed around two A.M. She had downed the shot at a "Not of
Legal Drinking Age"–themed after-party for Marissa and Luke's re-
hearsal dinner that one of the groomsmen had hosted in his palatial
hotel suite. The shot in question had been Concord grape flavored and
sugar-free. They were in their thirties, for god's sake, far too old to suffer egregiously for a little whimsy. It had been a couple of years at least
since Lily had ventured much past the two A.M. mark. The effects of her
nocturnal adventures were painful.

She stumbled out of bed, washed her face, and rinsed out her mouth.
Her head begged for water and caffeine, while her stomach gurgled its
desperation for food. Unread notifications on her phone from the previous night alerted her to a rumor of Jordan's dalliance with one of the
groomsmen, and intel that a former college classmate, Kate, had passed
out in the bathtub of the after-party hotel suite. She was now in desperate search of a chiropractor to fix her tweaked neck. Again, they were
in their thirties. By comparison, Lily's aftermath glowed with verifiable

adulthood. Here she was, hungover, but still upright in her own apartment, with her long-term girlfriend fast asleep on her side of the bed. It was enough to make Lily consider a commemoration of the moment with a live social media post, an action that would, of course, negate the maturity level that was the very reason for the occasion's noteworthiness.

Though she had wisely declined a two A.M. Jell-O shot, Alison would likely wake with a hankering for stimulants and carbohydrates, too. There were eggs in Lily's fridge and a half-empty package of ground coffee by the sink. Somehow the prospect of cooking breakfast and brewing her own drink seemed more exhausting than her plan to venture outside and pay someone to do it for her.

On the corner of Ninety-Seventh Street and Broadway, there was a café with a large selection of sweet and savory pastries; it was part of a Korean chain, though many patrons assumed it was French because it sold a variety of croissants and it had the word *Paris* in its name. Lily purchased a red-bean bun for herself, a pain aux raisins for Alison, and two oat milk lattes. Back in her kitchen, she fetched plates for the baked goods and filled two tall glasses with cold water. She downed one of them and refilled it. The digital clock on her microwave read 10:27 A.M. The wedding was at four and Alison needed go home before the ceremony.

Lily hovered beside her bed and admired Alison's placid face. She hated to wake her, but all would be forgiven once she plied her with food and coffee. Lily leaned over Alison and kissed her on the forehead.

"Sorry, it's late. But I got us breakfast."

After Alison left to change, Lily went for a run. On this cold and cloudy late-fall day, the park was fairly empty despite the leisurely weekend hour. Instead of the sweeping park drive, Lily ran a few laps around the dirt bridle path that circled the park's reservoir. The bridle path was generous in width and less scenic than its reservoir neighbor. As such, it was an ideal choice for those who prioritized the ability to avoid others over postcard views. In the course of one loop, there were three or four inclines of varying degrees of steepness, the tops of which afforded brief vistas of the reservoir and the skyline. Lily was certain that Central Park's architect had not specifically designed the bridle path's limited scenic moments with future runners' uphill fatigue in mind. Still, she was grateful for the universe's insistence that some people had to earn the same pleasures that others took as their due.

Midway through her first lap on the bridle path, Lily's phone vibrated in the pocket of her windproof outer layer. Assuming it was Alison with a question about pre-wedding preparations, she pulled over to the side of the path and glanced at her screen.

B: Could we talk?

B: This week.

B: About job stuff.

It was finally happening. B would offer her the editorial director position at her new brand. Lily would also see B in person. Every day. No more evasions. They would share actual breathing room and have lunch in B's massive office. They would run into each other in the office bathroom while primping for an evening event. When Lily texted her midmeeting, she would be able to observe B's immediate reaction. The gaps in their communication would be filled. Lily would have the unmitigated access she had sought over the past year and a half, so why the ice-cold bolt that shot across her chest?

It was completely natural that she might be scared. Massive career change was not a light matter. Lily sent B a reply.

Lily: Sure, sounds great.

Lily: I can come in any day.

Every important moment in her life, her college acceptance, a job interview, her first date with Alison, had been chaperoned by heart palpitations. Those shaky bouts were how Lily identified something as deserving of extra consideration. Ease was a mirage; the only salvation was the heart-pounding adrenaline of paralyzing fear.

It was nearly one P.M. Lily silenced her phone, restored it to her jacket's pocket, and resumed her laps around the bridle path.

Hours later, Lily waited on the corner of Sixtieth Street and Fifth Avenue for Alison's rideshare car to arrive. According to the tracking link on her phone, Eddie was seven minutes away from his destination. It was the last week of November and the city sparkled. Lights twinkled on lampposts and awnings and in store windows. Fragrant wreaths and golden menorahs appeared on street corners and in the lobbies of apartment buildings. The prospect of merriment was heavy in the air; it was the start of the most wonderful time of the year, assuming one had somewhere to go and people with whom to celebrate it. Otherwise, it was an arc of pure misery whose climax occurred precisely at 11:59 P.M. on New Year's Eve.

Marissa and Luke's wedding invitation had requested holiday black-tie attire. Lily wore an ankle-length emerald dress with long sleeves and bare legs. The dress's delicate weight was more appropriate for May flowers than November temperatures and she clutched her thick wool coat tighter around her body.

Eddie pulled up to the corner. Alison emerged from his car in a crisp black tuxedo and pressed white shirt unbuttoned to her sternum. Diamond studs sparkled in her ears. Lily gazed at her admiringly.

"You look fantastic."

"So do you. Aren't you cold?"

By way of answer, Lily hooked her arm into Alison's. She guided her toward the two-story wrought iron and gold gates at the entrance to the private club where Marissa and Luke's wedding was to take place. The club had been founded at the tail end of the nineteenth century; its first president was a man whose name still graced one of the largest banks in the country. Under a maroon canopy, two young men, in dark coats and leather gloves, checked off the names of various guests and then ushered them into the club's gracious courtyard, across the red carpeting, and through the front doors. Marissa and Luke had chosen to host their nondenominational wedding ceremony in the club's library.

An orange glow bloomed from the library's crackling fireplace. The decorations were minimal but effective: garlands of eucalyptus and magnolia leaves sprinkled with white lilies, and tall-stemmed candles in brass holders, enough to incinerate the club and its various inhabitants should the wedding not pan out as intended. Lily and Alison plucked programs from a stack on a table near the entrance. They selected two seats in the middle of the right section. A piano had been rolled into a corner of the library for the occasion, and at 4:05 P.M. a pianist tinkled the opening strains of a wedding march. Marissa had eschewed the standard cream, ivory, and bone stylings of her bridal cohorts. She wore instead a sleeveless bronze silk charmeuse gown that undulated like liquid metal down the library's makeshift aisle.

After the ceremony, for which Lily came prepared with a few tissues stashed in her black evening clutch, the guests processed up one flight to the President's Ballroom. Bouquets of lilies and magnolias at the center of each round table were framed by flickering candelabras. Renaissance-painted panels on the ceiling alternated with gilded moldings and Baccarat crystal chandeliers for good measure. Lily and Alison were seated at table thirteen, along with Jordan, Kate, and an assortment of other former classmates from Lily's college. The women deposited their handbags on their respective seats and strolled to one of the room's three bars. Rows of pre-poured flutes of champagne stood at an end of the bar like soldiers ready for battle.

"Champagne?" Alison asked. She reached for a flute.

"Of course," Lily said. For once, she was at ease in such an ostentatious setting, surrounded as she was by her peers and loved ones. Nobody here behaved like this was an everyday occurrence, the way guests at her professional events did. It was a special occasion—the most special occasion of a person's life, depending on whom one polled. And the implicit acknowledgment of this fact among the attendees imbued the party with the lightness of children playing dress-up, rather than the seriousness of adults whose self-esteem was based on the busyness of their calendars.

Flutes in hand, Lily and Alison migrated to a cluster of tables covered with self-service hors d'oeuvres. There was smoked salmon and dill on toast points; golden pigs in blankets; mini baked potatoes with dollops of sour cream and chives. A charcuterie platter, its many rolls of prosciutto, mortadella, salami, and Parma ham like the petals of a rose garden, was already on its way to utter annihilation. The guests at this party were not afraid to eat. Grazing complete, Lily and Alison drifted back to their table, where Jordan had taken a seat next to Alison's place.

"Where's your groomsman?" Lily asked.

Jordan narrowed his eyes. "He seems to have had a change of heart," he said. He glanced over two tables to the gent in question, who tended, obsequiously, to a redhead in black satin. "What does a guy need to do to get a second date?"

"Bisexuals are the worst," Lily said.

"They sure are," Alison concurred, and smiled in Lily's direction.

The caprese salad appetizers arrived. Their thick discs of red and white shimmered under liberal drizzles of olive oil. Between courses, Lily excused herself to go to the bathroom. In the burnished mirror above the sink, she eyed her reflection. She had placed her phone on silent before the ceremony and had assiduously restrained herself from checking it until now. There were a few junk emails and two text messages from B.

B: Let's schedule a call for this week.

B: I'll text you more about the position on Monday.

The initial interview would be over the phone. Of course it would be. That was fine. Lily supposed it was a step up from conducting an interview via text message. She stuffed her silent device back into her evening clutch and returned to table thirteen. The main course of lamb chops had arrived during her absence. She sipped from her near-empty champagne flute and sliced off a bite of medium-rare meat.

"How's work?" Jordan asked from across Alison's seat.

Lily swallowed. "Fine. Not great."

"She might have a lead on something new," Alison said. She placed a hand on Lily's leg.

Lily clasped Alison's hand in hers.

"Oh really?"

"We'll see," Lily replied. "It definitely sounds good on paper."

Soon it was time for the couple's first dance, to a 1960s ballad. Lily watched Marissa sway in Luke's arms. The two of them grinned comically at each other. Marissa was irretrievably happy. Lily squeezed Alison's hand and Jordan glanced over.

"When will I see you two up there?"

"We'll take a spin after dessert," Lily replied.

"That's not what I meant."

"I know."

A server came around with plates of vanilla buttercream cake slices. There were worse ways to pass a chilly November evening than at a wedding for two people one adored. That lasso of dread that had tightened around Lily when Marissa first shared her engagement six months ago had loosened its hold, if not disappeared altogether. Lily's personal feelings on marriage remained in flux; this discomfort was her existential fate. She was not like Marissa or the rest of her friends, save for Jordan. Her journey to romantic communion would never be a perfectly linear path toward an altar and eventual offspring. Lily's conflicted emotions could coexist with Marissa and Luke's joy. Marissa wasn't abandoning

Lily, because Lily had been alone from the start, by virtue of her desire for something different. Instead of resisting that aloneness or harboring anger at its existence, Lily chose acceptance—for herself and for the inevitability of her distance from everyone else. If her friendship with Marissa was as strong as she believed it to be, it would withstand the many changes these nuptials would bring. And if it wasn't, then Lily could still send Marissa off into her next chapter with genuine happiness.

The dance floor was crowded with couples and threesomes and larger groups, who moved in rhythmic spurts. They bobbed and shimmied to the band's greatest-hits playlist. Lily couldn't help but think of the Alzheimer's gala she had attended and all the other galas with it. How isolated and uncomfortable she was at those events, as she watched the swirl of splendor throughout the evening, convinced that she had no place in its sparkling revelry. She was that rare species: an invited crasher. Lily never made it to the dance floors of those galas; she took the end of those dinners as an excuse to slip away unnoticed, as she had been for the previous few hours, while everyone else let loose in uninhibited and uncoordinated bouts.

Lily chewed a final bite of cake from her half-eaten slice. She folded her napkin. She stood up from her chair and turned to Alison, to whom she extended her hand.

"Shall we?"

* * *

AS PROMISED, ON Monday morning, B elucidated, by text, the details of the editorial director position for which Lily would be interviewing by phone.

B: This is confidential.

Lily: Of course.

B: As I told you, it's for the new skin care line.

B: My skin care line.

Lily: Okay.

B: It's going to be called Self.

B: As in care.

B: And I'm going to be the face of it.

Lily: Wow.

Of course she was.

B: The position is for an editorial director.

B: My personal editorial director.

B: The editorial direction for Self will be driven by my personal preferences and obsessions.

B: One and the same.

B: So that's the job!

B: If you want it.

B: Though you still have to interview for it.

B: Formally.

B: What do you think?

Lily stared blankly at her phone's screen. B waited for her reply. And Lily had no idea what to type. She began to construct a pro-con list hastily in her head. Pro: The position reported to B. Was that a pro? This list would never work if she debated the categorization of each item. The position reported to B. Pro. The position was not at a magazine. Pro. The position was in skin care, a red-hot industry whose growth had seemingly no end. Pro. The position had a director title, which would look impressive on a CV and would set her up for future leadership opportunities down the line, at B's company or otherwise. Pro. The sheer fact of working for B directly would also bolster her résumé and overall status. Pro.

As for the cons, well, without being too argumentative, the fact that the position reported to B could also be construed as a con. Ever since she had met B, Lily had watched her sense of self spiral and morph and swing high and low until she practically vomited from dizziness. She had nearly lost Alison and herself. Now she was going to risk her autonomy again to go work for a literal different Self. But what had been the point of the past twenty months if not this inevitable culmination — a perfectly engineered escape from the dying magazine world at the instigation of B, a corporate icon.

Lily: Sounds like a great opportunity!

B: Glad to hear it.

B: You took your time answering.

Lily: Sorry, my editor needed me for something.

Lily: I'm here now.

B: Good.

This was the right decision. Lily knew it was the correct move. No one would turn down an opportunity like this. So many pros, barely any cons. Never mind that the bubble of happiness that had floated in her body when B had first mentioned the job a couple of months back had yet to reemerge. And that instead, a cold anchor in her stomach weighed her down to the chair. This was the best that Lily could hope for — she deserved nothing less. Or more.

Buzz buzz.

B: How about an editorial test before the interview?

Lily: Sure.

B: I want you to pull your favorite close-up images of me from every public event I attended in the last three years.

B: Organize them by theme.

B: You know, smoky eye, bold lip, dewy skin, etc.

She couldn't be serious.

B: Then I want you to draft a story about my red carpet beauty looks.

B: However many words you think makes sense.

B: But I'd say a minimum of 1,000.

B: And create a themed slideshow of your choices from each event you pull from.

B: I want pithy, clever captions for each slide. That implicitly center flawless skin as the basis for any successful red carpet look.

B: So that it ties directly to the skin care line.

B: Sound fun?

Lily: Okay.

B: Think you can have it to me by the end of the day?

B: Then you and I can go over my notes in our interview call.

B seemed to ignore that Lily still had a job, for which she was paid. And that B had yet to hire her.

Lily: I'm on deadline for a couple of stories.

Lily: But I'll do my best.

B: That's what I expect.

B: The best!

On the surface, this was more a paid fan club president than an editorial director. That carte blanche B had initially described appeared to have left the table.

But B had assured Lily that she would never offer her something for which she didn't think Lily was a fit. This job, like all jobs, required a degree of trust on the part of a future employee, a faith that promises made, even those not outlined in a contract, would be promises kept. And trust was also a factor on B's side of this equation. Her skin care line was based on her image, and as the editorial director, Lily would have the responsibility of maintaining said image. The job had stakes for B, too. It was an enterprise of joint risk.

The time on Lily's computer monitor read 12:05 P.M. She opened a browser window and signed in to a photo agency server that the magazine used to pull images. She typed B's name into the search field. And she scrolled through images of B just as she had done so many times before. On that level at least, Lily's qualifications for this job were unassailable.

• • •

WEDNESDAY EVENING AT home, Lily jotted down notes on a pad of paper; a large document was open on the computer screen in front of her. Outside, the rain hurtled from the sky. Droplets of water click-clacked on the top of Lily's air conditioner box. She had finished dinner an hour earlier. Tomorrow, she was slated to speak with B about the editorial director job. Her time slot was at three P.M. B's assistant had informed her that B had a three thirty P.M. meeting, lest Lily believe that this would be a long conversation. She shifted on her sofa, unable to focus on the bullet points she brainstormed on the notepad in her lap.

It had rained prodigiously since Monday and Lily hadn't been for a run in two days. Her muscles itched for exertion. Her mind required a release, too.

Lily tossed her notepad to the side and slid her laptop closer. She was tired of forcing herself to conjure ideas that others demanded of her. She was done with people who told her what mattered. And she was finished with anyone, like Susan, Theresa, or Marc, who dictated who Lily was and what she was allowed to achieve. She typed away furiously now.

For weeks, her writing had slumped into a rest stop, exactly when she believed she had reached the conclusion to the story that had consumed her for so many months. Pages and pages she had written with growing confidence. She had poured out the very emotions that she was forced to hide when she stepped outside the safety of her apartment's four walls. The voice that remained on perpetual mute in public was suddenly alive and voluble when Lily touched her fingers to the keyboard. And as those words surged, Lily gained a deeper understanding of where she had gone wrong. For so long she had sought the key that would unlock the chains that anchored her tightly in place while others passed her by. She had waited, patiently, for permission to graduate to the next stage of life. But there was no key and no one would offer her the chance for which she yearned. The metal restraints were not of her design; still, it was up to her to wrench herself free, by any means necessary. And opportunity was hers to create. Or write, as the case may be.

Endings were never easy. They required a choice, which brought its own finality. And there was always the danger that choice would turn out to be a wrong move. But to linger in discomfort from fear of a poor decision was no longer an option. Her passivity had grown intolerable. Lily's fiction writing required action; so, too, did her personal trajectory.

Lily typed and typed without pause. Hours went by. She knew the conclusion she sought. She would write one first. And then she would make her own conclusion real.

Around two A.M., Lily backed up her finished document and closed her laptop. She grabbed her phone. She requested a rideshare car. Lily would go to B. She would have her ending.

In the car ride downtown, the empty roads molten like tar, Lily stared out the window. She contemplated the Hudson River's opaque, dark expanse. Maybe *ending* wasn't the right word. It was more like clarity. Or truth, she wanted some truth. Her truth. The truth was she was in love with Alison. The truth was B had offered her a job. Lily could imagine how her life would unfold next to Alison, an apartment in which they cohabitated, meals they cooked, friends they hosted, films they watched, walks they took. Each moment collapsed into the next, a nesting doll of shared experiences. Instead of terror at what such proximity might yield, the possibility of this entwined life filled Lily with comfort. It felt like home. And with this job under B, she saw a ream of blank pages. No words charted Lily's future course. No sentences coaxed her toward her next step. Empty white sheets waited for that first dash of ink.

The car deposited her in front of B's Tribeca building. She buzzed B's apartment.

"Hello?" came a voice from the buzzer's speaker. "Who's there?"

"It's me. Lily," said Lily.

"Lily?" came the voice. "What the fuck are you doing here? Are you crazy?"

"Maybe. I don't know. Are you really that surprised?"

The door buzzed. Lily pushed it in quickly. She headed up to B's apartment. The elevator reached the penthouse and the door slid open.

B loomed a few feet from the door, where she blocked most of the entrance despite her diminutive stature. She wore loose pajama bottoms and a white T-shirt; her shoulder-length brown hair streaked with gray highlights was wrapped in a haphazard half loop. Her brow was furrowed.

"I still don't know what the fuck you're doing here," she said by way of greeting.

Lily stepped out of the elevator. "I have something I need to tell you," she said.

"And you couldn't just send me a text?" B asked.

"It needs to happen in person," Lily said.

B stared at her intently. The corners of her mouth tugged outward, in a grimace or a smile, it wasn't clear. She moved to the side.

"Come in."

Lily entered the apartment. B's penthouse was not as Lily had imagined it—it was far colder. An abstract canvas covered in angular slashes and zigzagging black lines faced the elevator. The living area had a boxy gray sofa and a Lucite coffee table stacked with hefty tomes. The floors were made of poured concrete. All along, Lily had been aware of B's chilled emotional landscape. This had been a major facet of her appeal, the control she exerted over the caprice of feelings. Some part of Lily had wanted to believe, though, that in her texts with B, she had excavated an

257

unknown layer of vulnerability. That she had access to a hidden softness that B stashed away from the rest of the world. Wherever that softness might have existed, it was not within the walls of B's penthouse.

"You're lucky I'm awake," B chided.

"You're right. I should have called first," said Lily.

"Speaking of, don't we have a call scheduled for tomorrow?" B moved toward the living area.

"Yes, but this isn't something we'd cover in an interview."

B strode to her adjacent kitchen, washed her hands, and fetched two glass tumblers from a shelf. She took a bottle of gin and an ice tray from her freezer and a lime from her fridge. She sliced the lime in half, poured an inch and a half of gin into each tumbler, and garnished them with half a squeezed lime and an ice cube. She returned to the living area. B set one glass on the Lucite coffee table and sat on the gray sofa. Lily sat across from her, in a leather and metal chair that was as uncomfortable as it appeared. She swallowed a floral sip from the glass. She still couldn't stand the taste of gin.

"I've been doing some writing."

"You came all the way down here in the middle of the night to tell me you've been doing some writing?"

"No. I mean, not exactly."

"Okay."

"It's a book."

"That's nice."

"It's almost done. I'm near the end."

"Okay. What's it about?" B reached for her glass and sipped her gin.

"It's a novel about a young woman who lands a dream job working for an older, über-successful fashion designer. The young woman is an aspiring designer. Was languishing at another fashion label that never gave her any opportunities. She was about to give up and apply to law school. And then this older fashion designer shows up and offers her a job."

"Interesting."

"Yes. And this older woman boss is everything the young woman dreams of being. Confident. Smart. Glamorous. A tough leader who makes her own rules."

"She sounds impressive."

Despite B's blank face, Lily could sense that her internal gears whirred in curiosity.

"And at first, the job is thrilling. The young woman is learning a lot. Or so she thinks. As she spends more time working for the older woman, the young woman starts to have reservations about her choice."

"Why?" B crossed her legs and leaned back against the sofa. It was an unconvincing attempt at nonchalance.

"Because the older woman doesn't really want to mentor the young woman; she wants to control the young woman. She wants the young woman to worship her."

All this time, B had evoked in Lily so many emotions—excitement, frustration, anxiety—through the mere act of sending a text. And here B sat, in the flesh, and Lily felt nothing at all. B was an appealing but empty totem of aspiration, not so different from the magazine fantasy world that had previously fed Lily's dreams. To be near B was to remain perpetually in the shadows. And Lily was finally ready to step into the light.

B worried a strand of shimmery gray hair that had loosed itself from her half loop. "What does the young woman do?"

"She quits. And starts her own fashion label," Lily said. She stared at B straight in her dark, penetrating eyes. "She would rather fail at realizing her dream than spend the rest of her life feeding someone else's vanity."

"I see."

B's eyes twinkled.

"Your older woman fashion designer sounds fascinating. Wherever did you find inspiration for your protagonist?"

"The older woman isn't the protagonist. And I've met confident, successful women of all backgrounds. Plenty of manipulative egomaniacs, too." Lily smiled. "I had a wealth of inspiration to draw from."

B held Lily's gaze for a beat, then glanced down at the floor. She drained the gin from her glass. She stared pensively at its empty form. Lily swirled the contents of hers, then placed the glass down, barely drunk.

"It's still a work in progress," Lily added. "But I feel confident the story is going in the right direction."

B looked back up at Lily, her dark eyes softer now. She offered her a tentative smile. "So, you want to write fiction, do you?"

"Yes."

B's cheek muscles tensed, but her tentative smile held steady. "I'm sure we can work something out. If you want to juggle writing with this role. Let's discuss this more on our call."

"Thanks for the offer, but I've made my decision. There's nothing more to discuss."

Billie's lips parted, as though to emit a rejoinder. Then she seemed to think better of it.

Lily stood up from the chair, zipped her parka, and retrieved her phone from her pocket. It was 3:28 in the morning. She walked to the foyer and pressed the button for the elevator. She glanced back at Billie, who still sat on her sofa. Lily flashed her a wry grin.

"Batter up."

Epilogue

· · ·

Two and a Half Years Later

A TWELVE-PERSON LINE bisected the basement of a bookstore in SoHo. It was a larger group than Lily had ever envisioned would show up for a book reading, her book reading, let alone wait for her to sign a copy they had purchased for that specific purpose. She was still adjusting to the idea that her name was printed on the cover of a book that sat on the shelves of stores and, in some cases, in the windows of the shops themselves, and that this book would live in people's homes, in a pile by the owner's bedside or on the top of a coffee table. Eventually, the book might be stashed in a misplaced box in someone's basement. She was okay with that inevitability, too. Because to be forgotten, one had to exist in the first place. And that was itself an achievement.

A woman stood before her and brandished a copy of the book for Lily to sign. The woman was exceedingly tall. So much so that she nearly blotted out the rest of the line with her presence. She had long, gray hair and elegant fingers, with which she passed Lily the book, open to its title page. A warm smile spread across the woman's face. Tiny lines appeared at the corners of her eyes, like sun rays piercing a cloudy sky.

These wordless moments of appreciation filled Lily with hope. She had created something completely of her own volition. It was out in the world. And there were people who might take pleasure from it. The joy of that exchange was almost too much to bear.

Despite her euphoria, Lily was a knot of adrenaline. She had asked Alison and Marissa and Jordan to skip this event out of fear that a familiar face would worsen her nerves. So, Lily was alone here, at this table, at this signing, as she had been alone when she wrote the book. In the end, this was the relationship for which she had fought all along, without fully knowing it — the one in which she and her writing achieved communion, because she was in charge of the narrative.

. . .

AFTER SHE TURNED DOWN Billie's job offer, Lily continued to toil at the magazine while she revised her novel. When she landed an agent and sold the book, Lily finally worked up the courage to say something about her magazine story load. By that point, the pace of the digital demands had grown so relentless that Lily could barely see straight. Each piece blurred into the next, and as Theresa was always quick to remind her, no one read any of them. One afternoon, she knocked on Theresa's half-open glass door and Theresa waved her in.

"I have five minutes," Theresa said. "And then I have to run to another digital meeting."

"Speaking of," Lily said, "I wanted to ask if I could take a couple of stories off my plate. Maybe Marc could ask the new digital associate if he could take one on. And someone else could take one of my print pieces."

Theresa crossed her arms over her chest. "Why?"

"Because I'm drowning, Theresa," Lily said. "I have six stories for the next issue. And eight stories for the website. And I'm worried about the quality of my work plummeting."

"Then do a better job of writing them," Theresa said. "This isn't a workload issue. This is an attitude issue. You need to be a team player. You never used to be this difficult."

Lily had wasted so much of her career bending over backward to avoid this term, the preferred descriptor for the dismissal and punishment of women—especially nonwhite women—who dared to vocalize their opinions. She had believed that *easy* was the adjective to which she should aspire and that if she adhered to its parameters it would serve her career well; now she realized that *easy* was simply another way of saying "keeps her mouth shut and does what she is told." And Lily was not a trained dog whose obedience merited rewards. She was a human being who deserved the right to have a say in the stories she wrote.

So, Lily quit.

Annabelle had a seemingly bottomless list of wealthy friends with eponymous companies, such as candle lines, perfume collections, monogrammed jewelry, etc., whose websites, press releases, and seasonal look books required written text. This copywriter work kept Lily relatively busy for the first couple of months after she quit.

She began freelance writing for other magazines and newspapers as well, profiles of up-and-coming actresses, beauty stories, conversations with fashion designers. The work was similar to what she had done in her full-time capacity, but since she could decide what pieces she juggled, she was able to find a more fulfilling spark in each assignment to which she committed. There was also the fact that these stories no longer bore the entire weight of Lily's work identity. Sometimes, they were fun. Her favorite assignment thus far was another piece on the designer Antonio Russo. And other times they were just a job. Combined with the copywriting work and the first payment of her advance, this patchwork of gigs kept her afloat.

Lily had also come clean to Alison about her fiction-writing ambitions and the novel she had worked on in secret. Lily had been nervous about her confession. It was never easy to tell someone, someone who loved you, especially someone who loved you, that you wanted to be an author. It was like admitting that one had a drug problem that would invariably drain one's financial resources. The only thing worse would be to inform one's partner that one wanted to become an actor.

Alison had supported Lily's authorial aspirations, so long as Lily was realistic about the very possible prospects for failure. This wasn't a swipe at Lily's abilities; the book industry was brutal. Lily understood this. When she managed to sign with an agent, six months after sending out fifty or so cold queries, and when the agent, in turn, sold Lily's book a year later, she celebrated the victory for what it was: good luck combined with very hard work.

The novel was titled *The Cusp*. The plot had shifted from its original conceit and the book's tone and themes had undergone a transformation. When Lily had begun writing it, after her demoralizing digital meeting with Theresa years ago, the novel had been an escapist fantasy. Lily had imagined what she thought was a dream professional scenario, a fledgling fashion designer with a dazzling, powerful boss who nurtures the young woman's talent and buoys her toward inevitable success. And Lily had lived vicariously through the career she crafted for her fashion designer protagonist.

As her writing had progressed, Lily had realized that her approach to the arc of *The Cusp* was all wrong. For years, the stories that had captivated Lily had been built on fantasies. Lily wasn't suddenly immune to the draw of a good fantasy; dreaming would always have its place in her world. Still, Alison had told Lily on their first date that, eventually, she wanted to split the difference between profitability and goodness. Lily needed to find her version of this balance in her own work. She needed to split the difference between the seduction of make-believe and the hard truths of reality. If her fiction was going to pursue these goals, she had to stop ignoring the disempowerment of her novel's central plot. Lily had confronted the fatal flaw in *The Cusp* and in her own personal narrative. There was no struggle if the boss gave the young woman exactly what she wanted; there was no earned achievement if the young woman relied on a de facto fairy godmother to remedy her situation. Instead, the fashion designer protagonist—and Lily—had to do what real-life women have to do. She needed to save herself.

On the subject of saving oneself and one's relationships, Lily had experienced another epiphany on the topic of cohabitation. Now that she was a freelance entity, she worked from home full-time. When her upstairs neighbor began an extensive renovation, Lily's tiny but once calm environment became borderline apocalyptic. Endless hammering, drilling, pounding, and sawing reverberated through Lily's apartment for eight hours a day. One afternoon, during the loudest phase of the renovation, Lily called Alison in gasping tears and told her she had lost her mind.

"Why don't you work from my place?" Alison replied.

Ten-hour workdays at Alison's apartment quickly transitioned into two weeks of full cohabitation, with the occasional excursion back to Lily's place on the weekends. These fourteen days passed by in a blur of unimaginable ease. The women cooked together and ate together and slept side by side, two curved parentheses that encapsulated a shared thought. When the cacophony of the demolition phase abated, Lily moved back home.

The first morning that Lily woke up alone in her apartment after that two-week stint, the empty left side of the bed, with its unruffled sheets and dent-free pillow, no longer whispered freedom. Its blankness spoke of an incomplete phrase. Lily had grown so accustomed to guarding her autonomy from the nastiness around her that she had ignored the possibility that some people in her circle might have her best interests in mind. She had been so dead set on solitude as the only way to preserve her identity; she hadn't counted on the fact that Alison's version of Lily might be a kinder and more generous portrait than the selfhood to which Lily so stubbornly clung. And that living with Alison—and with Alison's version of Lily—might grant Lily some of the peace for which she had so desperately thirsted.

"I've been thinking about the past couple of weeks," Lily said to Alison over dinner one night not long after that two-week stint at Alison's apartment. "How nice it was. Being together all the time."

"It was," said Alison as she spun a forkful of spaghetti.

"Maybe we could make that more regular. More permanent. If that's something you would like?"

"Are you asking me to move in with you?"

"I was asking to move in with you. If you'll have me."

"I have something I need to tell you, too. That I've been meaning to tell you for a few days. But I didn't know how."

"Okay."

Lily's stomach dropped. Alison was definitely moving to the suburbs. She had finally given up on the city, on Lily, on her punishing job. She had cashed out and bought a house in some tiny, bucolic enclave with lots of trees and kids playing in yards. Lily couldn't blame Alison for one second, though she didn't think her recent epiphany extended beyond the borders of the five boroughs.

"I interviewed at this firm downtown that specializes in nonprofit consulting."

"Oh wow. That's so great."

"I really liked everyone I met there. And the work they do. They've made me an offer. And I think I'm going to accept it."

"Amazing. I'm so happy for you."

"It's a number I haven't seen since, well, ever. It's a major pay cut. This is all to say, yes, I would love for you to move in with me. And also, I need you to move in with me—it's the only way I can afford this apartment."

There was another, unspoken reason why Lily was eager to abandon her previous stance on cohabitation. She wanted to prove to Alison and to herself that the Lily who had isolated herself at home, the Lily who had isolated herself in her phone and in her conversations with Billie, was gone. Because she was gone. And so was Lily's fixation on Billie. Because Billie wasn't real. She was a blank canvas that Lily had collaged with projected traits and motivations. If a real Billie existed, Lily had never met her.

It had occurred to Lily that her stubbornness around the digital world during that year and eight months had been laced with contradiction. On the one hand, there was the advent of social media and its impact on the long-standing print realm of magazines. And on the other, there was her constant texting with Billie. Lily had felt so threatened by the creeping fingers of digital media's grip on her livelihood, and yet she had had few compunctions about allowing a purely texting relationship to consume her daily life. It made her not so different from the followers who fawned over influencers' feeds. Billie had been no less a stranger than the filtered and buffed social media stars whom Lily had helped elevate to prominence. The only difference was numbers: Lily had been follower one and only—at least so far as she knew. And she had let Billie influence her, almost to the point of no return.

The morning following her middle-of-the-night visit to Billie's apartment, Lily went dark. She deleted Billie's information from her phone, though Lily had an inkling she would hear from her again, one way or another. A woman of Billie's ilk was not accustomed to being excised; she was the only person who was permitted to vacate her relationships. Three weeks later, nearly to the day, Lily's phone vibrated while she was at work, typing away at a transcript. The messages were from a number not in her contacts. She knew, instinctively, that it was Billie.

Billie: Hi there.

Billie: How's your writing?

Billie needed to come out on top. Her self-esteem demanded it. Lily knew that. And she would not give Billie the outcome she sought. Lily felt smug and in control because of her silence. It was in such marked contrast to the frazzled, anxious state in which she had perpetually existed when she had been at Billie's beck and call. This must have been how Billie had felt every time she issued a "Totally" or "Gotta run" in opaque reply to one of Lily's more probing queries. Billie had been drawn to Lily's attention rather than to Lily herself. This whole thing had been a long, twisted game for Billie, a renewable source of fuel for her ravenous ego.

Lily could understand the appeal. The rush of pleasure in withholding the very thing she knew that someone else so desperately ached for was heady and intoxicating. She could envision how someone might want to extend this high for as long as humanly possible. How a person might continue to up the ante on a willing supplicant's emotional investment only to cut them off, every so often, to remind them that ultimately, they owed the supplicant nothing.

But Lily was not Billie. She was not Lily with a B, contained within Billie's chilly borders. Lily was her own person. And while she wasn't so stoic as to deny herself the momentary indulgence of wielding power over someone who had once held Lily in her thrall, she would not extend this match beyond its natural ending point. She reentered Billie's contact info into her phone. And then she blocked her—for good.

• • •

THERE WERE ONLY two people who remained in the book signing line, though Lily had hardly had a chance to pay attention, so engrossed had she been in preventing her hand from cramping. As a twenty-something guy in stovepipe jeans with a puffy pompadour stepped up to the table, Lily saw that his voluminous hairstyle had blocked the petite woman in line behind him. It was Billie, her sharply sculpted face and casually sophisticated air exactly as they had been a few years back.

Lily's chest began to pound. She tried to inhale deeply but subtly, so as not to show that she was rattled. That was exactly what Billie wanted, evidence that she could still influence Lily, that even if Lily never responded to another text from her again, vestiges of Billie's dominance remained intact.

It was Billie's turn. She looked Lily straight in the eye as she approached the table with the nonchalance of a person about to place a morning coffee order with a barista. She handed Lily her copy of *The Cusp*.

"Congratulations."

"Thanks." Lily started to sign her name.

"Aren't you going to inscribe it?"

"Sure. What would you like me to say?"

"Isn't that up to you? You're the writer, after all." Billie's molten eyes sparkled mischievously.

"I guess I am." Lily paused. Her pen hovered above the title page. "Did you read any of it?"

Billie smirked and ran a hand through her silvery brown hair. Her white shirt collar was popped up as though to fend off potential assailants. "I did. Though I haven't finished it yet."

"Oh, no?"

"No, I have a couple of chapters to go." Billie smirked again. "Don't tell me how it ends."

"I already told you how it ends."

Lily wrote her message, signed it, and blew on it to dry the ink. She closed the book and handed it to Billie. There was no one else in line. The store clerk had finished folding up and storing all the chairs.

"Are you doing something to celebrate?"

"Just taking myself out for a drink."

Billie frowned in curiosity. "No friends or girlfriend to treat you? What's the fun in taking yourself out?"

Always looking for that sore spot to finger. This woman never fucking changed. "I'm extremely good company."

Billie smiled and shook her head lightly. "Is that your way of saying you don't have a girlfriend?"

Lily couldn't restrain a snicker. "Why do you care?"

"I don't. I was just making conversation."

Lily shrugged on her trench coat and slung her bag over her shoulder. She waved goodbye to the store clerk. She headed toward the store's staircase. Billie followed behind her. The women said nothing to each other as they walked upstairs and across the bookstore's ground floor to the exit. Lily paused when they were outside on the sidewalk.

"Where are you headed? I could walk you to your bar," Billie said as a change of tack.

"I don't think that's a good idea."

"You'd rather drink alone?"

"Yes, I would."

Billie held Lily's gaze. A gentle crease appeared between her eyes. "That's it, is it?"

"Why did you come here?" Lily's neck itched and warmed beneath her coat's collar. "So you could have the last word?"

Billie glanced down at the damp sidewalk. The headlights of passing cars danced across its murky surface. A trio of young women clomped by; they laughed loudly and demonstratively.

"No. I—" Billie paused, uncharacteristically at a loss. "I wanted to see you."

"Why?" That warmth built in intensity. It spread up Lily's neck to her chin. Lily pressed a cold hand to her cheek.

Billie's eyes flickered up and down Lily's trench coat, her crossed arms, the impatience that radiated from her taut legs.

"You look great."

Lily said nothing.

"I'm always going to wonder. Aren't you?" Billie continued.

"No," Lily said. "Anyway, better to wonder than to lose."

"Lose what?"

"Myself."

"I thought you were a better multitasker than that."

Lily uncrossed her arms. She stuck her hands into her pockets. "Just because I'm good at something, doesn't mean I want to spend the rest of my life doing it."

Billie's eyes softened. "It was fun, though, wasn't it?"

Lily shook her head. This conversation had already taken too long.

Billie gestured at the copies of *The Cusp* in the bookstore's window. "Don't you think you owe me a drink? I mean, I'm the reason you have this book. If it wasn't for me, you never would have found the courage to go out on your own. I told you I always love saving other women."

That wry grin returned to Billie's face. Lily matched Billie's expression with one of her own.

"You're right. I do owe you something," Lily said. "A proper goodbye. Goodbye, Billie. I wish you the best."

And with that, Lily turned and walked east toward Mulberry Street down those rain-slicked sidewalks. She never looked back.

Acknowledgments

• • •

This book exists thanks to so many people to whom I am deeply grateful.

To Tia Ikemoto, thank you for seeing the potential in this book and for your faith in me. (And for a perfect title.) You are tireless, patient, and wonderful. And thank you to everyone else at CAA, including John Ash, who helped with *Ellipses*.

To Amber Oliver, thank you for your early support of this book, for advocating on its behalf and on mine. I am so grateful for your enthusiasm for *Ellipses* and for your sensitive, smart insights.

To Emi Ikkanda, thank you for your incisive questions, your sharp notes, and your thoughtfulness. *Ellipses* and I are both very fortunate to have benefited from your thorough, intelligent editing.

Thank you to so many others at Dutton and Penguin Random House, especially Claire Sullivan, Aja Pollock, Christopher Lin, Lindsey Tulloch, and Nicole Jarvis. To Stephanie Ross, thank you for *Ellipses*'s beautiful cover. And thank you to Dawn Hardy.

To those who read a draft of my manuscript, Jill Kargman, Sarah Conde, Aimee Cho, and Molly Wright, thank you for your encouragement, feedback, and time.

ACKNOWLEDGMENTS

To the passionate, dedicated staff at *Women's Wear Daily* and *W Magazine* during the formative years of my career, thank you. In particular, thanks to Bridget Foley and Anamaria Wilson, who together gave me my first opportunity to write professionally.

To the countless people who have paved the way, through their artistry, work, and bravery, so that those who come after them may have greater opportunity, thank you.

To the many talented teachers in high school, college, and graduate school from whom I have learned so much. Special thanks to the Sarah Lawrence College MFA writing program, where I had the freedom to grow as a writer.

To those who offered advice and/or moral support, publishing related or otherwise: Peter and Amy Bernstein, Stephanie Tran, Kemper Donovan, Adam Milch, Julia Phillips, Carolyn Ferrell, Lauren R., Jake Pellegrini, Mike Monagle, Sabhbh Curran, Tanja Goossens, and Flora Hanitijo.

To Jennifer Barton for the absolute gift of over three decades of unconditional friendship and love.

To my parents; my brother; Yima; Sook Sook; and the rest of my family for creating a home where education, books, and the arts were prioritized and valued deeply. And for giving me a lifelong model of generosity.

To Dana, the kindest, smartest, and most supportive—my favorite person. I am lucky to love you.

About the Author

. . .

VANESSA LAWRENCE is a writer, editor, and native New Yorker. For nearly two decades she covered the arts, fashion, beauty, design, and New York society as a staff writer for publications including *Women's Wear Daily* and *W Magazine*. She has a BA in history from Yale University and an MFA in creative writing from Sarah Lawrence College. *Ellipses* is her debut novel.